TESS THORNTON

A RIVAL FOR THE Cowboy

RIDGEVIEW RANCH
BOOK 1

To request permission, contact the publisher at: EagleCreekPressBooks@gmail.com

Paperback ISBN: 978-1-957082-39-4

Library of Congress Number: Pending

First Paperback Edition September, 2024

Cover Art by: GetCovers

Photography and Graphics Courtesy Of: Shutterstock.com, Depositphotos.com, Twenty2 0.com, Elements.envato.com

Editing and Layout by: Eagle Creek Press, Inc.

Printed in the USA

Publisher: Eagle Creek Press,

EAGLE CREEK
PRESS

Contents

The Ridgeview Ranch Brothers Series

Chapter One

Cole

Reno, Nevada

My glove was sticky with nervous sweat inside when I tugged it off to adjust my reins. I wiped my palm on my jeans, swallowed, and rubbed a quick circle on Lynx's neck.

"Easy, girl," I muttered. My voice was gravelly, so I cleared my throat and tried again. "Easy now."

Wasn't doing much good. The bay filly's head was up, and she was hopping from one front foot to the other, jigging sideways and chomping the bit. I kept having to bump her back into line with my leg. Rookie horse, rookie rider—we made quite the pair.

Far as I could tell, Lynx was the only horse in the whole warm-up pen acting half-crazy. Everyone else looked bored, just moseying along the rail, loose-rein and casual. Meanwhile, I was clinging to the filly's side like a twitchy jockey, trying to keep my butt glued in the saddle while she spooked at her own shadow. I jerked my hat lower and prayed no one was laughing too loud. Time to head into the main arena for our pattern.

A couple riders gave me sympathetic glances when we went by. They'd all been here before, showing young horses for the first time. But when I passed the row of bleachers against the fence where Emily sat with her eyes glued to the ring steward, I made sure to stare straight ahead.

Last thing I needed was Little Miss Perfect watching me get publicly humiliated. She already made me look bad enough.

We circled around to take our place at the gate to start our pattern, number 213 pinned neatly on both sides of my saddle blanket. Far as Lynx cared, it might as well have been a "REJECT" stamp on my rear.

I kept catching myself rolling my eyes skyward, and it took some effort to level my head. Wasn't the horse's fault she was wound up, I scolded myself. Barely three years old, first time off the ranch, four hundred-mile haul, new routines. I was lucky Cody even trusted me to show her.

I blew out a breath and focused on relaxing my own muscles. That usually helped get a young horse to settle, too. But then Lynx jumped and swung her butt toward the rail, and I almost came out of the saddle. So much for that idea.

From his vantage point leaning on the fence by the gate, my boss Cody was probably laughing at me. Or worse, trying real hard not to. This year was my shot to prove myself after barely eking out of the rookie ranks last fall with just a top-ten finish in a local jackpot show. Cody kept saying I had potential, that horses took to me well. All I knew was Copper sure took to Emily in a hurry, and now I was battling an uncertain filly determined to run me into the dirt.

The crackly loudspeaker had announced the first two riders, and then it was us. "Number 213, Cole Langton aboard Playin it Smart, bred and owned by Walker Ranch."

I peeled Lynx away from the rail and aimed us for the center. Every step in, she jigged and spooked worse with the clapping and whistles urging us on. I gritted my teeth and murmured soothing phrases that were as much for me as they were for her.

Far as patterns went, it wasn't a tough one. I loosened the tension in my rein hand and touched my heel to Lynx's side. Time for this green broke filly's first dance.

As my old man always used to say, go big or go home...

We tipped down the center of the arena, Lynx's hooves pounding an uneven cadence. I steadied my reins, sat deep, and tried for that illusion of graceful control.

First stop was decent. The filly hunkered quick as I cued, skidding fifteen feet or so. I kept her still for the count, though she fought me, head flung up and neck arched. The four spins we sort of fumbled through, hopping more than pivoting clean. But soon as I touched my spur, Lynx broke forward, eager to move those fresh legs.

I had to smile. However wacky she felt under me, she sure wanted to work. I shaped a fast circle to the right, big and round as I could make it in the confined space. She offered to change leads a stride early, but I held her straight until my marker.

Then came the left lead circles, and that's when things unraveled. We overshot our first turn, Lynx's shoulder bulging out. My reins rasped as I corrected too quick, and she threw her head, stiffening up. I tried easing her back around, keeping my legs soft, but now she wanted to gape her mouth and pretend she didn't know what I was asking.

"Easy," I whispered, hating the desperate thread in my tone. The filly wasn't quite right yet. She needed another year to bake, and I was rushing her too much...

I had to remember to ride her like the greenie she was. Shouldn't expect she'd be anywhere close to Copper's level yet. They were the same age, but she'd been more nervous, hotter, and she was behind him by a good four months. Might as well be a year. Hardest thing now was keeping my own jumpy nerves from frazzling us both.

We finally swung onto the last required pass down center. It wasn't pretty, what with Lynx still distracted and poking along. But if we scratched out one decent sliding stop to polish off the run, maybe no one would notice too much.

Fifty feet from the far end, I sat deeper and let the reins slip. The filly perked and drove forward willingly. I smiled in front of my gritted teeth.

"That's my girl, easy now..." I adjusted my hat as the filly's feet shifted under me. The dry work part of our go was over, and it was just the cow work to go. Her favorite part. Now to let her sit a second and blow before I signaled the gate crew that...

Crap. They'd taken my hand on my hat as a cue. My grin froze as Lynx's ears pricked wildly right as her hips coiled under. Her stride bolted unevenly, and I caught a flash of white barreling at the closed arena gate.

Oh, blast. They were opening it up, already letting our cow in for the second half of our run!

"Steady!" I yelped, but Lynx was already hopping sideways, shying from the gate crew rattling their levers and pulleys. She skipped again as the panels squeaked apart, making the gap for my worst nightmare to come bolting out.

I should have felt her tensing, knew she wasn't ready. If I'd just gotten her a little more broke back at home... Taken a second before trying to keep my fool hat in place...

No time for should-haves. I had a half second to get this filly back under me. As the black cow made its dart toward freedom, I gripped hard with my knees and threw everything I had into cutting Lynx to the left to head off our cow.

Big mistake.

Her slide went from decisive and controlled to a panicked scramble. We plowed past the end marker in a spray of dirty chalk. Lynx was still trying to spin away from the cow while I hauled the reins sideways. Our turnaround was sloppy, missing the cow by a good ten feet. And then, the black baldy split right by us. *Too slow, too slow!* I wheeled her about and asked her to jog quietly, letting her catch up without getting too excited.

The cow was wandering by then, careless about the wreck its entry had caused. Jaw tight, I just tried getting us to the gate without any more trouble. But when I asked the filly to jog, she ignored me completely. She wanted out of there just as bad I suddenly did.

I guess I couldn't blame her. The cow work was a bust before we even boxed the dumb critter. Wasn't the horse—it was me pushing too much gas. Me not riding the horse under me, but the horse I *wanted* her to be. I should have backed her off from trouble right when I felt it gather.

The rest of our time ticked off the clock until the judge rang the bell to dismiss us, and I was more than ready for it to be over. As we passed Cody along the rail, I stared hard at Lynx's ear and tried not to imagine the look on his face. Didn't matter. Show was over for us. I patted the filly's neck anyway as we exited the loud arena.

"Good girl," I muttered, swallowing the frustrated break in my voice. "We'll get 'em next time."

If Cody even let me leg up on one of his prospects again after that disaster...

Emily

I pressed my lips out to keep them from drawing into a thin line. Squinting against the glare of arena lights, I watched Cole circle to line up his entry. Even from my perch halfway up the bleachers, I could read the tension singing through the young filly he rode. She had talent and try—I'd seen that myself back home in practice runs—but this atmosphere overwhelmed her.

And maybe Cole too, from the desperate set to his shoulders. I sighed softly. Of course, Cody would trust him with a prospect here. Never mind that more consistent riders—heck even half our students back home—would have shown Lynx off better after all the hours I'd put into exercising her. If Cole wanted to play with the big boys, today would test what he was really made of. My toes curled inside my boots as I ticked through the pattern in my head, anticipating each mistake before they happened.

The filly scotched, then overshot her first stop by a good eighteen feet, likely from Cole cuing too quick, then second-guessing himself. His timing worsened on the spins, and Lynx just looked baffled. At least when I'd been that green as an exhibitor, I'd been drilled at home. I didn't have hundreds of eyes tracking each error, because Cody fixed all my mistakes in the schooling arena through patient repetition. But for some reason, he let Cole start showing without teaching him a little more strategy for handling his nerves at home.

I drew a short breath as Lynx bobbled again—Cole was seesaw-ing up there, letting the atmosphere eat him instead of riding calm through her trouble. The filly was a sweet goer for all her greenness, but I knew how quickly that could sour if she got the wrong idea of what showing was about. Risky giving her to someone without seasoning.

Jaw tight, I watched Cole throw a panicked yank sideways right as their cow burst free for its suicidal bolt across the arena. A sharp whistle slipped through my clenched teeth—he was going to undo months of patient training if he couldn't ride smarter. As their pattern ran long and tortured, other riders lined up along the rail for their crack at the boxing class. Lots of shaking heads and a few chuckles. Cole didn't stand a chance in the placings. My sympathy twinged for the burning cheeks Cole hid under his hat brim against the eyes of the world he was so hungry to impress.

I blew out an exasperated huff as they made their shambling exit. Disappointing, but at least no real harm done yet, if Cody could get Cole back to basics at home before permanent damage set in. Though for his pride, the blistering defeat was likely hurt enough. At least Lynx hadn't lost her spark for the game—she deserved far better partners to nurture that blistering talent she had.

With a shake of my head, I rose to head back to the stall area, mentally cataloging the skills we apparently still needed some tough love to drill. If Cole hoped to ride with Cody, he had plenty yet to learn.

I found Cole at Lynx's stall, at the end of the row draped with red curtains and boasting the big Lazy W brand. The rest of our show string were napping or eating, but Lynx was dripping sweat and in need of a good rub-down and cool-out before she got turned loose. Cole was yanking roughly at the cinch, ears crimson. My steps slowed.

Maybe now wasn't the best moment to review his ride. But he spun right as I scuffed my boot in the dirt, immediately on the attack.

"Come to tell me more ways I screwed it up? Saves Cody the trouble."

I rocked back slightly, blinking. "Just making sure you're okay. Rough ride for anyone—"

"I don't need your sympathy." He gave Lynx's girth another jerk, pulling it completely loose, and slung the sweat-soaked cinch up over the saddle. The filly shifted, eyes rimmed in concern my way. "Shouldn't you be getting high and mighty Copper pretty for his victory parade?"

The dig flushed my neck with embarrassment on behalf of the horse. "That's unfair, Cole. You know Copper and I have worked hard. I just meant—"

"Go bother someone else." He spun his saddle down off Lynx's back, slinging it angrily across his shoulder. "Don't you have better things to do?"

The dismissal slammed me back a step. I threw a bewildered look at Cody, who stood stone-faced outside his stall holding his champion horse Rust. He shook his head once, tired disappointment hanging off him.

Cole was already stomping off for his grooming kit so he could take Lynx for a rinse down. I almost called out to stop him, hating leaving things ragged between any member of our team. But Cody subtly waved me off before leading Rust toward the warm-up pen. Handling Cole fell on his shoulders. I had my own stuff to worry about.

I patted Lynx's shoulder in sympathy. "He doesn't really mean it," I whispered in her flickering ear. If only excuses could heal the harm of careless tempers. With a sad glance after Cole, I turned slowly toward

Copper's stall. Winning suddenly felt far less important than guarding each step we took to get there.

I slipped inside and greeted the gentlemanly stallion with a finger tracing that perfectly round star in the center of his forehead. "Are you ready for your turn, big guy?" I slipped a halter on him and smiled as he immediately nosed at my shoulder for an apple slice I didn't have.

"You goof," I laughed, giving his golden neck a hug in apology. Copper flattened an ear coyly my way, sending me a little patient side-eye. Hard to believe such a clownish lug was actually a thickly muscled stallion who had taken his trial run in the breeding shed just last month. I kept scratching his silky hide as I moved to tie him in the corner of his stall before fetching his saddle. He leaned into every rub, eyes blinking sweetly shut in bliss.

We made quite the pair—both of us craving connection like water in the desert. Only I couldn't afford to let Copper's friendly manners slip, even a tiny bit. He was still a stallion, and this was April—the time of year when even the best-mannered studs tend to lose their marbles. Too much rode on this show going perfectly, and with Cody trusting me to help season one of his best horses... well, I wasn't taking any chances. Copper had to mind his manners.

As I hefted the saddle pad and custom leather onto his back, Cole trudged back from the wash rack with a soggy Lynx in tow, his patented scowl dug deep. I paused to offer congratulations on surviving their trial by fire, but Copper chose that moment to wheel and nip affectionately at my hat.

"Copper!" I gasped, jerking away with a frown. The stallion snapped upright, clearly shocked by my sharp tone. Behind him, Cole shook his head and led Lynx on with an exaggerated eye roll.

Heat flooded my cheeks. Now Cole would think that single nip meant Copper was getting dangerous or disrespectful. And there

wasn't time before our class to clarify that the sweet stallion simply
forgot himself for a moment. We'd school a little harder on his ground
manners. I wanted to rub his nose in apology for snapping at him, but
that was the last thing I should do to discourage him from getting a
little too friendly.

"You're okay," I murmured. "We got this." Cole's disgust still net-
tled, but I shoved it roughly aside. Champions rode for themselves and
their horses—not to please bitter critics. And that was what I aimed
to be—a champion. I had the best coach in the country and, in my
opinion, the best colt this side of anywhere. It was just a matter of time.

Chapter Two

Cole

The sun was slanting low and blinding me as I pulled the trailer into the driveway at Walker Ranch. I'd drawn the short straw, so I got stuck with the whole nine-hour drive home by myself with the second trailer, while Cody and Emily tag-teamed driving the first. That was fine by me. I wasn't much in the mood for chatter.

Cody whipped his trailer around in the parking area and backed it up to be unloaded, and once he was clear, I turned around and backed my rig in beside him. I'd hardly put the truck in park when I saw Emily popping open the rear door of the trailer to start unloading horses. I snorted as I grabbed my hat and got out. Figured, she'd run to unload her precious Copper first.

The trailer I was hauling was a little smaller than the main Walker Ranch show trailer. It was still set up with a living quarters in front—Emily stayed there when we were at the shows—but it only had space for three horses. We tended to haul the stallions in that trailer, since there were only two of them in our show string at the moment. That way, they didn't have to stand beside any mares on the road.

That meant Lynx was in the trailer Cody had just parked, so I crossed over to help Cody unload that bunch. He was just walking off with a handsome chestnut mare when I got to the door, leaving my girl as the next one to unload. I stepped up to unlatch the divider and rested a hand on Lynx's hip before I swung it open.

"Easy, sweetheart," I soothed. "Don't get in a hurry this time."

As I latched the trailer divider out of the way and reached for her halter rope, the bay filly bunched her muscles, looking like she was ready to rush backward out of the trailer like she used to do when we first started taking her places. But I smoothed a hand over her back and she paused, then sighed and dropped her head, letting me guide her.

"Good girl," I praised her. "You might just turn into a civil lady someday." Not that I minded the fact that she was half wild hare. I kinda liked her that way, really. But nobody likes a horse that panics in the trailer.

As Lynx backed down the ramp, my gaze crossed the yard toward the stables. Emily was already heading back for another horse, and she glanced over to see who still needed to be unloaded. As soon as her eyes hit mine, she jerked them away and made a beeline for the other trailer to unload Rust.

I huffed and shook my head. Good grief, she couldn't even look at me. I mean, it wasn't like we were great friends or anything, but it was getting weird how she'd been avoiding me since yesterday's class at the show. We'd been perfect bookends—she and Copper won, and Lynx and I ended up way at the bottom. She must've figured the loser would rub off if she talked to me or something.

Lynx's feet hit the gravel and I let her take a second to look around and figure out where she was. She had these subtle little tells, funny quirks that the other horses in the Walker Ranch show string didn't have. She liked it when I waited for her, and sometimes needed a minute to chew on things before I gave her something else to think about. I'd learned quick enough that if I just gave her that extra second or two, she was happier and more composed. She'd never be like Copper the Golden Boy, who always seemed ready to roll with whatever anyone asked of him, but she could fake it alright.

"Ready, girl?" I turned her toward the stables, letting the leadrope swing easily between us until Cody came out of the barn aisle, stopping me up short.

"I'll bed her down," he said, holding out his hand for Lynx's rope. "Why don't you head on home?"

I blinked, and my stomach clenched. "I got this."

Cody sighed and pushed his hat up his forehead a little to give me a long look. "I'm pretty sure they need you back home. Evan and Marshall can get the feed and gear unloaded, and the stalls are already ready for the horses. Get on home before it gets much later."

I clenched my jaw, but I let Lynx's leadrope slide through my hand as Cody tugged it from me. "I'm fired? Look, Boss, if it's about that class—I screwed up, alright? I know I—"

He held up a hand. "You're not fired, Cole. But you need a break—need to get your head space right. I never should've let yesterday happen. Neither one of you were ready."

Well, that was hard to argue with. Except I hadn't figured it for Cody's fault. No, that honor was all mine. I swallowed and stared at my boots. "I'll be early tomorrow. Got some ground to make up, some things to fix and—"

"You're not listening to me," he interrupted. "You're not coming to work tomorrow. I'm turning Lynx out with the broodmares for a few days, just to let her relax for a bit, and you're staying away, too. If you're going to train horses, Cole, you need to learn when to back off."

He turned away, leading Lynx, and I just stood there gaping after him like a fish out of water. "So... Wednesday?" I called after him.

"No. I'll let you know," was all he said.

Well, that... I sniffed and stuffed my hands in my pockets. That kind of felt a lot like being fired. He really wouldn't even let me rub down "my" horse and put her gear away? Just gave me the boot the minute we got home? I scuffed my feet on the concrete of the aisle as I turned around. There wasn't much else to do but get my crap out of the truck and trailer and...

My head came up just then as Emily led Rust by me. The stallion's deep mahogany coat glowed in the setting sun as he walked past, and he had eyes only for his stall. Never even glanced my way.

And neither did Emily. She *had* to have heard Cody telling me to leave and not come back. My head swiveled as she walked on, but all she gave me a view of was her intensely curly blonde hair spilling out of the back of her ball cap, and the sway of her hips as she marched down the barn aisle.

Served me right, I guess. What made me think I could play with the big dogs on my first out? It just... well, it'd be nice if I didn't have to be humiliated in front of the most beautiful girl in town. But what did it matter? Not like she noticed me, anyway.

Emily

"What's the matter with Cole?" I asked casually as I clipped the latch on Rust's stall.

Cody stopped, peering inside at his champion horse and not looking at me. "Nothing. I just sent him home, is all."

I glanced at my boss with a question in my eyes, but he either didn't see it or chose to ignore it. I cleared my throat. "The, uhm... the chores...? Cole usually helps put stuff away."

"What's not already done will get done tomorrow. He needed to go home, and so do you."

What I *needed* to do was finish my job. I swallowed and drummed my fingers on the edge of Rust's stall, trying to think of something nice to say. "I guess Cole had a pretty rough ride yesterday."

"He wouldn't be the first." Cody thinned his lips and moved away, taking his hat off and dusting it against his jeans. "I'm heading home."

"Tell Morgan and Nikki hi for me," I said.

Cody's only reply was a grunt and a wave of his hand, but his steps quickened as he left the barn aisle. I couldn't blame him. If I were him, I'd want to get home to my wife and baby daughter, too. But all I had to look forward to was my busybody mom, who was probably not even home from work yet. Or if she was, she'd brought work home with her.

Yeah, I didn't mind staying a little longer.

Cody was right about chores. It looked like Lizzy and Dustin—Meg and Audrey's kids—had already been through the barn, bedding down all the show horses' stalls, giving the water buckets a fresh scrub and leaving neat little piles of horse treats in the feed bins for each of them. The tack could sit in the trailer overnight, and the barn was already quiet. There wasn't much for me to work on. So, I did what I always did when I wasn't sure what to do with myself. I slipped into Copper's stall and leaned against the door, just watching him eat.

This was where I found the room to breathe—just "my" horse and me, inhabiting the same space, letting the peace of the moment soak into my soul. The steady munching sounds of him working through his pile of hay, the soft earthy aromas of horse and fresh shavings and sweet alfalfa... I closed my eyes and let my chest rise and fall in a deep sigh.

Copper wasn't one to let himself be admired in silence, though. After a moment, he pulled his head out of the feed bin and wandered over to me, one of his ears half-cocked and his eyes soft and mellow.

"Hey there, you big lug," I murmured, giving that floppy ear an affectionate tug. He leaned his head into my hand, enjoying the little ear massage... and then he sneezed all over me.

"Thanks a lot." I grimaced, trying to brush off my shirt. Didn't do much good. Copper stretched out his chin, finding the palm of my hand and begging me to scratch his jaw and throat. He really was nothing but an overgrown cheeseball, and I never could resist his goofy ploys for attention.

After a few minutes, though, he went back to his hay, leaving me to just lean against the wall with my arms crossed. I watched him for a little while longer, but it was clear that the stallion was relishing his dinner, and I was just hanging out for nothing. "Well..." I sighed and opened the door. "See you tomorrow, buddy."

He just sneezed into his hay and kept eating.

By the time I got into my car, the sun had long since slipped behind the mountains. It was a fifteen-minute drive into town, which was just long enough for the last of the weekend's adrenaline to wear off and the bone-weary exhaustion to sink in. I dragged myself up the steps into the cozy little apartment above my mom's clothing resale shop on rubbery legs.

My first instinct was to faceplant on my bed fully clothed, shut out the world, and will the jumble of messy feelings from the Reno show to fade. But Mom would be waiting up, bursting to hear every detail about our wins. The thought of her bubbly pride in my growing success bolstered my last heavy steps toward the door, and I jangled my keys in my hand as I turned the knob.

"There she is!" Mom dropped an armload of funky scarves and flew at me, almost bowling me backwards in a giddy hug. She smelled like her signature lily of the valley perfume laced with dust. I laughed and returned the squeeze.

"You act like I've been gone for months! It was just the weekend."

Mom held me at arm's length, mock pouting as she surveyed my flushed face. "Well, forgive a mother for missing the company of her only chick still in the nest. And after your big win too!" She twinkled, tugging me toward the oversized paisley loveseat wedged between a rack of beaded cardigans and an antique side table. "Come, sit down and tell me about your show."

"Where?" I glanced at the loveseat and scooped up a pile of newly tagged t-shirts. It looked like Mom had brought her new aquisitions upstairs again to wash, iron, and price before she hung them up in her shop tomorrow. She always did that, even though she had a perfectly fine work area in the back of the shop. She said she liked being there when I came home, but what it really meant was that our apartment was always cluttered with second-hand clothes and boxes of household goods that didn't belong to us.

I wedged myself into the loveseat and Mom plopped down beside me, a wad of scarves still bunched in her lap. "I want to hear all about Cowboy and his blue ribbons! How'd our golden boy do?"

I smiled wryly, patting her hand. "Copper, Mom. The horse's name is Copper."

"Oh, potatoes, potahtoes!" She waved airily, too keyed up to sit. "You know I can barely keep all those ranch names straight. The important thing is, my baby girl wowed those California judges again!"

If only the success *had* been in California, land of movie stars and Rodeo Drive. Last weekend had been little more than an early spring schooling show in northern Nevada, but I didn't correct her. "Copper did great, yeah. He's such a natural in the show pen."

"Because he has a great trainer," Mom insisted. "Cody didn't put you in charge of the ranch's best horse for nothing."

I cracked a thin smile. Cody had his reasons for letting me train and show Copper, alright, but they weren't reasons Mom would understand. "Sure. Hey, mind if I hit the shower? I'm beat."

"Oh! Of course. I made cinnamon rolls for when you're done."

I pushed up from the loveseat, dodging a tower of folded jeans that were perched precariously on the armrest. "Thanks, Mom, but I just want to crash."

"Not until you message your sister. She's been trying to reach you for days." Mom plucked up the top scarf from her stack and started to fold it again. "She said she was starting to think you were in a car wreck or something."

I sighed and rolled my neck. "I'll shoot her a text. Good night, Mom. Love you."

I trudged slowly toward the bathroom for a quick shower, tugging my phone from my pocket to finally answer Lauren's flood of unanswered messages.

"Sorry I didn't answer. Busy weekend. Call you tomorrow."

I tossed the phone on the bathroom counter and stripped down, then stepped under the stream of hot water. As I lathered the travel grit away, I practiced my sunniest voice. Mom wasn't going to let me off that easily. No, no, tomorrow morning, she'd corner me at the breakfast table and demand to know all about how wonderful Copper was, see the pictures and videos from the show, and ask how "that nice young Langton boy" was doing.

Cole Langton was the last person I wanted to talk about right now. He was... ugh, he was maddening, that was what he was. He couldn't even be gracious when he had a victory—which wasn't all that often—and he was surly as an old cuss when he was losing. The most civil conversation we'd had in the last two years of working on the same ranch was, "Hey, did you feed the weanlings yet?" followed by "No, it's your turn."

Yeah. We weren't friends, and were never going to be.

Which was a shame, because he was kind of cute. If a girl liked guys who growled more than they smiled and had that lean, chiseled look of a working cowboy. But who would like that?

I ducked my head under the water to try to mat down my frizzy hair and blot out all thoughts of grouchy cowboys. This weekend, I'd brought home a victory for Walker Ranch and added some laurels to Copper's resume, as well as mine. That was enough to camp on for one evening. The rest could wait for tomorrow.

Chapter Three

Cole

The truck's tires crunched on the familiar gravel as I pulled into Ridgeview Ranch. Home sweet home, where at least the cows didn't challenge my horse and the horses didn't expect me to be some kind of prodigy. I huffed a sigh and killed the engine, letting my forehead thunk against the steering wheel.

Through the windshield, I spotted Gage hefting hay bales onto the flatbed. He glanced up at the sound of my arrival, tossed me a nod, and kept right on working. Typical Gage—more grunt than gab. Fine by me. Last thing I wanted was to jaw about Reno.

I climbed out and grabbed my duffel bag full of dirty clothes. And, of course, I hadn't zipped the bag, so half of them had spilled all over the floor. I started stuffing them back inside, and it wasn't long before a second set of footsteps scuffed up—lighter than my brothers', but just as purposeful.

"Well, hey there, stranger!" Mom's voice lilted across the dusty lot, edged with her signature don't-you-dare-try-to-dodge-me tone. "How was the show?"

Dang. No escaping the post-game recap. I focused real hard on the zipper and tried for casual. "Oh, you know. Typical show. Lots of hurry up and wait."

Silence stretched a beat too long. I could feel Mom's eyes drilling through my skull, sussing out all I wasn't saying. Before she could pry loose the gory details, the thud of hooves spared me.

Trent and some brunette I didn't know rode into the driveway, horses lathered like they'd put in a solid day's work. Mom gave me a single pat on the shoulder and that smile that was more threat than promise—the one that said, "We'll talk later." She headed back toward the house as Trent pulled up. He swung down easy and looped an arm around the girl's waist soon as her boots hit dirt.

"Cole, hey! Meet Cassie."

I tipped my hat, then shot a questioning glance back at my brother. Where had he dug this one up?

"You missed the high school rodeo finals over in Pocatello last weekend," he said, all cocky and cheerful. "Cassie here was the outgoing Queen, so she had to buzz the arena carrying the American flag, and, uh..." Trent winked. "Her horse threw a shoe."

I turned back around to keep stuffing loose clothes into my duffel bag before this girl accidentally got a view of my dirty socks all over the place. "Good thing you were there to rescue her, I guess," I mumbled.

"Sure was. Cassie, this is my little brother, Cole. Don't mind him, he's usually a surly cuss when he's had a bad day."

I growled at Trent one more time but tipped my hat at Cassie again and mumbled something halfway polite. I wasn't in much of a mood for pleasantries, with my cheeks still burning from Reno. The way Trent grinned like a fool at this girl he'd just met only added coal on the flames. She wasn't holding back, either.

I wished like crazy that someday, some girl would look at me like Cassie was mooning at Trent.

"Where've you been?" I asked, nodding toward his sweaty horse.

"Just showing Cassie the northern pasture, but while we were out there, we found a hole in the fence and had to run about fifty pairs back in. Chase just went out there with his truck and some tools to fix it. Could probably use your help 'fore dark if you want to ride out. I was going to, but..." Trent grinned and adjusted his arm around Cassie's waist.

"Maybe."

That was a lie. All I wanted to do was sink into a chair and pound some dinner leftovers. Chase probably already ate, but my stomach was starting to sing a chorus. I zipped my duffel bag and swung it over my shoulder, but as I glanced up at the house, I changed my mind. Mom would be in there waiting for me, and with no one else inside to deflect her questions...

I dropped my duffel bag. "Guess I'm on it. Be good to put some elbow grease in anyway, after sitting in a truck all day." Work might not cure all ills, but it sure beat words.

"Thanks, Cole!" Trent grinned and was already turning for the barn, eager to show our place off to his new girl. The sound of her giggles was almost louder than my pickup when I started it back up to roll toward the pasture.

I found Chase wrestling with a stubborn fence post, sweat dripping down his face as he strained to get it level. He had a splintered rail propped beside him and a sledgehammer in hand, looking fit to take out his frustrations on the first thing that moved wrong. Perfect setup.

I killed the engine a good ways back and coasted in quiet, parking where Chase was too busy to notice. Then I crept up behind him, making sure to stay out of swinging range. One little blow to tickle his right ear... I leaned in, my lips puckered to breathe down his neck. "*Cha-ase*," I whispered right under his hat.

"Jumpin' Jehoshaphat!" Chase lurched so hard he fumbled the hammer, nearly clocking himself in the shin before he caught it. I was too busy clutching my sides to help, tears near streaming, I was laughing so hard.

"Cole, you hare-brained..." He chucked a dirt clod at my leg, but he was grinning, too. "Here, make yourself useful 'fore I tan your hide."

"What makes you think I came out here to help you?"

"Because if you don't, I'll use this hammer on your head, where it might do some good. Go pound in that stake over there so I can set the cross braces."

He tossed me a spare mallet and pointed to the two-by-four he was getting ready to screw into his new post. The other end would be screwed into the ground stake after the new fence post was leveled, and then Cole would drop a bag of concrete down into the hole to set the thing. One guy could get it done on his own, but two made it go so much faster.

I took the mallet and set to work, and once I had it in the ground, I went back for the screw gun. "Ready?" I asked.

Chase held the level up to his fence post and gave it a slight nudge. "Not quite... okay, now."

I bent down and screwed the two-by-four into the ground stake, then stood back and watched Chase tweak the post.

"You moved it," he complained, squinting at his level as he held it against the post.

"And cows can't tell if that thing is plumb straight or not. It'll hold the fence just fine. Go get your concrete bag and call it good."

"No, I still have to get it straight in the other direction." Chase set his level down and propped up another two-by-four, this one jutting out at ninety degrees from the first one.

"Oh, good grief. We're going to be here all night. Set that post, and move on! I've been on the road all day, and I'm hungry."

"I'm not going to just slap something up," he grumbled. "This is how Dad always did the fences, and every fence he built still looks great."

"Except the one you're fixing right now," I pointed out.

"Yeah, and you know why? Because Gage and Trent originally put this line up. They did a crap job of it, too. Only lasted five years. Go screw that other stake to the two-by-four."

I sighed and trudged over to the other side of the post, grumbling all the way. Still, it did feel dang good to be putting back something solid after letting Lynx down. At least there was *something* I was good at, even if all it was was helping my brother level a fence post.

Finally, Chase was satisfied. Or, at least he didn't object when I went to the back of his truck and just grabbed a bag of concrete mix to dump into the hole. This was how Dad always built his posts—no mixing water in, because the moisture from the ground would set this concrete on its own, and Chase would come back out tomorrow or the next day to remove those stakes holding the post level. It was definitely the slow way to build a fence, but Chase wasn't the guy to hurry a job well done. And I knew better by now than to fight it.

"Not bad," Chase allowed as we stepped back. He wiped his brow and squinted at me, easy smile fading to something more searching. "So. Gonna make me dig out how those fancy judges treated my little brother last weekend?"

I winced inwardly. Reno was still scraping raw across my ego and apparently showed plain on my face. "They're just like all the others,"

I muttered, kicking a stray pebble. "And couldn't tell their rear ends from an oakum bucket far as scoring goes."

Well, okay, that wasn't *entirely* the truth, but it sounded good, especially when you figure who I was talking to. It wasn't exactly my best showing, but I still couldn't figure what Copper had over Lynx. I mean... you know, besides the fact that he stayed calm and did his job in the show ring. Lynx was pure athleticism—she'd work circles around that lazy golden boy in a heartbeat, just as soon as she had a little more time to settle in.

But it wasn't just Lynx. She might not be ready for the prime time, but plenty of other horses last weekend were. And yet, those judges had sure picked Emily and Copper to drape in glory while I slunk out the back with my hat pulled low. Not that Emily wasn't pure grace on a horse... I had to close my eyes, and my mouth felt like cotton when I let the mental image hit me again. Her slim posture in the saddle, the way her hands played the reins like a sweet violin, and her waist would twist just so as she worked with her horse's movement...

I cleared my throat and blinked the stars out of my eyes. Being pretty as all get-out doesn't make a someone good horse trainer, but for some reason, everyone figured she had both going for her. Bloody unfair.

Chase's low whistle jarred me from my bitter spiral. "Not good, huh?"

I shook my head a little. "What?"

"The show. Reno." He snapped his fingers in front of my face. "Pasture, fence post... do you even know where you are?"

"Yeah. Yeah, I was just... thinkin'."

"Not about something good. And from the look on your face, you don't want to talk about it."

I shrugged. "Not really."

His voice was soft with something too close to pity for my pin-pricked pride. He slung an arm around my shoulder and gave me a bracing jostle. "Hey, we've all been there. 'Member when Gage tried his hand at bulldoggin'? Nearly got his leg broke bad enough Mom woulda gelded him. But he went right back out soon as—"

The roar of Gage's beat-up diesel cut him off. My eldest brother pulled up alongside our handiwork and leaned out the window, one arm propped on the door.

"Quit twiddlin' and get a move on 'fore the grub gets cold. Mom's putting supper on the table."

I shared a grin with Chase. Gage was a lot of things—strong, stoic, one heck of a roper. But verbose wasn't in his wheelhouse. "Fine by me." I popped open the door of my own truck and started it up before he could ask any prying questions.

Soon as we hit the house, the aroma of mama's famous pulled pork hooked my nose and reeled me through the front door. She was setting out her welcome home spread—coleslaw, mashed taters dripping with butter, and piles of that tender, smoky pork. My absolute, number one favorite.

The whole clan was circled up—Trent and Cassie all googly down at one end, Chase wedged in beside Gage and across from me, and a space left open between us for Mom. Like always.

Things hadn't changed much in the last three years, if you didn't count the occasional girl one of my brothers would bring home to dinner. But none of them ever stuck around too long, a fact that got Mom's hackles up from time to time. "I don't understand it," she'd say whenever one of us broke up with (or got dumped by) his latest flame. "Y'all are handsome, you take showers, and your daddy taught you to get a girl's door. You're not getting any younger, you know, and I want grandbabies!"

She was mostly kidding, but not completely. Gage was twenty-eight, after all, and the rest of us—Trent, Chase, and me, in order—were all spread out in two-year intervals. You'd think one of us would've got leg shackled by now, but it hadn't happened yet.

Conversation flowed between bites, jokes, and jabs bouncing across the table. If Cassie's laugh pierced my eardrums once or twice, I masked my wince with a long swig of Mom's sweet tea. Sounded like she knew something about horses, which was handy, but her rapid-fire questions about everything from cattle counts to tractor engines got old fast. Probably because I was in a mood, but I made myself a little private bet that she'd be out of here as soon as she got her first taste of real work. Not too many of the girls we'd ever met could hack it. Still, the sparkle in Trent's eyes said he aimed to let her try.

Mom was being super nice, trying to ask Cassie all kinds of questions about herself and managing not to let her eyes glaze over when Cassie answered. Chase and Gage kept it interesting, though, regaling her with sanitized tales from our rougher years. Gage even roused himself to talk through his infamous near-miss wrangling a half-wild bull, a story that always made Mom go a little red in the face.

Soon as dinner wound down, I hopped up quick to clear plates, eager to escape before talk turned back to Reno and all I couldn't bear reliving just yet. But Mama caught my eye over the stack of dishes thrust in my hands.

"Put those down and give me a hand with dessert," she ordered, sweet but steely under the smile.

My stomach bottomed out. No mistaking what that meant—one-on-one time. I trailed her to the kitchen, defeat dogging my steps. She waited until the door swung shut, then leaned back against the sink and pinned me with the full wattage of her Mother Knows look.

"Alright, out with it. No point keeping all that disappointment bottled up tighter than a ticked-off rattler. What happened this time?"

Dang, but moms had a knack for prying straight to the sore spots. I slouched against the fridge, sighing heavy as all my frustration came bleeding out.

"I tanked, Mama. Let Lynx down when it mattered. Asked too hard, couldn't keep steady. She's likely ruined on shows now, all 'cause of me. And Emily..." I broke off, hating how the next words tasted. "Let's just say she proved her star ain't fadin' anytime soon."

"Oh, Cole. That's tough to swallow, no mistake. But one stumble don't break the race."

She pushed off and crossed to me, laying one work-worn hand on my cheek. I leaned into her touch like a little kid, eyes stinging.

"Folks 'round here believe in you, son. Your brothers, me, that fancy trainer of yours. We know you're up to it. You've put your time in, proved you're serious. And now that you finally get a chance to get out more, are you gonna let one misstep steal that?"

I swallowed hard. Put like that, I sounded like a right fool for letting Reno cloud out everything Cody and the Walkers had invested in me. For forgetting the faith of the people gathered just in the other room to welcome me home.

Slowly, I shook my head. "No, ma'am."

"Atta boy." She gave my cheek a pat and turned for the cobbler cooling on the stove. "Now, best you serve this up 'fore Gage comes looking and finds us both blubbering in here."

My laugh was more sniffle than humor, but I mustered up a grin as I took the laden tray. "Can't have that. Man might string more'n two words together from the shock."

Chapter Four

Emily

I wrapped the towel around my head as I padded into my room. All I wanted to do was close my eyes and escape to sweet oblivion, but I couldn't put off calling Lauren any longer. There was already an answer to my text waiting when I got out of the shower, and she'd never let me hear the end of it if I didn't call her.

I just didn't think Lauren quite understood what it meant to get up at four-thirty in the morning. She definitely didn't understand how wrung-out physical fatigue could actually feel good, or how I didn't need an hour of boring TV shows to put me to sleep at the end of the day.

Settling onto my bed, I dialed Lauren's number and waited, the phone pressed to my ear. She picked up on the second ring.

"Em! So, you *are* alive. I was starting to think you'd fallen off the face of the earth!"

"I'm so sorry, Laur," I sighed as I kicked back on top of the covers. "The show was crazy busy. We hauled eight horses to Reno—some of them were just there for the experience, and they needed extra exercise, plus all the chores... I can't usually just get away."

"It's okay, I get it. But next time, a little more than a cryptic text assuring me that you aren't stranded in the middle of the road somewhere would be nice. So, tell me about the show! How did you and Copper do?"

I grinned into the phone. "Copper was amazing, as usual. We had some really solid runs and brought home a few ribbons."

"That's fantastic, Em! I'm so proud of you," Lauren gushed. "So, what's next?"

"What's next?" I propped up a little on the pillow, scrunching my wet hair so it would dry in manageable ringlets rather than staticky frizz the next day. "More work, that's what's next. More training, some extra schooling runs because Copper was starting to anticipate the cow. Then we have another show in two weeks, and—"

"No, I mean, 'what's *next*?' Like, is he famous now? How long will it take? Are you getting offers to work for the really big stables in Texas?"

I chuckled and found a sock to tug onto one of my feet while I held the phone against my shoulder with my cheek. "Oh. Good grief, no. Copper's hardly more than an upstart, and I'm even less than that. I'll be lucky if those big places even hear my name in the next ten years, let alone want to hire me to lope their colts around for them."

"Oh, come on. You always did sell yourself short. What about the horse? Mom says everyone reckons he's something special."

I shrugged at the wall. "He is... to me, at least. Copper has a couple of seasons to prove himself, I guess, before he's pigeon-holed beyond any hope of greatness."

Lauren snorted. "What does that mean?"

I rolled my eyes up to the ceiling and flopped a corner of the covers over myself. "Never mind. Hey, how's the new job? You get all mad when I don't tell you anything, but I hardly even know who you work for."

"Biggs, Carson, & Walls, Incorporated," she recited robotically. "That's how I have to answer the phone."

"What, they've got you answering phones now? I thought you managed their PR."

"Which basically amounts to keeping their social media updated and filling in for the executive secretary whenever she decides to leave early for the day. Which is like every day lately."

"Aw. You'll get your big shot one of these days. I bet a Fortune 500 Company already has their eye on you. How's Dad?"

"Same as always. He took me out to lunch yesterday, but I don't see him much."

I fingered the fraying corners of my quilt and frowned. "And Sandy?"

Lauren coughed. "You mean besides spending all his money on cosmetic surgery? Best if Dad and I don't talk about Sandy. We just fight."

I sighed, but I couldn't help a little smile. Lauren was no more of a fan of Dad's girlfriend than I was. "Sorry."

"Ah, don't worry about it. Hey, speaking of fighting, what about that Cole guy you work with? How did he do last weekend?"

My smile faded, and I let out a heavy sigh. "Not great. He had a rough go with his horse. And he's been in a mood ever since, barely acknowledging anyone, especially me."

"What, like it's your fault that he messed up?"

"He didn't really 'mess up,'" I found myself arguing—no idea why, though. "I mean, yeah, he made mistakes, but some of it was just that Lynx is really fresh and needs some seasoning."

"Tell me you would've had the same problems with that same horse."

"Of course I wouldn't h..." I blinked and clamped my teeth shut for a second before an evasive answer popped out of my mouth. "Well, it doesn't matter. Lynx isn't my style of horse."

"Whatever. You don't need to defend him, Em. It's not your fault he had a bad go and it's not your fault he's not talking to you."

"I know that," I mumbled, picking at a longer thread that was working loose from the edge of the quilt. "I'm not taking it personally."

"Uh huh."

"I'm *not*. I just wish it didn't make things uncomfortable on the ranch."

"I can imagine. But hey, enough about ranch drama. Tell me, when are you coming to visit me in San Diego? I miss my little sister!"

I blew out a huff as I flopped back on the pillow. "I don't know. My calendar's stacked with shows until like November. Any weekends we aren't gone to a show, they're doing stuff on the ranch, and—"

"So, what, you work there nonstop? Even the kids flipping burgers at the fast food joint get a day off now and then."

"They don't have a thousand animals to keep alive," I shot back.

"Neither do you. You just work there, remember?"

I chewed the inside of my lip. She was right... I had to keep reminding myself of that. But there was something about all the work and worry and the hard-won splendor of life on a cattle ranch that felt so *right* to me that it didn't seem possible to walk away at the end of the day, letting the rest fall on the Walkers' shoulders. I had to do my part, right?

I sighed and forced a smile onto my face, because Lauren would hear it if I was frowning. "Sure. Hey, you must have some more interesting stories than I have. Did you ever eat at that new sushi place you told me about? And what about that guy from work you said you were going to go out with... David, right?"

There was a weak chuckle from the other end. "Let's just say both are on the 'do not repeat' list."

"Ouch. I thought he was a nice one."

"Yeah... nice to everybody... and I do mean *every*body."

"Oh, I'm sorry, Lauren. If it makes you feel any better, you're still ahead of me by like... a thousand."

She laughed. "Only because of population ratios. None of these guys would even look at me if my gorgeous sister were here. I'm serious, I need you all to myself for at least a weekend. Schedule it!"

"I'll try," I promised. "I might be able to get out there in late June for a couple of days."

"You'd better! We'll hit the beach, drink overpriced cocktails, and forget all about stubborn cowboys and unruly horses for a weekend."

We said our goodnights, and I hung up feeling both comforted and a little melancholy. Lauren and I might lead different lives, but she'd always be there to lend an ear and a word of encouragement when I needed it most.

Setting my phone on the nightstand, I burrowed under the covers. And I didn't remember anything else until my alarm went off at four-thirty the next morning.

"Again. This time, soften your hands."

I dropped the reins on Copper's neck and stretched my fingers out as Cody reset the training flag. "My hands *were* soft. It's him. He's jerking into the turn before I'm even ready."

"And just like before, you're either letting him do it and not making him wait for you, or you're setting him down too hard and just making him mad. Slow your mind down."

I blew out a shaky breath and gathered up my reins again. "Okay," I muttered to the young stallion. "Wait for me this time, will you?"

Copper's ears swiveled and then locked on the training flag. It was set up on a pulley line to run back and forth down the arena fence, and Cody was holding a remote control to make it stop, reverse, and change speeds. It wasn't exactly like working a real cow, but it was really useful for teaching Copper how to use his body correctly. We could go as slowly as he needed to while we built that muscle memory into him.

Except today, "slow" was the last thing on my horse's mind.

The flag moved to the left, and Copper lurched and wheeled after it before I even had a chance to get him balanced right.

"Right leg!" Cody called. "If he does that with a real cow, he'll lose it!"

"I'm *trying*!" I gritted out. "You didn't warn me at all!"

"I shouldn't have to warn you. You have to be a step or two ahead of your horse."

The flag stopped, and Copper slid to a nice, balanced stop parallel to it, his nostrils twitching as he waited for it to move again. Oh, he loved this game. That was actually why I was having so much trouble with him today. He just wanted to chase the flag and forget that he was supposed to be listening to me at the same time.

I gathered the reins softly, asking him to rock his weight back over his haunches this time, rather than just lurching forward into an ugly, uncontrolled rush. The next turn was better—he was on the correct line, and he didn't have to scramble so hard to get into position. It was actually easier for him, and I felt him yield to my cues a little better.

But when the flag changed direction again, it all fell apart.

"Always to the left," Cody said as he flicked the motor off.

"Yeah, I know. I can't figure it out!" I risked a glance back at my boss, but all I could see in the shade of his cowboy hat was a cryptic smile.

"You can't, huh?" Cody dropped the flag remote into his pocket and turned his attention to the young horse he was schooling today. He didn't say anything more to me for several minutes as he patiently walked the bay gelding in a few quiet circles.

"So?" I demanded at last.

Cody glanced up, almost as if he'd forgotten I was there. "So, go think about it. And cool off your horse while you're at it."

"Can I just have one more try?" I pleaded. "We just got started for the day, and I know I can get this right. Should I try a different bit? We just changed saddles on him, maybe this one doesn't fit him as well as we thought. What is it?"

"He's done for the day. Take him out to the field on a slack rein, let him relax for a bit before you put him away."

"Well... should I saddle Lynx next?" I asked. We had been home from the show for three days now, and the filly had just been turned out to pasture all that time. If she was going to the next show, shouldn't she be getting ready for it?

"You let me worry about Lynx. Get Copper out in the fields, and don't hurry back."

I bit back a retort and nodded, steering Copper out of the arena. What was that all about? And what was it my boss was refusing to tell me?

My shoulders slumped in frustration as I guided my horse through a gate and out toward the fields where a couple hundred cows grazed. Evan Walker was driving the tractor, and he waved at me in passing, but I couldn't summon much of a smile as I waved back.

Cody's coaching had become more frustrating lately. I couldn't put my finger on it. He kept making me guess things, expecting me to figure out stuff when it would be easier for him to just tell me what he was seeing. Wasn't that the whole point of riding under a master, someone who could teach you how to get better?

I growled under my breath and brushed a tangle of sweaty hair out of my eyes as a breeze kicked up. Copper was playing with the bit and trying to sneak bites of the tall grass as we waded through it. I just sank a little deeper into my seat and let my gaze scan the peaks in the distance. Somewhere between the rise of the foothill slopes and the back meadow pond, my pulse finally slowed, and I stopped being frustrated with my boss. That meant it was probably time to turn back and figure out what my next job for the day was.

As we rode through the lush pasture, I spotted Dusty and Luke Walker in the distance, checking on the herds. It seemed rare these days to find the brothers working together. Usually, they spread themselves a little thinner, either working with one of the hired hands or sometimes even with their wives. I waved at them, but I didn't plan to stop until I heard one of them shout back at me.

"Emily!" Luke called. "Hey, do you have a minute?"

I turned Copper toward them and nudged him into a little jog. "What's up?"

Dusty was coiling his rope and trailing behind Luke as they turned their horses toward me. Luke looked more urgent, jogging to meet me. "Boy, are you a Godsend. Has Cody got you working colts this afternoon?"

I shook my head. "Beats me. He just told me to take my time cooling Copper out, and he won't tell me what I'm supposed to do next."

"Good, because I need a favor. Audrey's stuck for someone to pick up Lizzy. She just got a call from the school, but she's in the middle of a tricky root canal."

I glanced at Dusty. Really, with all those Walkers around town, there wasn't someone to pick Lizzy up from school?

Dusty piped up. "I just called Jess, but she's tied up, too, and so is Kelli. I could go, but we were really trying to get this bunch moved today. If Cody doesn't have you doing something else, would you mind? I'll make Cody keep you on the clock and all."

I shrugged. "No, I don't mind. But what about Audrey? Doesn't she work at the school?"

Luke gave a chuckle and a cryptic smile. "Check your watch. It's only one-thirty."

Oh. I narrowed my eyes. "So... what you're saying is that Lizzy did something to get herself suspended. Again."

Luke cleared his throat. "Apple don't fall far from the tree, you know. I really appreciate it, Emily. Hey, don't go too hard on her, will you? Audrey will make up for it, I promise."

"Right." I lifted my reins and rolled Copper back over his hocks. "Tell Lizzy I'm on my way."

Chapter Five

Cole

I wiped the sweat from my brow as I made my way across the ranch. Summer sure did come out full force in the last week. And with it was usually plenty to do—set irrigation pipes for the hay fields, brand and sort the spring calves, move the herds out to our leased grazing lands.

But my mind wouldn't focus much on the ranch. My phone felt heavy in my pocket, and I found myself checking it every few minutes, hoping to see Cody's name flash across the screen. Nothing. Just silence and the sinking feeling that I'd ruined my shot at proving myself.

All I could do was try to clamp down on that doubt and get back to work. Except I wasn't sure where to start. Chase was mending a fence line, his strong hands deftly twisting the wire to the newly sunk posts. Said he didn't need any help. Trent was pushing a group of yearling calves to a new pasture, but he'd be finished by the time I even saddled a horse to go join him. And Gage, well, he was under the tractor changing the oil, and I knew better than to get in his way.

So, what did that leave for me? Everything I thought to do had already been done. By them. The ranch ran like a well-oiled machine, and I was just a spare part, not quite sure where I fit.

That was why I'd taken the job with Walker Ranch in the first place, really. I didn't hire on with the aim to become a horse trainer. I'd started with them to do the grunt work—hired muscle that wasn't really needed around Ridgeview. There just wasn't enough work—or enough money—to keep all four of us brothers employed at our family ranch. And being the youngest, well that left me as the most logical one to find work somewhere else.

So, when Blake Walker ran into my mom at the grocery store and said he wasn't going to go on the road with the show horses anymore, I landed the job as the guy who wrangled the heavy stuff. The guy who hauled hay and groomed horses and did the dirty work so the fancy Walker Ranch show horses and their riders could look their best.

But then, Cody had "seen something" in me.

Yeah, right. He'd just felt sorry for me, and wasted everyone's time.

I kicked at a loose rock and sent it zinging across the driveway, right into the white rail fence that ringed the front pasture. The fence that was peeling and sagging a lot more than I remembered.

I squinted and walked over to it, flaking a bit of paint off the top rail. The wood underneath felt squishy. When did that happen? Well, at least I knew what to do about it. I headed into the shop where we kept all the extra paint, but I only found one dried-up bucket. The scrap lumber pile was depleted, too. No way to fix the fence without a run to the hardware store. I frowned.

That's when I started to notice more little things—the things that had always been there but I'd never really seen. The sagging roofline of the old barn, the rust eating away at the hinges of the gate, the way the paint peeled off the house in strips, like wounded skin.

How had I missed it? The slow decay, the signs that our ranch wasn't thriving the way it used to. What in blazes had my brothers been up to this last year or better? Grumbling to myself, I found some grease for the gate hinges, as well as some rust sealant, but there wasn't much I could do about the way the rust was eating holes through the bottom part of the gate bars. As I returned the stuff to the tool shop, I happened to glance at the floor. It was dry now, but there was a stain on the ground about five feet across that proved the roof had leaked fairly recently.

What the...? How had *no one* fixed this? I'd just go have a word with Mom and see what had been happening this past year. I trudged back to the house, my stomach growling. Maybe I'd grab a sandwich while I was there.

I slipped in the back door, leaving it hanging open, and was halfway to the fridge when I heard it—the faint rustling of papers, the click of a pen. Mom was at the computer, her back to me, engrossed in what looked like a stack of bills. She was clicking away with her mouse on the screen, then she set the bill aside to reach for the next one in the stack. Then she froze.

I paused, watching her. The way her hand hesitated over a particular letter, the slight tremble in her fingers as she set it aside. Separate from the rest.

I swallowed hard, a sense of dread creeping up my spine. Should I say something? She didn't even know I was there yet. I crossed back to the door to close it, loud enough to make my presence known.

Mom startled, turning to face me with a smile that didn't quite reach her eyes. "Cole! I thought you were out with Chase, fixing fences."

I shook my head, the words heavy on my tongue. "He said he didn't need me and told me to go help Trent. But Trent only had a few head to move, since we sold half the stock last year."

The silence that followed was thick, uncomfortable. I watched as Mom's gaze drifted back to the letter, the one she'd tried to hide.

I stepped forward, blocking her view, forcing her to look at me. "Mom, are we in trouble?"

She took a deep breath, her shoulders sagging. Then, slowly, she reached for the letter and held it out to me. "You might as well know."

I unfolded the paper, my heart pounding as I scanned the words. It was from the Department of Fish and Wildlife, stating that the grazing lands we had leased from the state for the last twenty years had been identified as potential breeding grounds for the spotted owl. Meaning...

Meaning that Ridgeview Ranch had just been gutted when it was already down.

I clenched the letter in my fist, the gravity of the situation sinking in like a stone in my gut. We didn't have enough grazing land without it. We *depended* on that lease.

Mom laughed then, a rueful sound. "The spotted owl." She sighed. "I remember when Moyers lost their grazing rights over this. Your father was furious, tried to find a lawyer to help them argue the case, but there was nothing to be done."

"As if those hills aren't already full of deer and elk!" I snarled. "What do they think a few cows are going to do? The cows don't even go into the old-growth parts of the woods because there's no grazing there!"

Mom shook her head. "Cole, don't. You won't accomplish anything."

I threw a hand out in exasperation. "Why is this just now coming out? I thought our lands were cleared. We were supposed to be fine!"

"You know why. It's because of the fires two years ago. Lots of timber got destroyed. If I had to guess, I'd bet they don't even know what's going on with the owl population. They're just throwing out blanket statements right now."

I screwed my mouth into a scowl and fought to keep my voice steady. "What are we going to do?"

She sighed, pointing to a line in the letter. "It only says 'potential' breeding ground. They still have to send the game wardens out to evaluate."

I cut her off, the truth bitter on my tongue. "We both know how that's going to go. We'll lose our grazing rights, and with them, the whole bloody ranch."

Mom smiled weakly, nodding. Her eyes wandered then, taking in the walls of the house Dad had built for us, the home that held a lifetime of memories. I could see the fear in her eyes, the unspoken worry. I hadn't said anything that she wasn't already thinking.

We really might lose it all. The ranch, the house, everything.

I wanted to comfort her, to find the right words. But before I could speak, she straightened, her voice too bright. "Could you run into town for me? Pick up a few things? Since you're not working on anything else."

I recognized it for what it was—a distraction, a temporary escape from the heaviness in the room. And I was more than happy to oblige. At least it gave me *something* to do.

"Fine," I sighed, already walking to the hook by the door for my keys. "Just give me a list."

Emily

My eyes scanned the front walk of the middle school as I parked the car. I knew Lizzy Tracy pretty well by now. Her mom had died a couple of years back, leaving her to her aunt Audrey, who had married Luke Walker about that same time. And Lizzy and Luke were two peas in a pod. Everyone who worked on the ranch knew that if there was a crackpot scheme afoot, it was probably hatched by one of those two.

Which is why it was probably a good thing for Lizzy that she was going home to face Luke first, before Audrey Walker got home. He'd get her to at least *pretend* remorse over whatever she'd done so she wouldn't be in so much trouble with her aunt.

And there she was, sitting on the bottom step, her backpack at her feet and a smug grin on her face. I sighed. Yep, pretty typical.

"Hey, Emily!" Lizzy chirped as she climbed into the passenger seat, tossing her bag into the back. "Guess what? I won't have to go back to school for the rest of the summer!"

I blinked, taken aback by her nonchalant announcement. "What do you mean? School doesn't end for another week."

Lizzy's grin widened, a glint of mischief in her eyes. "Didn't you hear? I got suspended. And with only a week left, they won't bother having me come back until fall."

I rolled my eyes as I put the car into gear, trying to keep my tone neutral as I asked, "What did you do to get suspended this time?"

She crossed her arms, her demeanor suddenly defensive. "I wasn't the one who started it, you know. It was Robby Feldham."

I waited, just keeping my eyes on the road. "Uh-huh."

"He was picking on Dustin in the hallway, trying to pull his books out of his backpack and calling him names. You know how Dustin gets when he's upset, and Robby just wouldn't stop."

My heart clenched at the thought of sweet, gentle Dustin being bullied. He was autistic, and while he had made great strides in social interaction, he was still an easy target for cruel kids like Robby.

Lizzy continued, her voice laced with righteous indignation. "I couldn't just stand there and watch. Dustin's my cousin, even if it's just by marriage. I had to do something."

I braced myself, almost afraid to ask. "And what exactly did you do?"

Lizzy shrugged, a hint of satisfaction in her eyes. "I stuffed Robby's head into his locker. Then, I went straight to the principal's office and told them what happened. I know the drill by now."

I groaned inwardly, picturing the scene. Lizzy had her priorities right, I couldn't deny that. She was fiercely protective of Dustin, but her methods tended to be a bit... unorthodox.

"You should have seen Robbie's face when a *girl* grabbed him by the front of his shirt!" Lizzy hooted. "Hah! He doesn't know I've been bucking hay bales and helping doctor calves. Taking him down was *way* too easy."

"You, ah... you might not want to brag about that," I cautioned her.

"Oh, I won't. Not to Aunt Audrey, anyway, but I'll tell Luke. He'll give me a high five, I bet."

"He probably would," I muttered.

"Mrs Delaney won't let me come back until fall, that's for sure," Lizzy continued, sounding almost proud. Then, as if suddenly remembering something, she perked up. "Hey, can we stop and get Italian sodas on the way back to the ranch? Aunt Kelli says they just got a new flavor in. I'm buying."

I scoffed, incredulous at her audacity. "Lizzy, you're in trouble. You can't expect me to reward you with treats."

"But you're not my mom. Why should you care?" She pulled a few crumpled bills from her pocket, waving them in front of me. "I've got enough for both of us. And besides, I bet Uncle Luke already told you to go easy on me, didn't he? Aunt Audrey is going to give me an earful when I get home anyway. Might as well enjoy myself while I can."

I shook my head, torn between frustration and a grudging respect for her bravado. I was about to launch into a lecture on consequences when my phone buzzed with an incoming text.

It was from Cody. "Hey, Em. If you're still in town, can you swing by the hardware store and grab some more electrical tape before heading back? I didn't realize we were so low, and we need to re-braid some of these manes today."

I scowled at the screen, annoyed by the additional errand. I'd wanted to get on some more colts this afternoon, but it didn't look like that was happening. As if sensing my hesitation, Lizzy leaned over, reading the message.

"You know," she said slyly, "Kelli's Coffee Wagon is right there in the same parking lot as the hardware store. We could kill two birds with one stone. I won't tell anyone if you won't."

"Kelli would rat you out," I reminded her.

"No, she wouldn't. Kelli is awesome, and besides, she's probably not even at the Coffee Wagon right now. I bet she's at the ranch with Marshall and the baby. Come on, Emily!"

Lizzy wasn't going to let this go. Truth be told, a cold drink did sound pretty good right about now.

"Fine," I relented, putting on my turn signal. "We'll stop at the hardware store. But I'm going in alone, and if you happen to sneak out and buy a soda while I'm gone, that's not my responsibility."

Lizzy grinned, settling back into her seat with a satisfied air. "Works for me."

As we drove towards the other end of town, I couldn't shake the feeling that I'd just been played. But then again, that was Lizzy's specialty—finding the loopholes and exploiting them for all they were worth.

When we pulled into the hardware store parking lot, I spotted Kelli's bright yellow coffee wagon, its chalkboard menu promising a rainbow of Italian soda flavors. Lizzy was practically vibrating with excitement, her earlier transgressions seemingly forgotten in the face of sugary bliss.

I parked the car, turning to face my young charge. "Alright, here's the deal. I'm going into the store. I'll be back in ten minutes. If, during that time, you happen to acquire a soda by some means unknown to me, I won't ask questions. But," I held up a finger, my tone stern, "this is a one-time thing. And it doesn't change the fact that you're still in trouble when you get home."

Lizzy nodded solemnly, but I could see the glimmer of triumph in her eyes. "Got it. And, ah... what if two sodas should happen to make it back to the car? Should one of them be strawberry?"

I narrowed my eyes. "Make it a raspberry, and I'll drive extra slow on the way back to the ranch."

She grinned. "Deal."

I stepped into the cool, air-conditioned store and made my way to the electrical aisle, scanning the shelves for the specific type of tape Cody had requested. He liked the plain old black stuff, using it to tie off the long braids in the manes of the show horses because it didn't break the ends like a rubber band did. But it looked like they'd reorganized the shelves since I was here last, because I found just about every kind of electrical connector in the world except the stupid tape.

I didn't dare leave Lizzy unattended for too long. Who knew what kind of mischief she could get into, even in the few minutes I was inside? She'd already proved time again that she couldn't be trusted to supervise herself. Where was... *there!*

I spotted the tape and reached for it, and I was already headed for the cashier's desk when I collided with a solid form rounding the corner. Startled, I stumbled back, an apology already forming on my lips.

"I'm so sorry, I wasn't looking where I was going and—" I stopped short, realizing who I'd bumped into. "Cole?"

He looked flustered, his face redder than usual as he hurriedly stepped back, putting space between us. "Emily. Hey. Sorry about that."

He was looking down, avoiding my gaze, his hands shoved deep into his pockets as if he didn't trust them not to betray his discomfort. That was weird. When had he ever been too shy to stare me down? "No worries. I should have been paying more attention."

An awkward silence stretched between us, the hum of the old fluorescent lights suddenly deafening. I held up the pack of electrical tape, more to fill the void than anything else. "Cody sent me to grab some more of this."

Cole stared at me blankly for a moment as if the words weren't quite registering. Then, suddenly, recognition dawned on his face. "Right. Yeah. Tape. For the manes."

I glanced at his cart, taking in the can of paint, fencing wire, and paintbrush. "Fixing some fencing?" I asked, more to keep the conversation going than out of genuine curiosity.

He nodded, still not quite meeting my eyes. "Yeah. Just some repairs around the ranch."

I sensed there was more to it than that, but I didn't push. Cole and I hadn't spoken at all since the show in Reno, and we weren't great friends to begin with. "Well, I'd... I'd better get going." I started to move past him, ready to head to the checkout, when his voice stopped me.

"Hey, Emily?" I turned back, surprised by the note of uncertainty in his tone. "Has Cody... has he said anything about having me back out to work with the horses?"

My heart clenched at the raw hope in his eyes, the way his voice wavered just slightly. I wished I had better news for him. "I'm sorry, Cole. I don't know anything. Cody hasn't mentioned it to me."

His face fell, just for a moment, before he managed to shutter his expression. But in that brief instant, I caught a glimpse of something hungry and broken in his gaze, a desperation that tugged at my heartstrings.

He started to turn away, his shoulders slumping almost imperceptibly. Before I could stop myself, I blurted out, "It sounds like we're washing and braiding the show horses' manes this afternoon. It's a big job, you know—takes hours, and I'm sure Cody wouldn't mind having an extra set of hands."

Cole paused, his back still to me. For a long moment, he didn't respond, and I wondered if I'd overstepped. Then, slowly, he turned to face me, his eyes finally meeting mine.

"No. I don't think he wants me there." But I could see the glimmer of hope in his eyes, the way his fingers twitched at his sides as if itching to get back to work.

"I'll still ask. It goes a lot faster with another person there."

A flicker of a smile crossed his face, gone as quickly as it appeared. He tipped his hat, a gesture that felt strangely formal given the circumstances. "Thanks, I guess." With that, he turned and walked away, leaving me standing in the aisle, the pack of electrical tape clutched to my chest.

And for some reason I couldn't explain, I really, *really* hoped my boss would agree to bring that pain in the rear back to the ranch.

Chapter Six

Emily

I pulled the truck into the driveway at Walker Ranch, the freshly raked gravel popping under the tires. Lizzy sat beside me, still sucking down the last of her Italian soda like it was the best thing she'd tasted in her life. She kept stealing glances at me, trying to read my expression, but I kept my face neutral. Luke was standing out front, arms crossed, waiting for us. The minute he saw Lizzy, his brow furrowed.

"Got yourself in trouble again, huh?" he asked, trying to sound stern, but there was a hint of curiosity in his voice.

Lizzy shrugged, slurping up the last bit of her drink with a loud, unapologetic noise. "Wasn't my fault. Dustin was getting picked on."

Luke's expression softened, and I could see the stern facade slipping. "And what did you do about it?"

Lizzy's eyes sparkled with that mischievous glint she always got when she was proud of herself. "Shoved Robby's head in a locker."

I bit back a smile. Lizzy had guts, I'd give her that. And a fierce loyalty to her family that I couldn't help but admire. Just then, Evan walked up from the barn, his face as unreadable as ever. He was Dustin's stepfather, and I could tell he was interested in hearing what had gone down.

"What happened?" he asked.

Luke was trying with all his might not to smile, but he was failing. "Lizzy popped a kid for picking on Dustin."

"Is that so?" he asked quietly, his eyes narrowing slightly.

Lizzy grinned and nodded. "Yup!"

"Huh." For a moment, Evan just studied her. Then he glanced at Luke and gave Lizzy a small, approving nod before turning back to his work without another word.

Luke, however, broke into a crooked grin. "Well, if anyone asks," he said, reaching out to fist-bump Lizzy, "the other kid had it coming."

Lizzy grinned wide and threw a triumphant look my way. I just shook my head, trying to hide my amusement. "You two are impossible," I said, pushing open the truck door. "I've got work to do."

Luke chuckled, still grinning as he led Lizzy back toward the house. "You know you got detention now, right? Reckon you and me can go prune the roses before your aunt gets home. And, hey, if you happen to give her a bouquet of them, make sure I get some of the credit, okay?"

"Okay," she chirped.

I walked across the yard to where Cody was standing at the wash rack, his show horse Rust tied up, mane and tail all soapy. The smell of shampoo and wet horse drifted on the warm breeze.

Cody lifted his chin in greeting. "Hey, Emily. You mind grabbing the next horse and getting it started? We've got fifteen to wash and braid today."

"Which one do you want?" I asked, wiping my hands on my jeans.

"Doesn't matter," he said, his focus on rinsing Rust's mane. "But I do need Lynx brought in from the broodmare pasture. You could go get her."

Right. Speaking of Lynx... I hesitated, the words catching in my throat. "I, uh... ran into Cole at the hardware store."

Cody didn't say anything right away, but I saw his cheek tighten in a half-smile, like he was expecting this. After a moment, he simply said, "Oh?"

I shifted my weight, feeling a bit uncomfortable under his steady gaze. "He seemed pretty eager to get back to work," I offered.

Cody nodded slowly, his hands working through Rust's mane as he rinsed out the last of the shampoo. "Reckon he's had enough of a break," he said casually.

I waited, hoping he'd say more, maybe give me a clue about what he was thinking. But he didn't. He just kept working, not looking up. The silence stretched between us, and I found myself lingering longer than I meant to. After a minute, Cody glanced up sharply. "You gonna get a horse bathed or just stand there all day?"

I straightened, my face flushing. "Right. On it." I turned and headed to grab Lynx's halter.

The walk to the broodmare pasture was a good ten minutes, the sun beating down and the air thick with the smell of dust and dry grass. When I got there, Lynx wasn't where I expected her to be. She was hiding behind the other mares, moving further back every time I got closer, using the foals as cover.

"Come on, Lynx," I muttered, the frustration bubbling up. "Don't be difficult."

But Lynx wasn't having it. She kept dodging behind the others, staying just out of reach. My patience wore thin as the minutes ticked by. This wasn't like her—she was usually easy to catch. Maybe she needed more time off, or maybe... maybe it was something else. Something to do with Cole. I *knew* he was going to burn this horse out!

By the time I finally managed to get a halter on her, I was sweating and more than a little irritated. "Stubborn mare," I grumbled as I led her back to the barn. The walk back felt longer, my frustration growing with each step. I could still feel Cody's eyes on me, that half-smile like he knew something I didn't.

When I reached the wash rack, Cody was still working on Rust, and I decided I wasn't in the mood to deal with Lynx anymore. Not right now, anyway. I led her back to her stall to cool off and grabbed Copper instead. His palomino coat gleamed in the sunlight, but it was his white mane and tail that needed extra care. We had a whole regimen for the white manes and tails, and it took a long time to really do it right.

I set to work, pulling out the old braids and untangling his long, white mane. It was soothing, the familiar motions helping to calm my nerves. By the time I was done with Copper, I figured maybe—just maybe—I'd be over my irritation with Lynx... and Cole.

But I wasn't making any promises.

Cole

I tossed the hardware bags onto the passenger seat and slid into the driver's side, the truck's vinyl seats already baking from the late morning sun. I checked my phone again. Still no reply from Cody. I'd sent another text ten minutes ago, just after that awkward run-in with Emily on aisle six. Maybe she'd put in a good word for me.

Or maybe she'd just clamp her teeth for the heck of it. Figured. Why would she stick her neck out for me?

"Come on, Cody," I muttered under my breath, gripping the steering wheel so tight my knuckles turned white. "Just throw me a dang bone." But so far, not a peep.

I started the truck and pulled out onto the main road, heading back to Ridgeview Ranch. The screen of my phone stayed blank in the cup holder. I hated this feeling—this waiting around, like my whole life was on pause until someone decided I was worth giving a chance to. I'd bought everything on Mom's list—rust sealant, primer, spray paint, and a few extra things that had nearly drained my checking account. But at least I could do something useful. I couldn't afford to sit on my rear, hoping for a miracle.

The drive back was too quiet, the kind of quiet that lets your mind wander into places you'd rather it didn't. I kept sneaking glances at my phone at every stop sign, every red light, praying for that little ping that'd let me know Cody was giving me a shot. But every time, nothing.

"Rats," I muttered again, a little louder this time, slamming my palm against the wheel. I couldn't just wait around all day, hoping for something that might never come. I needed to do something, keep my hands busy, keep my mind from spiraling.

When I got back to the ranch, I jumped out of the truck, grabbed the bags, and headed straight for the equipment shed. My boots scuffed through the gravel, my frustration boiling over with each step. The old gates behind the barn caught my eye, rusted and leaning against the fence where they'd been dumped months ago. They needed work—just like me.

I dropped the bags on the ground and pulled on a pair of old gloves. I could at least get these gates cleaned up, rust-treated, and painted. Make myself useful. Maybe it'd be enough to keep my head on straight.

I grabbed a wire brush and started scrubbing, putting all my frustration into each stroke. The more I worked, the more I felt like I was scrubbing away at something inside me, too. Then it was time for the rust sealant. I yanked the gloves off for the delicate work, and poured some of the milky liquid into a cup, then slapped it on with an old paintbrush. This part always fascinated me—how that stuff could go on looking and smelling like Elmer's glue, but then turn to a hard, shiny, black finish. My hands always turned black, too, but I didn't mind. It meant I was doing something.

My phone buzzed in my pocket, and my heart jumped. I yanked off a glove, grabbed the phone, but it was just a weather alert.

"Figures," I grumbled, shoving the phone back into my pocket, my heart sinking back into that all-too-familiar pit of disappointment.

An hour passed. I moved on to the primer, spraying it on in smooth, even strokes, covering the raw metal until it gleamed in the hot sun. My hands were black with grime, sticky from the rust sealant, and then coated with the primer. The sun beat down, sweat mixing with the dirt on my face, but I kept going. I couldn't stand just hanging around, feeling useless.

Finally, I grabbed the paint. I focused on each gate, careful to make the coat even and smooth. The steady hiss of the spray can was almost calming, a distraction from the constant knot in my stomach. Just as I was getting into a rhythm, my phone rang. I nearly dropped the paint can in surprise.

It was Cody.

I fumbled to answer, my hands slippery with sweat and paint. "Hey, Cody."

"Hey, Cole. Got a minute?"

"Yeah, sure." I tried to sound casual, but my heart was down in my boots. "What's up?"

"Got a full afternoon ahead, and I could use an extra hand. Think you can come down and help groom the show horses?"

I blinked, unsure if I'd heard right. "You mean, like, today?"

"Yeah, today. Right now, if you're free."

"Yeah, I'm free. I'll—I'll be there. Let me... I got some stuff to put away."

"Just whenever you can get here," he replied. "See you in a bit."

I hung up and just stood there for a second, the phone still in my hand. I couldn't believe it. Did Emily actually say something? Or maybe Cody just needed someone, and I was the first name that came to mind. Either way, I wasn't about to question my luck. Not now.

I scrambled to put the paint away, my hands shaking with a mix of adrenaline and excitement. It took longer than I wanted to clean up, and by the time I was done, my hands were black with rust treatment and paint. I tried scrubbing them with a rag, but it was no use.

"Crap," I muttered. The last thing I wanted was to show up looking like I'd been rolling in tar. Those show horses were worth more than my truck, and Cody wasn't gonna be happy if I got paint in their manes.

I found an old bucket and filled it with water, scrubbing my hands with a stiff brush until most of the grime was gone. It wasn't perfect, but it'd have to do. I didn't have time to be picky. I wiped my hands on my jeans, took a deep breath, and headed back to the truck.

Emily

I grabbed the purple shampoo and squeezed a generous amount into my hand, rubbing it into Copper's long, white mane. The shampoo foamed up, creating a bright lavender lather that I worked through each strand. This whole process took twice as long as a normal bath, but Copper deserved the extra effort. The purple shampoo and conditioners were the best way to brighten his mane and tail, bringing out that clean, crisp look the judges loved. I'd done it a hundred times, but today, my mind kept wandering back to Cole.

As I gave Copper the final rinse, I heard the familiar sound of an old engine rattling down the driveway. I didn't have to look up to know whose truck it was. The whining fan belt was a dead giveaway. I glanced over as Cole's beat-up truck pulled in, the fan belt screeching like nails on a chalkboard.

I shook my head, a faint smile tugging at my lips despite myself. "He really ought to fix that thing before it strands him somewhere," I muttered under my breath. Luke would probably love to tinker with it, and Jess—well, she could have that old truck running like new in no time. But Cole? He'd always said he didn't need the help. Didn't look that way to me.

But then, as if the truck's whining wasn't enough to announce his arrival, Lynx let out a shrill whinny from her stall. I dropped the shampoo bottle, startled. Lynx hardly ever cared if I was around, and here she was, screaming like her life depended on it. What in the world was that about?

I looked over my shoulder, half-expecting to see another horse passing by outside or something. Maybe the screech of Cole's fan belt just hurt her ears. But no—there was nothing. Just Cole, getting out of his truck, his hands in his pockets as he strolled past the wash rack. He glanced my way, his eyes drifting to me for just a second before he gave a small nod and kept walking.

I blinked, a bit taken aback. That was about the most cordial greeting I'd ever gotten from him. Maybe he was thanking me for talking to Cody about bringing him back. Or maybe it was just a fluke, and he hadn't even meant to acknowledge me. Still, I couldn't help but notice the change.

Down the barn aisle, I heard Lynx again, her whinnies now more like soft, happy grunts. I leaned around the corner, curious despite myself. There was Cole, standing with his back to me, cradling Lynx's head over her stall door, his hands gently massaging her ears. He was speaking to her in low, soothing tones, his voice too soft for me to make out the words.

I swallowed, feeling like I was intruding on something private. It was almost... intimate, the way Lynx responded to him. Her eyes were half-closed, leaning into his touch like he was the only person in the world she trusted. And maybe he was.

I turned back to Copper, feeling a twist of something I couldn't quite name—was it jealousy? Frustration? Lynx barely tolerated me on a good day, but here she was, practically melting under Cole's hands.

I scrubbed harder at Copper's mane, my mind swirling with thoughts I didn't want to examine too closely. Maybe Lynx did need more time off, or maybe she just liked Cole better. Either way, it didn't make sense to dwell on it. I had work to do, horses to bathe and braid. I couldn't let this get under my skin.

But even as I focused on getting Copper's mane just right, I couldn't shake the feeling. Lynx seemed to love Cole. And somehow, that felt like a slap in the face.

I'd be darned if I let it show, though.

Chapter Seven

Cole

The next morning, I showed up at Walker Ranch just like I always did, hoping I wasn't reading too much into Cody's words from last night. "See you tomorrow," he'd said after we finished bathing the last of the show horses. He didn't mention anything about why he'd sent me home earlier in the week. Didn't give me any hint if I was on thin ice or back in his good graces. Just a casual "See you tomorrow," and then he turned and walked away.

Emily had flashed me a look when Cody said it—something I couldn't quite read. Was it surprise? Amusement? Maybe a bit of both. I tried to shrug it off, but it nagged at me all the same. This morning, I figured if Cody didn't want me here, he would've said something. So here I was, trying to act like I belonged.

I grabbed a broom and started sweeping the barn aisle after the regular morning chores, just like old times. The horses shifted in their stalls, rustling in the quiet of the early morning. The smell of fresh hay and saddle soap hung in the air, and for a moment, it felt like everything was back to normal. Like I hadn't almost lost this chance altogether.

Lizzy was there, too, sweeping along beside me. She was chattering away, something about some new show she was watching, or maybe it was a book. I wasn't really paying attention. I was still stuck in my own head, wondering what Cody had planned. Lizzy, suspended from school, seemed happy enough to have a distraction, and she sure wasn't short on words.

"So then, the dragon turns into this huge—hey, Cole, are you even listening?"

"Hmm?" I blinked, pulling myself out of my thoughts. "Yeah, yeah. Big blue dragon, right?"

Lizzy rolled her eyes. "That was ten minutes ago. This is the *green* one. You're worse than Luke sometimes."

"Hey now," I chuckled. "I'm doing my best here."

She shook her head, but I could tell she wasn't really mad. Lizzy was like that. Always talking, always moving. Kind of like Lynx, come to think of it. Never could stand still for long. I liked having her around, even if she did talk my ear off. Better than being stuck in my head all morning.

I finished sweeping up a pile of hay and dust when I saw Cody coming down the aisle, his stride purposeful. I straightened up, my grip tightening on the broom handle. Was this it? Was he gonna tell me to head home again?

"Cole," Cody said, nodding toward the end of the barn. "Go catch Lynx. I've got some exercises I want you to work on."

I nearly dropped the broom. "Right. Okay." I quickly leaned the broom against the wall and gave Lizzy a quick smile. "Thanks for the help, Lizzy."

She grinned. "No problem. You gonna go ride Lynx now?"

"Yeah. Sounds like that's the plan," I said, trying to keep my voice steady, like this was just another normal day. But inside, my heart was pounding. Cody hadn't given me any explanation, hadn't said a word about what had happened earlier in the week. Just "Go catch Lynx."

I hustled down to the tack room, grabbed Lynx's halter, and then headed out to the corral where she was catching some morning sun. Lynx came trotting up to the fence when she saw me, ears pricked, like she knew something was up. She watched me approach, her dark eyes tracking my every move.

"Hey, girl," I murmured, sliding the halter over her nose. She nickered softly, nudging my shoulder as I led her back to the barn. I couldn't help but smile. "Ready to get back to work? Sure hope we make the boss happy today."

I threw the saddle over Lynx's back, tightening the girth and adjusting the stirrups. My hands moved on autopilot, years of practice guiding each motion, but my mind was racing. I needed this to go well. I needed to prove that I was worth keeping around.

With Lynx saddled and ready, I led her out of the barn and into the morning light. The sun was just starting to rise over the hills, casting long shadows across the ranch. I could see Cody waiting by the training pen, arms crossed, watching us approach.

I took a deep breath, squared my shoulders, and headed over. Time to show him what I could do.

Emily

The hay truck bounced over the ruts in the field, and I gripped the wheel a little tighter, glancing down at my phone balanced on the seat beside me. The text from Cody lit up the screen: *Saddle Copper and meet me in the big outdoor arena as soon as you're done.*

A ripple of nerves shot through me. I'd been replaying his coaching from yesterday over and over in my mind, trying to pick apart every word, every expression on his face. I knew there was something he wanted me to fix, something he saw that I hadn't yet. And now, with him asking to meet in the arena first thing, my mind raced with what it could be. Finally, he was going to tell me!

I pushed down on the gas pedal, urging the old truck to go just a little faster. The yearlings huddled in the corner of the field, their heads popping up as I approached. I didn't waste any time dumping the hay. Usually, I'd spread it out a bit more, but not today. Today, I needed every second.

As soon as the hay was on the ground, I swung the truck around and headed back toward the barn, the engine grumbling in protest. I didn't care. Cody wanted me riding Copper now, which meant he had something particular in mind. Something I needed to work on. And I was more than ready to find out what it was.

I pulled up to the main barn, barely giving the truck a chance to settle before I jumped out. My boots hit the gravel, and I was running, heading straight for the tack room. Copper's saddle was where I'd left it, his protective boots hanging on the hook beside it. I moved everything to the saddling area, then hurried to his stall. He nickered softly as I approached, his ears flicking forward.

"Morning, handsome," I said, slinging the saddle over his back. My hands moved quickly, almost on autopilot, tightening the girth, adjusting the snaffle bridle. I was running through the motions, but my mind was already in the arena, trying to anticipate what Cody would ask me to do.

I slipped Copper's protective boots onto his legs, making sure they were smooth and snug, then paused. The sun was already starting to climb, and it was going to be hot out there today. I swapped my ball cap for a wide-brimmed cowboy hat, jamming it down on my head. No sense in getting sunburned when I needed to be focused.

With Copper ready to go, I flung his reins over my shoulder and led him out of the barn. The big outdoor arena was just up ahead, the gate open, the sandy surface raked smooth from yesterday. But when I got closer, my heart sank. Cody wasn't there yet.

Instead, I saw Cole. He was already in the arena, Lynx moving beneath him in that stretchy, flowing gait she had when she was warming up. Cole sat the saddle easily, his hands relaxed on the reins as he guided her through a set of circles.

I sighed, feeling a knot tighten in my stomach. Of course, Cole was here already. He was back in the game, just as determined as ever. And here I was, itching to prove myself, to get Cody's feedback and fix whatever needed fixing. Now, I'd have to wait.

"Just my luck," I muttered, giving Copper a pat on the neck. I walked him into the arena, keeping to the far side to give Cole plenty of space. I didn't want to distract him, didn't want to give him any reason to think I was watching him, even though I couldn't help but notice how easily he moved with Lynx, like they were in sync.

I shook my head, trying to push the thoughts away. This wasn't about Cole. This was about me and Copper and figuring out how to be better.

I just hoped Cody showed up soon. I wasn't sure how long I could stand to be out here, waiting, with Cole working his horse like he belonged here, and me feeling like I was still trying to prove that I did.

Cole

Lynx moved beneath me like she was floating, each hoofbeat land-ing square and confident. I could feel the strength in her stride, the eagerness in the way she pushed off the ground. She felt good to-day—maybe a little *too* good. I had to keep my leg light, barely touch-ing her sides, or she'd get ahead of me, eager to show off. But she was listening, her ears swiveling back to me every few strides, waiting for the next cue. When I sat deeper in the saddle, I felt her roll her hindquarters under herself, quivering like a coiled spring, ready to explode into motion the second I gave her the signal.

I turned her out of a warmup rollback along the fence, and that's when I saw Emily. She'd just come through the arena gate, leading Copper. The sun hit her just right, catching the halo of her curly golden hair, making it seem like it was glowing. My eyes were drawn to her, and I couldn't seem to look away. The wide-brimmed hat framed her face perfectly, setting off the blue of her eyes, even from across the way. I couldn't help but notice the way she moved—confident, purposeful.

She glanced my way, and for a moment, I forgot to breathe. It was like the whole world narrowed to just her and that moment. Lynx stopped underneath me, sensing my distraction, but I didn't even notice. My breath stalled in my chest, and my mouth went dry. Why did I care? Why was I staring? I had no idea. But there was something about the way she looked in that morning light that caught me off guard. It wasn't the first time I'd seen Emily in that hat, but right now, she seemed... different. More vivid, somehow. More alive.

I blinked, trying to shake it off, but I was rooted to the spot. Why did she have to look at me like that? Like she saw something I didn't even see in myself? Lynx shifted beneath me, sensing my hesitation, and I finally snapped out of it.

"Gol-durn it, Cole," I muttered under my breath, tearing my eyes away. I really didn't need to be staring at Emily. Not today. Not any day, really. Especially not when I had a chance to redeem myself in Cody's eyes. I blinked a few times, trying to shake off whatever had come over me, but my heart was still thudding in my chest like I'd just run a mile.

I watched as Emily checked her cinch, then swung up into her saddle with that same smooth grace she always had. Copper moved out beneath her, and when she finally met my gaze again, she pressed her lips into a thin line—a civil greeting, nothing more. But it was more than I usually got from her. Then she nudged Copper into a long, low trot to warm up his muscles.

I swallowed hard, turning my focus back to Lynx. *Focus, Cole. You gotta focus.* I gave her a gentle nudge, guiding her into a series of warm-up circles, getting her loosened up, feeling every little movement she made, every shift of weight. We circled the arena, sometimes crossing paths with Emily and Copper. We were used to avoiding each other by now. No big deal. Just another day working the horses.

But every time we came close, I couldn't help but notice how Emily seemed to hold her breath, her shoulders stiffening just a fraction. Maybe she was just annoyed about sharing the arena with me. Couldn't blame her for that. Not with our history.

We warmed up like that for a good half hour, Lynx settling into a nice rhythm, Copper moving strong and steady under Emily. The horses were more than ready to get down to business, but Cody was nowhere to be seen. I kept glancing toward the barn, wondering what the heck was taking him so long.

Just as I was starting to think he'd forgotten about us, Cody finally showed up, riding down from the barn on Five Iron, his old retired show horse and Walker Ranch's head stallion. His little girl, Nikki, sat in front of him on the saddle, clutching the horn with one hand and holding a little stuffed horse in the other. Cody didn't look like he was ready to work at all.

Emily and I both stopped our horses, exchanging a quick, curious glance. What was Cody playing at? We watched as he rode up to the arena, looking more like he was out for a Sunday stroll than about to run us through our paces.

I could feel the tension building in my shoulders. I'd been gearing up all morning, ready to prove myself, to show Cody that I could handle whatever he threw at me. But now, seeing him with Nikki and his laid-back demeanor, I wasn't so sure what was coming.

Chapter Eight

Cole

Cody was all smiles as he rode up, Nikki perched in front of him on the saddle. He barely glanced our way, just strolled along on Five Iron like he didn't have a care in the world. His hat was pulled low, and he was murmuring something to Nikki, pointing out a bird fluttering in the branches of a nearby tree. He didn't seem the least bit interested in us or what we were doing.

I shifted in the saddle, Lynx's muscles coiled beneath me, ready to go. I could feel her eagerness, just waiting for a signal. Emily sat nearby on Copper, just as confused as I was. We both watched Cody, waiting for him to say something, to give us some kind of direction.

Finally, I cleared my throat. "So, uh, what do you want us to work on today, boss?"

Cody looked over at us like he'd forgotten we were even there. "Your horses good and warmed up?"

Emily answered before I could. "They've been warmed up for a while now."

Cody nodded, eyes still ahead, like he was looking for something in the distance. "Good. Time to get to work." But he just kept walking

Five Iron around the perimeter of the arena, his focus back on Nikki and their little father-daughter adventure.

I glanced over at Emily, and I could tell she was just as baffled as I was. What was Cody playing at?

"Are you bringing Five Iron out of retirement?" Emily finally asked. "Should I set up the training flag?"

Cody chuckled and shook his head. "Nah, the old man just likes to flex his muscles now and again. And I don't trust just any horse on the ranch to give pony rides to Nikki." He pointed at something on the ground, probably a beetle or a rock, and Nikki giggled, clutching her little stuffed horse tighter.

There was a tense silence between me and Emily, the kind that makes your skin prickle. I didn't want to be the one to break it, but I couldn't stand not knowing. "So, uh, what are we doing today?"

Just then, I heard the rumble of a truck turning into the driveway. It headed straight for the arena. Cody seemed to notice, too, and turned Five Iron toward the gate. A moment later, I saw it was Morgan, his wife. She pulled up alongside the fence and leaned out the window with a smile.

"There's my girl!" she squealed, and Nikki threw her ams out to greet her mama.

Cody swung down from the saddle, his movements slow and easy, like he had all the time in the world. He had this way about him—like nothing ever rattled him, not even with the pressure of running the Walkers' training stable, helping Morgan with White Pines, being a new dad, and all the expectations that came with everything. I watched as he sauntered over to the fence and carefully handed Nikki over to Morgan, who took her with a warm, familiar laugh. She balanced Nikki on her hip and leaned in to plant a quick kiss on Cody's cheek.

"Sorry I took so long this morning," Morgan said. She cuddled Nikki against her shoulder, her hand brushing her daughter's hair back from her face.

Cody grinned, that easy, laid-back smile that always made it look like everything was just fine in his world. His eyes never left Morgan's face, like he was soaking her in. "Ain't a problem," he drawled, and then he leaned in closer, pressing a kiss to her lips—full and unhurried, like he didn't care that Emily and I were sitting right there, watching the whole thing.

I felt a flush creep up the back of my neck. It wasn't like I wasn't used to seeing Cody and Morgan together, but there was something about the way they were looking at each other right now, like we didn't even exist, that made me want to look away. It was like they were in their own little world, a bubble where nothing else mattered. I shifted in my saddle, suddenly feeling like I was intruding on something private.

I risked a glance at Emily. She was sitting stiffly on Copper, her eyes darting between Cody and Morgan, a crease forming between her brows. She looked just as baffled as I felt—maybe even a little annoyed. I couldn't blame her. This wasn't what either of us had expected when we showed up ready to work.

Morgan finally pulled back, her cheeks a little flushed, but she wore a bright smile as she waved over at us. "Good morning, you two!" she called out, her voice light and cheerful, like she hadn't just made everything awkward.

Emily managed a polite smile and a nod, but I could see the tightness in her expression. "Morning," she said, trying to keep her tone even.

I just nodded back, trying to hide the fact that I was looking for a way to disappear. It wasn't that I minded seeing Cody and Morgan happy—it was just... well, it was just a lot.

Morgan climbed back into the truck with Nikki and drove off, leaving a cloud of dust behind. Cody climbed back on Five Iron and moseyed over to us, still wearing that easy grin, like he had just devoured a pint of ice cream.

Emily and I shared another look, and I could see the question in her eyes as clear as day. What the heck was going on?

I finally took the plunge. "So, what are we doing now, boss?"

Cody pushed his hat back on his head, squinting at me in that way he did when he was about to drop some news he knew I wouldn't like. "*We*," he said, drawing out the word, "aren't doing anything. I'm gonna work Five Iron. I want you two to go out and rotate the working calves."

Emily blinked, her brows knitting together. "Rotate the calves?" she repeated. "But the bunch we have in now has only been in for a week. They're just starting to settle and get good to work with."

Cody grunted, giving her a slow nod. "You're right. But I want you to go do it anyway."

I stared at him, my mind drawing a blank. Rotate the calves? *Now?* And he wanted us to work *together?* Without him around to keep us from snapping at each other? What was he thinking?

I looked over at Emily. She didn't look any happier about it than I felt. She had her lips pressed tight, a look of frustration flickering in her eyes. I let out a slow breath and shrugged, deciding not to question Cody any further. He had his reasons, and there was no point in arguing.

"All right," I said, turning Lynx toward the gate. "Let's get to it."

Emily sighed but nudged Copper forward. We both rode out of the arena, heading toward the pens. I could feel the tension between us, thick as the dust kicking up under our horses' hooves. This was going to be a long morning.

Emily

Cole and I rode side by side, steering our horses around the perimeter of the holding pen where the yearlings were milling about, their ears flicking in every direction. We'd been tasked with rotating the calves, moving this bunch back out to pasture, and bringing in a fresh group. It was straightforward enough work, but I could already tell we were going to have problems.

Cole was keeping his distance, sitting back on Lynx like he was afraid to get too close. He gave the calves way too much room, letting them drift wherever they pleased. It was driving me nuts.

"You're giving them too much space," I said. We'd been getting along so far, or at least trying to, and I didn't want to ruin it. But it was clear his approach wasn't working. "If you don't close in a bit, they're gonna scatter."

Cole shot me a sideways glance, his jaw tightening. "I'm not rushing them, if that's what you mean," he replied, his tone defensive. "You keep crowding them, and they're gonna panic."

"I'm not crowding them," I snapped back. "I'm just keeping them moving. If we don't keep them together, they'll bolt for the open field, and then we'll be chasing them all morning."

"Yeah, well, maybe if you didn't rush them, they wouldn't feel the need to run," Cole muttered, his eyes narrowing as he guided Lynx into a slower circle.

I bit my lip, trying to keep my temper in check. "Look, I'm just trying to get this done the most efficient way. We don't have all day, and I'd rather not be out here longer than we need to be."

Cole's grip on his reins tightened. "Maybe you should mind your own business and let me handle it my way."

"I *am* minding my business!" I retorted, feeling my patience snap. "My business is making sure these calves don't get run into the ground, or worse, break out because someone's too slack on the reins."

Before Cole could reply, one of the calves broke from the group, darting toward the open field. I felt a surge of frustration. "See, this is exactly what I was talking about!"

But then, quick as lightning, Lynx exploded, her ears pinned, and her body coiled tight. Cole had left enough space for Lynx to work her magic, and she did just that—cutting the calf off in a few swift, sharp moves. She darted in front of it, pushing it back toward the herd with the kind of finesse that only came from stupid amounts of talent and experience. Cole barely had to move a muscle; Lynx did it all on her own.

I bit down on my tongue, watching as the calf rejoined the group, Cole's smug grin spreading across his face. He didn't say a word, but he didn't have to. His expression said it all.

I clenched my jaw, swallowing back the sharp words I wanted to hurl at him. Fine. So he got lucky this time. Didn't mean his way was better. I focused on my own horse, urging Copper forward, trying to drown out the sound of Cole's silent gloating.

We kept working in tense silence, pushing the new bunch of calves back toward the corrals. The air between us was thick with unspoken words, each of us too cantankerous to break the quiet. My tongue was on fire with all the things I wanted to say, all the ways I wanted to call him out for being such a stubborn mule.

Just as I was about to open my mouth, I saw Cole's shoulders shift, that familiar mischievous glint sparking in his eyes. I'd seen that look before—usually right before he pulled some sort of stunt. I braced myself, trying to keep my focus on the calves and the task at hand.

He moved Lynx in closer, sidling up next to Copper. I watched him out of the corner of my eye, trying to pretend I wasn't paying attention. But I knew better. He leaned over just enough to snatch the end of Copper's reins, giving them a playful tug that sent my stud sidestepping and tossing his head, caught off guard.

"Cole!" I yelped, pulling the reins back through his grip, my knuckles tightening around the leather. Copper danced beneath me, snorting in protest. My heart jumped to my throat, a mix of irritation and a little bit of panic.

Cole just grinned like a fool, his eyes gleaming with mischief. "What's the matter, Em? Just thought I'd help you with your steering."

I glared at him, my patience wearing thin. "You call that *helping?* You're gonna spook him messing around like that."

"Aw, Copper can handle it," he said, his voice light and teasing. "He's got a good head on his shoulders. Might even help him get sharper, you know?"

I could feel my face heating up, a mix of anger and embarrassment prickling at the back of my neck. "We're out here to work, Cole, not to play games."

He shrugged, clearly unbothered. "A little fun never hurt anyone. Might even lighten the mood."

"Maybe you should focus on getting the job done instead of goofing off!" I snapped back, jerking Copper's reins to get him back on track. I could feel my temper boiling over, and I knew I needed to rein it in, but Cole just had a way of getting under my skin.

"Easy, Em," Cole said, still smirking. "No need to get all riled up. We're just moving some calves."

"Yeah, well, maybe if you took it seriously for once, we'd actually get somewhere!" I shot back. "You think this is some kind of joke?"

He didn't answer right away, just let out a low chuckle that made my blood boil even more. I focused on getting the calves back in line, feeling Copper's muscles bunch under me as he settled down again. We worked in tense silence after that, the weight of our unspoken frustrations hanging heavy in the air.

Cole kept his distance, steering Lynx a little wider, giving the calves more room to move. I kept a tighter line, trying to keep them grouped together, moving them toward the gate. Every time we crossed paths, I could feel his eyes on me, like he was waiting for me to say something, to call him out again. But I wasn't going to give him the satisfaction.

By the time we finally got the new bunch of calves back toward the corrals, my nerves were shot. Cole had done his best to rattle me, and darn it, he'd succeeded. I could still see that smug look on his face from when Lynx had effortlessly turned that calf back. It was like he was just waiting for me to mess up, to prove that he was right and I was wrong.

And then, as if to push things just a little further, Cole reached out and nudged the brim of my hat down over my eyes.

"Cole!" I shouted, jerking my head back, my hat falling crooked over my face. I straightened it quickly, my hands shaking.

He laughed, that low, teasing chuckle that made me want to scream. "Sorry, Em. Didn't see you there."

I shot him a glare that could have melted steel. "You think you're so funny, don't you?"

He grinned wider, clearly enjoying himself. "I like to think I have my moments."

"Well, you don't. Just... don't touch me, okay?"

He shrugged. "Fine by me."

We didn't say much else on the way back to the barn. The silence between us was thick and heavy, every hoofbeat echoing my frustration. When we got to the barn, we both slid off our horses, unsaddling them without a word. I could feel the heat of his presence next to me, the tension still simmering between us.

Cody walked by, giving us a quick glance. He didn't say anything about the obvious friction between us. He just nodded and said, "Go saddle up your next mounts—Slick for you, Cole, and Bunny for you, Emily. Time for some reining drills."

I glared daggers at Cole as I dropped Copper's stirrup from the horn and pulled my saddle off, my blood still boiling. Cole just stared back, his expression deadpan, not giving me an inch.

"Fine," I muttered under my breath, turning to grab Bunny's tack. "Let's get this over with."

Cole didn't say anything, just kept working in silence. But I could feel his eyes on me the whole time.

Chapter Nine

Cole

By the time I pulled up to the house, the sun was dipping low over the ridge, painting the sky in shades of orange and pink. I could feel the exhaustion in my bones, but it was a good kind of tired—the kind that comes from a long day's work where you've actually accomplished something. I'd been working more closely with Emily than I had in a long time, and while it hadn't exactly been smooth sailing, there was a weird sense of satisfaction in knowing we'd gotten through it without too much bloodshed.

Still, I couldn't help but feel a gnawing confusion about what Cody wanted from me. I'd been back at Walker Ranch for a couple of days now, but he hadn't said much beyond basic instructions. It was like he was testing me, but for what, I had no idea. And working with Emily... well, that only added another layer of uncertainty. Was Cody trying to see if we could actually manage to work together without killing each other? Or was it something else?

I climbed out of the truck, stretching my back, my muscles aching from twelve hours in the saddle. The house was already buzzing with activity. I could hear Gage's voice drifting out from the kitchen window, talking with Mom about something. Inside, Chase was sprawled out on the couch, one arm slung over the back, his eyes half-lidded like he was watching but not really seeing.

"Hey," I said, kicking off my boots by the door and stepping inside. "Long day?"

Chase glanced up, a half-smile on his face. "Could say that. How's the horse whispering going?"

I rolled my eyes. "Don't know about any whispering, but I managed not to get kicked in the head, so I'd call it a win."

Chase chuckled, setting the remote down. "Progress, I guess."

I dropped down onto the couch next to him, feeling the weight of the day settling over me. Chase was the one I usually talked to about this stuff—when I needed to get something off my chest. He wasn't much of a talker, but he'd always been good at listening, even when he didn't have all the answers.

"You ever get the feeling like... you're supposed to be doing something, but you don't know what it is?" I asked, my gaze fixed on the TV screen, not really seeing it.

Chase snorted. "All the time, little brother. Welcome to the club."

"Yeah, but with Cody... it's different. He hasn't said much to me since I got back. Just keeps giving me these tasks and watching." I rubbed the back of my neck, trying to work out a kink. "I don't know if he's testing me or what."

"Could be," Chase said, leaning back, his expression thoughtful. "Or maybe he's just trying to see if you're gonna stick around this time."

I shot him a look. "I didn't leave! He's the one who sent me away."

"Okay, maybe he was testing to see how hungry you are. How bad you want it."

I screwed my mouth into a scowl. "I ain't going anywhere. Not yet, anyway."

"Good to hear. You making any progress with that chick you work with, or still iced out?"

"Yeah, progress," I muttered, rubbing my shoulder. "More like arguing."

Chase chuckled. "You and Emily ever gonna learn to get along?"

"Not likely," I said, shaking my head. "But it'd help if I knew what Cody was up to."

"Reckon he'll tell you when he's ready."

"Huh." I grabbed the remote from him to flip the channel—he wasn't watching anyway. "Yeah, I reckon."

Before Chase could snatch the remote back, we heard Gage's voice raising from the kitchen. He sounded upset—more than usual.

"We're running out of options, Mom," Gage was saying, his tone sharp. "If we lose more grazing rights, we're gonna have to sell off more cattle. We're already stretched thin. We can't keep going like this."

Chase and I exchanged a look. Gage wasn't one to get worked up over nothing. We both got up quietly and moved toward the kitchen, leaning against the doorway to listen.

Mom was sitting at the table, her hands wrapped around a mug of coffee. "I know, Gage," she said, her voice calm but firm. "But there's only so much we can do. The state's got their rules, and they're not bending over backward to help ranchers like us."

Gage ran a hand through his hair, clearly frustrated. "Their rules are putting us out of business, Mom. They care more about a bird than they do about people. It's not right."

She sighed, looking down into her coffee like it might have the answers. "I get it. Believe me, I do. But fighting them isn't going to get us anywhere. We have to figure out another way to make this work."

Gage threw up his hands. "What other way? We've already cut back on expenses. We're selling off cattle. We're running out of land to graze on, and now they want to take more? It's impossible."

Mom didn't answer right away. She just sat there, staring into her coffee, and I could see the lines on her face looking deeper than usual. I hated seeing her like this—worried, not knowing what to do.

Chase cleared his throat, stepping into the kitchen. "Maybe there's something we haven't thought of yet. Maybe we could lease some land from one of the neighbors."

Gage shook his head. "You think we haven't tried that? Everybody's in the same boat. Nobody's got any extra grazing land to spare. And if they do, they're charging an arm and a leg for it."

Mom looked up at us, her eyes tired. "We just have to hang on a little longer, that's all. Maybe something will change. Maybe as the forests recover, they'll ease up on the restrictions."

"Maybe," Gage said, but I could hear the doubt in his voice. "But what if they don't? What then?"

Mom shook her head. "We've got a meeting with the state rep next week, but I don't know if it'll do any good. They're set on protecting those owls, and we're just... stuck."

"And we already have proof that our cows don't compete with the owl nesting!" Gage growled. "They won't listen!"

Mom just thinned her lips, and there was a heavy silence in the kitchen. I felt like I should say something, but I didn't know what. I wasn't in much of a position to change what the state said about the spotted owl, and I sure as heck didn't have any bright ideas about how to keep the ranch afloat.

Chase leaned against the counter, glancing between Mom and Gage like a ring master at a boxing match. "We'll figure it out," he said, but even he didn't sound too sure.

I looked over at Gage, who was still standing there, arms crossed, looking like he wanted to punch something. I could see how much this was eating at him, eating at all of us. The ranch was more than just land and cattle. It was our home, our way of life. And watching it slowly slip away—it hurt.

Mom finally stood up, setting her coffee mug down. "Why don't we all sit down for supper," she said, trying to change the subject. "We'll talk more about this later. No sense in fretting over it all night."

I nodded, but I couldn't shake the feeling of helplessness. As we moved toward the table, the thought crept into my mind again—maybe I could help by doing something else. If I got a job in construction, I could be making good money. The valley was trying to rebuild after the fires, and every construction crew around was looking for hands. It wouldn't be glamorous, but it'd be steady pay. Money we could use.

But then, there was this thing with Cody and the horses. I'd started to see what I could do—what I wanted to do. And it sure as heck wasn't swinging a hammer all day.

The thought of leaving the ranch and everything I'd just started building at Walker Ranch didn't sit right with me, either. I wanted to help. I just wasn't sure how.

Later, after supper, when I finally climbed into bed, I still couldn't shake the unease. My mind kept turning over everything that had happened today—Emily, Cody, the ranch. I stared up at the ceiling, my thoughts tangled and messy. I needed to make a decision, but every option seemed like a bad one.

I rolled over, trying to get comfortable, but sleep wouldn't come. I couldn't help but wonder if there was a way to make all of this work. And if there wasn't, what the heck was I gonna do next?

Emily

By the time I pulled into the parking lot behind Mom's shop, I was feeling just about done with this day. I cut the engine and sat there for a moment, the car ticking as it cooled down. The narrow alley behind the store was cluttered with old clothes racks, boxes, and who knew what else—like everything around here, it was all just a little too chaotic. I sighed, pressing my forehead against the steering wheel for a moment before I finally hauled myself out of the seat.

Climbing the stairs to the apartment above the store, I could hear the muffled sounds of Mom working in the shop below. She was talking to someone, her voice light and cheerful, like she didn't have a care in the world. I wished I could be more like that, but all I could think about was how I still had no idea what Cody was thinking, and Cole was as infuriating as ever.

I opened the door to the apartment and stepped inside. It was the same as always—cluttered with a mix of old furniture, thrift store finds, and Mom's half-finished projects. The tiny kitchen was filled with stacks of dishes and papers, a pile of laundry spilling over onto the floor. I kicked off my boots and dropped my bag on the only clear spot on the couch.

"Emily, that you?" Mom's voice called up from below.

"Yeah, it's me."

"There's a frozen dinner in the freezer if you're hungry," she said. "Just pop it in the microwave for a few minutes."

I walked over to the freezer and pulled it open, staring at the sad selection of frozen meals. I wasn't in the mood for any of it. I shut the door a little harder than necessary, leaning against the counter. "You gonna be up soon?"

"Still got a lot of work down here," she replied. "I'll be up in a bit. Don't wait for me."

I nodded, even though she couldn't see me, and walked back to the living room. I flopped down on the couch, kicking a pile of magazines onto the floor to make room. The cushions sank under me, and I stared at the ceiling, feeling a wave of frustration wash over me.

I pulled out my phone and scrolled through my contacts, my thumb hovering over Lauren's name. She always knew what to say to calm me down, to make sense of things when I couldn't. I hit the call button and listened as it rang, hoping she'd pick up.

"Hey, this is Lauren! I can't come to the phone right now, but leave a message, and I'll get back to you soon!"

I hung up before the beep, letting out a heavy sigh. Just my luck. I tossed my phone onto the coffee table, staring at it like it might suddenly ring with some magic solution to all my problems.

After a moment, I picked it up again and shot off a quick text. Maybe Kate was around. We hadn't gotten together in ages—really, not since the show season started.

You free to hang out?

Her response came almost immediately, a little ping lighting up my screen.

Heck yeah, girl! What's up?

I smiled a little, feeling a bit of the weight lift from my shoulders. Kate always had a way of making me feel better, even on days like this.

Just need to get out of here. My mom's working late, and I'm going stir crazy.

Same here. My dad's watching the game, and it's LOUD. Wanna hang at your place?

I looked around the apartment—the cluttered counters, the overflowing laundry basket, the mess of papers and projects Mom always seemed to be working on but never finished. The thought of inviting Kate over made my skin crawl. I loved her to death, but I wasn't about to let her see this mess. Not tonight.

Nah, let's go somewhere else. How about the tavern?

There was a pause, and then another ping.

Ooo, good call. Meet you there in 20?

Perfect. See you soon.

I shoved my phone back in my pocket and stood up, brushing off my jeans. The thought of getting out of this cramped, cluttered apartment sounded like exactly what I needed. I grabbed my keys off the table and headed back down the stairs, not bothering to let Mom know I was leaving. She'd be down in the shop for hours yet, and I didn't feel like trying to explain.

As I stepped outside, the cool evening air hit me, and I took a deep breath. Maybe some time with Kate would help clear my head, help me figure out what to do next. At the very least, it would be a distraction from everything else.

The tavern was already buzzing with the early evening crowd—locals unwinding after a long day, a mix of families and ranch hands gathered around tables, laughter and conversation filling the air. The scent of sizzling burgers and fries drifted through the open door, mixing with the faint smell of sawdust and peanuts.

I pushed through the double doors, stepping into the warm, cozy space. The old wooden floors creaked under my boots, and I could see a group of kids playing by the jukebox in the corner, their parents keeping a watchful eye from the nearby tables. A few folks were tossing peanut shells on the floor, something that always made the tavern feel laid-back and a little rough around the edges. It was the kind of place where everyone knew everyone, and you could always find a familiar face.

I spotted Kate right away, sitting at our usual booth near the back, waving me over with a big grin. She had already ordered a soda, the tall glass in front of her with a bright red straw sticking out. Her scrunchy dark hair was pulled back into a high ponytail, and she was wearing a denim jacket over a plain white tee—simple, but she made it look good.

"Hey, girl!" she called out as I made my way over, sliding into the seat across from her. "Rough day, huh?"

I let out a long breath, leaning back against the booth. "You could say that. Thanks for coming out."

"Are you kidding?" Kate laughed. "Anything to get away from my dad and his yelling at the TV. The man gets so worked up about the stupidest things."

I smiled, grateful for her easy way of lightening the mood. "Well, thanks anyway. I needed a break."

A waitress came by, setting down a bowl of peanuts and a couple of menus. "You two want something to drink?" she asked, her pen poised over a notepad.

"Just water for me," I said, glancing at the menu. "No, maybe some iced tea."

"I'm ready for another root beer," Kate said, flashing a grin. "Gotta stay on brand."

The waitress nodded and walked away, and I turned back to Kate, who was already cracking open a peanut and tossing the shell on the floor.

"So, what's going on?" Kate asked, popping the peanut into her mouth. "You seemed kinda stressed in your text."

I sighed, running a hand through my hair. As per usual, it was all frizzy again because I'd been out all day in the sun without moisturizing it. "It's just... everything. Work's been tough. Cody's got me and Cole working together more, and it's like oil and water. I swear, we can't get through five minutes without bickering."

Kate raised an eyebrow, her grin widening. "Cole, huh? That the tall, dark, and broody one?"

I rolled my eyes. "I guess you could say that. He's just... infuriating. Always has to do things his way, always pushing my buttons."

Kate laughed. "Sounds like someone's got a crush."

I shot her a look. "Please. The last thing I need is a crush on Cole Langton."

"Oh, come on," she teased, leaning forward. "You can't tell me you don't think he's cute. I mean, he's got that whole rugged cowboy thing going on. I wouldn't kick him out of the barn."

I snorted, shaking my head. "Yeah, well, he might look good, but he's a pain in the neck. Besides, I've got enough on my plate without adding 'managing my feelings for Cole' to the list."

Kate laughed again, her eyes dancing with amusement. "Fair enough. But seriously, what's going on with Cody? You said he's been acting weird? I haven't seen anything around White Pines that seems off."

"Yeah," I said, frowning. "He's got me doing all these different things with the horses, but he won't tell me why. And then he keeps throwing me and Cole together, like he's trying to see if we'll kill each other or something."

Kate nodded thoughtfully, chewing on another peanut. "Maybe he's trying to see how you handle pressure. Or maybe he's trying to get you two to work out whatever's between you."

I snorted. "Whatever's between us is a whole lot of nothing. And I'm fine under pressure—it's Cole who's the problem."

"Sure, sure," Kate said, still grinning. "But hey, if it gets you more time in the saddle, it can't be all bad, right?"

"Yeah, I guess," I said, still feeling a bit frustrated. "I just wish I knew what Cody was thinking. It's hard to know if I'm doing the right thing when he won't say."

Kate shrugged. "That's ranch life, isn't it? Half the time you're just guessing and hoping for the best."

I laughed, nodding. "Ain't that the truth."

The waitress came back with our drinks, setting them down with a smile. "Ready to order?"

"I'll have the bacon cheeseburger, extra pickles," Kate said. "And fries. Lots of fries."

"I'll take the same," I added, handing back the menu. "Thanks."

As the waitress walked away, Kate leaned back in the booth, her eyes on me. "So, other than work, what else is going on?"

I shrugged, taking a sip of my iced tea. "Not much. Just trying to keep my head above water. You know how it is."

Kate nodded. "Yeah, I hear you. My dad's still giving me grief about White Pines. Thinks I should be doing something more 'important' with my life. Like being an equine therapist isn't important."

I could hear the frustration in her voice, and I knew it wasn't just about her dad. She cared deeply about her work and the people she helped. It wasn't just a job for her—it was her calling. "He just doesn't get it," I said softly. "But you're doing great, Kate. I see how much those kids and vets love you up there. And Morgan always brags about you, what a heart you have for therapy. She's tough to impress."

"Thanks," she said, her smile a little softer now. "It's just... hard, you know? Even when she says I'm doing great, I always feel like I have to prove myself."

"I get it," I said, feeling a pang of understanding. "Believe me, I do. I work for her husband, remember?"

Kate giggled. "Keepin' it in the family!"

We sat in comfortable silence for a moment, each lost in our own thoughts. I was grateful for Kate's company, for the way she could make even the toughest days feel a little lighter. The jukebox started playing an old country song, and a few couples got up to dance, their boots scuffing against the floor.

Kate nudged me with her elbow. "Think we'll ever have it figured out?"

I smiled, shaking my head. "Probably not. But we can keep trying."

"Cheers to that," she said, raising her glass. "To figuring it out, one day at a time."

I clinked my glass against hers, feeling a bit of the tension ease from my shoulders. Maybe things weren't perfect, but for now, I had a good friend, a decent meal on the way, and a moment to breathe. And sometimes, that was enough.

Chapter Ten

Cole

I swung my leg over Lynx's back and settled into the saddle, feeling the leather creak beneath me. It was still early, the sun just starting to climb over the horizon, casting long shadows across the arena. The cool morning air smelled like dust and hay, with just a hint of the honeysuckle growing wild along the fence line. I took a deep breath, trying to focus on the task at hand. Today was going to be a long day.

Clinic days were always a bit of a circus—twenty riders all bringing their own horses, their own egos, and their own expectations. But it helped keep the bills paid. After the fires tore through the valley, and Walker Ranch had to figure out where to cut back, Cody had come up with this idea to keep the ranch's show-horse budget funded. Hence, the outside horses we'd taken in for training, and these community clinic days we would cram in between our out-of-town shows. And hence, my promotion from stall grunt to training apprentice.

Cody had everyone all lined up at one end of the arena, giving a quick rundown of the day's schedule. I was supposed to be helping out, riding along, and giving pointers to the ones who needed it. Emily was doing the same on the other side, her back straight and her eyes scanning the line of riders like a hawk. She was good at this—better than me, probably. But I was determined to hold my own.

I glanced around, taking stock of the group. There was the usual mix—some older women in their fifties who'd come together like it was some kind of horsey girls' trip, a dad and his young daughter who looked like she was about twelve, a few teenagers who were probably here hoping to pick up some pointers for their 4-H shows. I could tell right away which ones were the serious competitors and which ones were just here for the experience.

"Alright, everyone," Cody called out, raising his voice over the sounds of restless horses and murmured conversation. "We're gonna start with some dry work this morning—working on reining maneuvers. We'll get into the cow cutting after lunch. Remember, today's about improving your skills, so don't be afraid to ask questions."

He shot a glance my way, and I gave him a nod, urging Lynx forward. We started at one end of the arena, and I watched as the riders tried to follow Cody's lead, practicing their circles, spins, and stops. Some of them had decent control, but a few were struggling—hands too tight on the reins, legs in the wrong position.

I rode over to one of the older women, who seemed to be having trouble with her turns. She was laughing, her face flushed with the effort. "You wanna keep your shoulders square," I said, trying to sound encouraging. "And keep your hands steady. Just a little lighter on the reins."

She looked up at me, her eyes twinkling. "Well, aren't you a handsome young man," she said with a grin. "I might just have to mess up a few more times so you keep coming over here."

I felt my face heat up a bit, but I kept my expression neutral. "Just here to help," I said, smiling back. "Let's try it again. Do less, and you'll get more."

She giggled, and a couple of her friends joined in, watching me with amused expressions. "You hear that, girls?" one of them called out. "We've got our own cute cowboy instructor!"

I gave them a polite nod and moved on, trying not to get too flustered. It was all in good fun, I knew that. This bunch were all regulars, and they were always a hoot and a half, especially during lunch breaks. But it was still hard to stay focused when you had a bunch of women old enough to be your mom... or your grandma... acting like schoolgirls.

I glanced over at the teenagers, noticing one girl in particular who kept staring at me. She was riding a flashy paint horse, her shoulders hunched up around her ears. Every time I tried to catch her eye, she looked away, blushing furiously.

I rode over, keeping my voice low and friendly. "Hey there. You doing alright?"

She nodded quickly, but her eyes stayed glued to her horse's mane.

"Alright," I said, trying not to sound too intimidating. "Just remember to keep your hands light. You want to guide him, not pull him around. Let him make the mistake before you put him back. That's how he learns."

She nodded again but didn't say anything. Her hands were shaking on the reins, and I could see her horse starting to get antsy.

"Has Cody suggested trying a softer bit on this horse?" I asked. "Might do him good, help him relax. He might like something with a roller to keep him busy."

She tried to smile, but she ended up just turning pink around the edges and staring at the back of her horse's head. "Uh, no, he... he didn't. That is, I... I don't think so." She gulped, tried to look up at me again, and then dropped her eyes to the arena sand.

I sighed. "Well, maybe Emily will have some suggestions." I was sure fresh out. How was I supposed to help the kid when she couldn't even look me in the eye?

"Emily," I called over, trying not to sound too desperate. "Mind giving her a hand?"

Emily trotted over on Copper, her expression calm but focused. "Sure thing," she said, flashing the girl a reassuring smile. "Why don't you come over here with me? We'll work on that turn together."

The girl nodded again, relief flooding her face, and I watched as Emily led her away, talking softly. I shook my head, feeling a mix of frustration and confusion. Why did some people make it look so easy?

I turned my attention back to the rest of the group, riding alongside them and giving pointers where I could. But every so often, my eyes drifted to the fields beyond the arena, where the Walker Ranch cattle were grazing. I couldn't help but think about home, about the grazing rights we were losing, and the bills that were piling up. It felt like there was a clock ticking down, but I didn't know how much time we had left.

"Cole!" Cody's voice snapped me back to the present. "Keep 'em moving, we're not here to sightsee."

"Right," I muttered, nudging Lynx forward again. "Sorry."

I tried to refocus, riding alongside a dad and his young daughter as they worked on their turns. The girl was determined, her little face scrunched up in concentration. "You're doing great," I told her, keeping my tone upbeat. "Just keep your eyes forward, and don't forget to breathe. See how he reaches forward and around when you look up? You stare at the ground, he does, too."

Her dad gave me a nod of thanks, and I could see the pride in his eyes. I envied him that—having something so simple and straightforward to be proud of. Sometimes, it felt like everything I was reaching for was just *out* of reach.

We worked through the morning, going over different maneuvers, each rider taking turns demonstrating what they'd learned. Cody rode between us all, giving pointers and correcting form. Emily and I did our best to keep things running smoothly, but every so often, we'd catch each other's eye. And it was the weirdest thing, but this sort of silent understanding passed between us. For all our differences, we both wanted the same thing: to do right by Cody, to prove ourselves.

By the time lunch rolled around, I was sweating through my shirt, my hands sticky with dust and leather. Cody called a break, and everyone started heading toward the tables set up under the big oak tree. There was a cooler of drinks and a spread of sandwiches, chips, and cookies—just what you'd expect at a ranch lunch.

I swung down from Lynx, loosening her cinch a bit before leading her to the shade. She was done for the day. I'd saddle another horse for the afternoon session with the cows. I'd wanted to ride her, because heaven knows she needed the cow practice, but Cody over-ruled me. "Keep her slow and precise today," he'd said.

And that was one of my problems. When your favorite horse is a stick of dynamite, and you were there for every second of the action, going slow was like watching paint dry.

I glanced over at Emily, who was pulling the saddle off Copper. She looked up, catching my eye again, and for a second, I thought she might smile. But she just gave a quick nod, her expression unreadable, before turning away.

I shook my head, feeling that familiar frustration bubbling up again. I still didn't know what to make of her—why she got under my skin the way she did, why I couldn't stop thinking about her. But right now, I had other things to worry about. Like how to keep my head in the game when my mind kept drifting back to home.

As I led Lynx over to the water trough, I tried to push all those thoughts aside. I needed to stay focused. Today wasn't just about proving myself to Cody—it was about proving something to myself, too.

Emily

After lunch, the sun was high in the sky, casting a warm, golden light over the ranch. The morning's reining work had gone well enough, and most of the riders seemed pleased with their progress. Now it was time for the real fun—the cow work. I could feel the excitement buzzing in the air as we moved into the larger outdoor arena where a group of cattle had been penned up, ready for their turn to play.

I led my fresh mount—a stocky sorrel we had taken in to train named Cosmo—into the arena, glancing around to see everyone getting back into place. Cole was already there on his new horse for the afternoon, a bay gelding named Frank, keeping a watchful eye on the group as they gathered at the far end. He looked calm, focused—like he was in his element. And from the way the ladies were watching him, I could tell I wasn't the only one who noticed.

The older women from this morning were still giggling amongst themselves, their eyes constantly drifting toward Cole. One of them, a lady in a pink baseball cap with rhinestones, was practically swooning every time he so much as glanced her way. I could see a few of the teenagers whispering to each other, stealing shy glances in his direction. Even the twelve-year-old girl kept sneaking looks at him, her cheeks going pink whenever he caught her eye. I bit back a grin. It was almost comical, the way every female in the vicinity was googly-eyed over him.

Okay, I had to admit it. Cole had that rugged cowboy charm that was hard to ignore. And when he wasn't being a stubborn turd, always thinking he knew best, he wasn't exactly bad to look at either. I just wished he didn't make it so difficult to work with him half the time. He could be so frustrating, always needing to be better than the next person, always pushing the limits. It was like he had something to prove—to Cody, to the world, to himself.

"Alright, everyone!" Cody's voice cut through my thoughts, snapping me back to the task at hand. "Let's get moving on the practice flag. We'll get your horses warmed up and working before we bring the live cattle in. Remember to keep your eyes on the flag, and your hands steady. Let the horse do the work."

I moved Cosmo into position and watched as Cody took the little twelve-year-old girl over to the mechanical flag, a simple contraption that moved back and forth to simulate the movement of a cow. It was a great tool for getting a horse's attention and teaching them to track, without the added chaos of a real cow. It was perfect that everyone got to watch Cody, the expert, helping probably our greenest rider on the flag. As soon as they were finished, Cody took her straight over to the live cows, and turned the flag work over to Cole and me.

Cole and I started helping the rest of the group get into a rhythm, moving their horses smoothly with the flag. I could see that most of them were doing alright, but there was one rider in particular who was struggling—a middle-aged man on a flashy, high-strung sorrel mare that looked eager to work. The horse was all fired up, practically vibrating with energy, but the guy kept pulling back, slowing her down, and you could see the frustration building in the mare. She was cow fresh, clearly wanting to do her job, but her rider wasn't giving her the chance.

I frowned, glancing over at Cole. He was watching the same pair, his brow furrowed in concentration. We both saw it—the way the mare kept fighting the bit, tossing her head, wanting to go but being held back. It was only a matter of time before that energy boiled over.

"Think we should say something?" I asked Cole quietly as we rode closer together.

He shook his head, eyes still on the rider. "Not our call. Keep him safe, teach him the moves. Beyond that, it's up to Cody to step in."

I nodded, biting my lip. He was right, of course. But I couldn't help feeling a little impatient. If Cody didn't see what was happening soon, things could get ugly.

Finally, Cody finished up with the rider he was working with and turned his attention to the man with the sorrel mare. He rode over, bringing him and his horse over to the live cattle. "Alright, let's see what you got," Cody said, nodding toward the pen. "Keep her steady, and don't let her run off with you."

The rider nodded, looking a little nervous as he moved his mare toward the pen. But the second she spotted the cow, the mare lit up, her ears pricking forward, her muscles coiling like a spring. She was ready to work.

But instead of letting her go, the man pulled back hard on the reins, trying to hold her in check. The mare tossed her head, fighting against the pressure. Cody's eyes narrowed, watching closely.

And then it happened. The mare's frustration boiled over, and she blasted forward, yanking the reins from the rider's hands. She tore after the cow with a speed and determination that caught everyone off guard, weaving and ducking with sharp, powerful turns that sent dust flying up in clouds.

Cody shouted, "Whoa! Easy now!" and signaled the rider to pull back. "Let's go back, one step at a time," he instructed, trying to regain control of the situation.

I clenched my jaw—that wasn't going to work. Ordinarily, it would, but not this time. The mare was too wound up, too frustrated from being held back. She needed to go. She needed to feel like she had the freedom to work. I thought back to earlier days in the show ring, and I remembered seeing this mare in action before. She'd been trained by one of Cody's competitors, and this guy bought her a few months ago. She was a little hot, a little edgy, but she was also an experienced horse that knew her job well, and just needed to be let loose.

I rode over to Cody, keeping my voice low so as not to draw too much attention. "Cody," I said, "I think she needs a different approach. Maybe let the rider park his hands on the horn and give the mare her head. Let her do what she's trained to do."

Cody turned and gave me a look—a stern, quiet warning to back off. "This isn't your call, Emily," he said, his tone sharp. "We're sticking to the basics."

I felt my cheeks heat up with frustration. I was just trying to help, to make things go smoother. Before I could say anything else, Cole rode up next to me. "I think Emily's right," he said. "That mare's experienced. The rider's fighting her too much, getting in her way. Emily's got it nailed."

Cody paused, looking between the two of us. For a moment, I thought he might tell us both to mind our business, but then he let out a slow breath and nodded. "Alright," he said. "Let's try it."

He called the rider over and explained the change. "Let her have her head this time," he said. "Just park your hands on the saddle horn and hold on. Let her show you what she can do."

The rider nodded, looking relieved to have a different plan. He adjusted his grip, planting his hands firmly on the horn, and gave the mare her head. The second he did, she shot her head down and low, her movements fluid and confident as she cut the cow with precision and speed. The change was immediate—the mare was focused, her frustration melting away as she got to do what she was bred to do.

The rider's face lit up, and I could see the tension leaving his shoulders. Cody watched closely, nodding in approval. "Good," he called out. "That's more like it!"

As the rider finished his turn and brought the mare to a stop, a round of applause broke out from the rest of the group. I couldn't help but smile, feeling a rush of satisfaction. It was a small victory, but it felt like a big one.

Cody rode over to me and Cole, a thoughtful look on his face. "You two were right," he admitted. "Good call."

Cole and I exchanged a look, both of us a little surprised to hear him say it. For a moment, we just stared at each other, and then, almost without thinking, I felt a smile tugging at my lips. Cole's expression softened, and he gave me a small nod, a hint of a smile playing on his lips as well. It was a rare moment of agreement, and it felt... nice.

As we rode back to the barn to unsaddle, the sun was starting to dip low in the sky, casting long, golden shadows across the arena. I glanced over at Cole, feeling a strange mix of emotions. Maybe he wasn't so bad after all. Maybe there was more to him than I'd given him credit for.

But then again, that didn't mean he wasn't still a stubborn turd most of the time.

Chapter Eleven

Cole

The last of the riders had packed up and left, their trailers rumbling down the long dirt drive of Walker Ranch, kicking up a haze of dust behind them. The sun was starting to dip low, painting the sky in streaks of pink and orange, but the heat of the day still clung to everything, the air thick and sticky. I wiped the sweat off my brow with the back of my hand and took a deep breath, feeling the exhaustion settle into my bones.

It had been a long, hot day. The clinic went alright, and Cody's nod of approval felt good—a small victory, at least. But even as I finished mucking out the last stall, a weight settled in my chest. I couldn't stop thinking about everything hanging in the balance—things here at Walker Ranch and back home. There was a lot riding on the decisions we were making, and it all felt like a race against time. I grabbed the pitchfork, ready to start hauling feed, when my phone buzzed in my pocket.

I pulled it out, squinting at the screen. It was Chase. I hesitated for a second, glancing around. I didn't want anyone overhearing this conversation. I ducked into the far end of the barn, where it was quiet, stepping behind a stack of hay bales.

"Yeah?" I answered, keeping my voice low.

"Hey, Cole, when you heading home? Gage and Trent are about at each other's throats over here."

I let out a frustrated sigh, rubbing a hand over my face. "I still got chores to finish up. Why? What happened now?"

Chase growled on the other end. "They had a meeting with the Fish and Wildlife agent this afternoon. Took him out to the grazing grounds, tried to show him there ain't any owl nests out there, but he's holding his ground. Says just because he didn't see any nests doesn't mean they're not there. He's sticking to the grazing restrictions, Cole."

I closed my eyes, leaning back against the barn wall, feeling the weight of the news settle like a stone in my gut. "You've got to be kidding me," I muttered under my breath, my fist clenching around the phone. That was the last thing we needed. "What's that mean for us?"

"It means things are gonna get tight," Chase replied, his voice low and strained. "Real tight. Gage and Trent are talking about selling some cattle, maybe even some of the land, if it comes to it. Mom's trying to keep them calm, but it's getting ugly."

I could hear the worry in Chase's voice, and it cut through me like a knife. "Look, just... hold things down until I get back, alright? I'll finish up here and head home as soon as I can."

"Yeah," Chase said quietly. "Just hurry, okay? We could use you here."

I hung up and took a deep breath, trying to keep my frustration in check. I knew Chase was right, but what could I do? It wasn't like I could change the state's mind about the stupid spotted owl. And no matter how hard I worked here, it wasn't going to put enough money in our pockets to cover what we were about to lose.

I stuffed my phone back into my pocket and turned to head back to the feed room, my thoughts a tangled mess. That's when I almost ran right into Emily.

She was standing just inside the doorway, her eyes wide with surprise. I stumbled back a step, my heart lurching in my chest. "Emily," I said, a little sharper than I meant to. "What are you doing here?"

She blinked, her face flushing as she glanced away. "I was... just getting some feed," she said, her voice quiet. "I didn't mean to eavesdrop. I—"

My cheeks heated, and I could feel the frustration rising again. Of all the people to overhear that conversation, it had to be Emily. "Well, you heard enough," I snapped, brushing past her to grab a feed scoop from the wall. "Fish and Wildlife are about to shut us down. So now you know."

She didn't move, just stood there, her eyes still wide, watching me. "Cole, I—" she started, then stopped, biting her lip. I could see the wheels turning in her head, trying to find the right words.

"What?" I shot back, dumping the feed into a bucket with more force than necessary. "Gonna tell me how I should handle it? Go ahead. I'm listening."

Her expression softened, and she shook her head slowly. "No, I'm not," she said quietly. "I just... I didn't know things were that bad. I'm sorry."

I snorted, not looking at her. "Yeah, well, it is what it is. Doesn't change anything."

For a moment, there was just silence between us, the only sound the distant lowing of cattle and the rustle of hay in the barn. I could feel her eyes on me, and it made my skin itch.

"I'm serious, Cole," she said, her voice a little stronger now. "If there's anything I can do to help—"

"There's not," I cut in, turning to face her. "This is my family's problem, not yours. Just... forget you heard anything, alright?"

Her face fell slightly, and she nodded. "Okay," she said softly. "If that's what you want."

I didn't know what I wanted. Not really. Part of me was angry that she'd heard, but another part of me... maybe a small part... was relieved. Like, maybe I didn't have to carry all this weight on my own.

"Look," I said, letting out a long breath. "I gotta finish these chores. You should probably head home."

She nodded again, but she didn't move right away. "Alright," she said, finally turning to go. But before she left, she paused, glancing back over her shoulder. "For what it's worth, Cole... I think you're doing the best you can. And that's all anyone can ask."

I stared after her, watching as she walked away, her footsteps light on the barn floor. For a second, I felt a flicker of something—something that wasn't frustration or anger. Something that felt a lot like... gratitude.

But I didn't have time to dwell on it. I had work to do, and I needed to get home. I shook my head, grabbing the feed bucket and turning back to the horses. There'd be time to think about all that later.

Emily

I turned the key in the lock and pushed the door open, stepping into the familiar clutter of our little apartment. The smell of lavender and old books greeted me, a mix of home and something else—something I never could quite name. So many other scents from so many other homes, all swimming in the over-riding aroma of fabric softener and ironing starch. My mom was sitting at the dining table, her brow furrowed in concentration as she scribbled away in her notebook, bills and envelopes spread out in front of her.

"Hey, Mom," I said, trying to sound cheerful as I set my bag down by the door. My voice came out a bit flat, and I could feel the exhaustion weighing down every step I took.

She looked up, her face brightening with a smile. "Emily! How was the clinic?" she asked, setting down her pen. "I bet you had a great time teaching today. You always do."

I forced a smile, nodding as I kicked off my boots. "Yeah, it was... fine," I said, but even I could hear how unconvincing I sounded.

Mom's smile faltered, and her eyes searched mine. "Just fine?" she asked, a hint of concern creeping into her voice. "You were looking forward to it so much. What happened?"

I shook my head, dropping my eyes to the floor. "It's nothing," I muttered, rubbing the back of my neck. "Just tired, I guess."

"Come on now," she said, leaning forward on her elbows, her expression softening. "You're always tired after a clinic day, but you're usually buzzing with excitement, talking a mile a minute. Something must've happened."

I felt my chest tighten, that familiar feeling of being cornered. I didn't want to talk about Cole, didn't want to betray his confidence. It wasn't my place to share his problems, especially not with Mom. "I said it's nothing," I snapped, sharper than I intended. "Can we just drop it?"

The hurt flickered across her face, and she drew back, her shoulders slumping. "Alright," she said quietly, picking up her pen again. "If that's what you want."

Guilt stabbed at me, and I took a deep breath, trying to find the right words to apologize. But the room suddenly felt too small, too cluttered. The piles of papers, the stacks of old magazines and books, the mismatched chairs crowding the table—it all pressed in on me, suffocating. I clenched my fists, the anxiety bubbling up in my chest like a wave I couldn't hold back.

"Mom, I..." I started, then my eyes darted around the room, unable to stop taking in the mess—the piles of papers, the half-opened mail, the empty coffee cup teetering on top of a stack of magazines. "Can't you—" I blurted out, my voice rising before I could stop myself. "Can't you just clean this place up a little? We live in a dump!"

The words hung in the air, sharp and cutting, and the look on my mom's face shifted from hurt to something deeper, something that twisted in my chest. I hadn't meant to say that. Not like that. I felt the heat rush to my face, humiliation flooding through me. I opened my mouth to apologize, but nothing came out. I needed to get out of there, away from the look in her eyes. Without another word, I turned on my heel and walked out of the room, my footsteps heavy on the old wood floor, leaving my mom sitting there, her expression stunned and sad.

I shut my bedroom door behind me, leaning against it as I squeezed my eyes shut. My heart was still pounding, and I felt like I couldn't catch my breath. How could I have said that to her? I knew better than anyone how much this shop meant to Mom—how it had kept a roof over our heads all these years. I might as well have kicked her in the gut.

I slid down the door until I was sitting on the floor, my back against the cool wood. I felt awful, like the worst kind of human being. First, I'd accidentally overheard Cole's private conversation—learning all about his family's troubles that he surely wanted to keep hidden—and then I'd gone and hurt my mom with my careless words.

I clenched my fists in frustration. Even if I went out there right now and apologized, it wouldn't change anything. The damage was done. I knew she wouldn't be able to un-hear it, no matter what I said. She'd still be thinking about it, wondering if it was true. I felt like I was stuck in this cycle of making things worse, one bad move after another.

I pulled out my phone, staring at the screen as if it might hold some answers. I could feel the heaviness settling in my chest, and I just wanted to escape into something, anything, that would take my mind off all of this. I started scrolling, looking for something to distract myself, but nothing held my attention.

Then, a weird idea popped into my head. What if I texted Cole? It was a ridiculous thought. Why would I do that? But... maybe just something simple, like saying, "Good job today." After all, he *had* done a good job. A great job. He'd really made a difference for some of the clinic riders, and the way he'd stood up for me to Cody had felt... nice. Better than nice, actually. It felt like, for a moment, we were on the same team.

Before I could talk myself out of it, I pulled up his number and typed out the text.

Good job today. You really helped those riders out.

I stared at the screen, my finger hovering over the send button. Was this a terrible idea? I couldn't decide. But then I just thought, what the heck, and hit send.

For a few minutes, there was nothing. I stared at my phone, waiting. Maybe he wouldn't respond at all. Maybe he'd think I was being weird. But then, my phone buzzed with a reply.

Thanks. You weren't so bad yourself.

I couldn't help but laugh a little at that. I could almost hear his voice, that dry, half-serious tone he got when he was trying to be humble. I knew it must have cost him a lot to even admit that much.

I chewed on my bottom lip, thinking. Should I leave it there? A nice little exchange, no pressure. Or... should I push my luck? Maybe this was a chance to show him that I wasn't just some rival or obstacle. Maybe I could be... what? An ally? A friend?

Taking a deep breath, I decided to go for it. What did I have to lose, really? I typed out another message, trying to keep it light.

How are things? I mean... how was it when you got home?

I hit send before I could change my mind, and then waited, my pulse thundering in my ears. There was nothing for a moment, and I started to think maybe I'd overstepped. Maybe I shouldn't have asked. But then, I saw the blinking dots, showing that he was typing back. My heart did a little flip.

And then... they stopped.

I stared at the screen, holding my breath. A second later, they started again. And then stopped.

I let out a frustrated sigh, about to put the phone down, when finally his message came through.

Easier to explain over the phone. If you want to hear all the gory details.

Well, now! I wasn't sure what I'd expected, but this wasn't it. And maybe... maybe this was better. I hesitated for just a second, then typed back quickly.

Sure.

I pressed send and waited, my stomach twisting with a mix of nerves and excitement. I didn't know where this was going, but I was curious to find out.

Cole

I stared at the phone in my hand, thumb hovering over the call button. What was I even doing? Why was I talking to Emily Carson about this? I could almost hear Gage's voice in my head, telling me I was crazy. Little Miss Perfect wouldn't understand, wouldn't get any of this. She'd never had to scrape by or watch her family struggle. What did she know about any of it?

But then again, she'd asked. She'd actually asked how things were at home. And for some reason, maybe because I was tired or because she'd actually seemed to care, I'd told her I'd call. I clenched my jaw, took a deep breath, and punched the call button before I could think better of it.

The phone rang once, then twice, and my heart started hammering in my chest. What was I even going to say? But then, she picked up on the second ring.

"Hello?" she answered, her voice cautious, like she wasn't sure what to expect.

I froze for a second, all the words I'd thought I'd say suddenly gone. "Hey," I managed, but my voice came out a little more clipped than I meant. There was an awkward pause, and I cleared my throat, trying to fill the silence. "Uh... I didn't think you'd actually pick up."

She gave a small laugh, and I could almost see her raising an eyebrow on the other end. "Well, you did say you'd call," she said. "So... here we are."

"Yeah," I replied, rubbing the back of my neck. "Here we are."

Another pause stretched out between us, the quiet almost deafening. I shifted my weight from one foot to the other, glancing around the barn. "So... today," I blurted, grasping for anything to break the tension. "Clinic went pretty well, huh?"

"Yeah, it did," she said, sounding a bit more relaxed. "People seemed to have a good time."

"Yeah, most of 'em," I said, and a small grin tugged at my lips. "Especially that lady with the pink rhinestone ball cap. I thought she was gonna ask me out right there in the arena."

There was a beat of silence, and then Emily's laugh came through the phone, light and a little breathless. "Oh, yeah. She was definitely smitten," she said, and I could hear the smile in her voice now. "I think you made her whole week when you took her hand to adjust her reins."

I chuckled. "Well, at least someone's having a good time," I said, trying to keep things light. "Maybe I should start charging extra for the charm."

Emily laughed again, and I could hear the tension in her voice melting away, replaced by something softer. For a moment, it felt easy. Like we were just two people talking, no rivalry, no pressure. But then there was a pause, and her tone shifted.

"So... your family," she said softly. "I know Chase a little, but I've never really talked to Trent or Gage. And I know your mom because she's worked with Morgan on some horse rescues, but... not in a while."

My stomach tightened, and I went quiet, trying to find the right words. But the truth was, I didn't have any. Not for this. Not for everything that was happening.

"Cole?" she prompted gently, and something in her voice—something soft, understanding—made the dam break.

"Mom hasn't done any horse rescuing for a while because we can hardly afford our own groceries."

"I... Oh," she sighed. "Is it...?"

I took a deep breath and let it all out. "It's bad, Emily," I admitted, my voice low. "My dad's death... the fires... now the grazing rights. It's all piling up. And we're losing ground, literally. Our grazing grounds are shrinking, and it's straining the family. Gage and Trent are always at each other's throats about what to do. Mom's trying to hold us all together, but... I don't know how much longer we can keep this up."

She was quiet for a moment, and I could hear the soft hum of background noise on her end. It sounded like a clothes dryer or something. Then she asked, her voice gentle, "What can you do?"

I hadn't expected that. Empathy. From Emily. Little Miss Perfect, who seemed to have everything together, who never seemed to struggle with anything. I wasn't sure what I'd expected her to say, but it wasn't this.

"I don't know," I admitted, feeling the words stick in my throat. "Tonight, Chase and I were talking about taking construction jobs. That's the first time Chase has even talked about leaving the ranch. I've been thinking about it for a while, but hearing him say it... it just made it all feel more real."

Another pause, and I could almost hear her thinking on the other end of the line. "Would that mean you'd have to stop training horses?" she asked, her voice quiet.

I swallowed hard, the thought hitting me like a punch to the gut. "I don't know," I said honestly. "Maybe. Probably. I mean, if we're both working construction, there won't be time for much else."

I could hear her swallowing over the phone, then she spoke again. "I hope you don't have to do that," she said softly.

I blinked, caught off guard. "Why?" I asked cautiously, not sure what she was getting at. "Why would you care?"

It took her a moment to answer, and I could hear the hesitation in her voice. "Because... you're good, Cole," she said finally. "You have a gift with the horses. I'd hate to see you give up on that."

I stared at the ground, her words sinking in. Did she really mean that? "I don't know," I said, my voice thick. "You're always ragging on me. You can't think I'm that good."

Her voice wavered a little, then steadied, more certain. "No, I do," she insisted. "You've got a sharp eye. You're good with the horses. And you've got something special with Lynx."

I was stunned into silence, not sure what to say. It wasn't often I got a compliment from Emily, and I wasn't sure how to take it. "Lynx is the one in charge," I said finally. "I'm just along for the ride."

She laughed softly on the other end, and I couldn't help but smile. "Sometimes that's the best way."

"Yeah," I agreed, feeling some of the tension ease out of my chest. "Maybe you're right."

We both fell quiet for a moment, and I could feel the corners of my mouth turning up in a small smile. Maybe this wasn't so bad. Maybe Emily wasn't so bad.

"Hey..." I gulped some air. "Do me a favor?"

"Sure."

"Don't say anything about this to Cody. If... you know, if it comes to that, I don't wanna have him hear it from somewhere else."

There was a small hum of agreement from the other end. "You got it."

"Well, I guess I'll see you tomorrow," I said finally, not really wanting to hang up but not knowing what else to say.

"Yeah," she replied, her voice soft. "See you tomorrow, Cole."

I ended the call, staring at the phone in my hand for a moment longer before shoving it back into my pocket. I didn't know what to make of any of this, but I had to admit, it felt... nice. Different. And maybe, just maybe, a little hopeful.

Chapter Twelve

Cole

I showed up early to Walker Ranch the next morning, feeling a bit lighter on my feet. After the conversation with Emily last night, I wasn't exactly sure where we stood, but it felt like a truce of sorts. Or maybe just an understanding. Either way, I wasn't about to question it. The air was crisp, the sun just beginning to climb over the horizon, casting a soft orange glow across the barn.

I went straight to the tack room, checking the leg boots I'd washed last night to see if they were dry, making sure everything was in order. I figured I'd get a jump on things, prove to Cody I was serious about pulling my weight. Just as I was double-checking the cinches, I heard footsteps behind me.

"Cole," Cody called, and I turned to see him standing in the doorway, arms crossed. "Got a job for you today."

"Yeah? What's that?" I asked, trying to sound eager. Cody always had that look about him, like he was sizing you up, testing you.

He jerked his head toward the door. "Need you and Emily to take the truck over to the Lambert place. I bought a load of ranch two-year-olds from them, need you both to bring them back here."

I blinked, surprised. "Both of us?" I asked. "Ain't that a one-man job?"

Cody shook his head, his expression firm. "Normally, yeah. But these young ones are fresh. Last thing I need is one of 'em spooking and causing a mess. You and Emily can handle it better together."

I nodded slowly. Fresh two-year-olds were always a gamble, especially if they hadn't been handled much. It made sense to have two sets of hands, but I couldn't help the twinge of nerves that shot through me. Working with Emily all day... that was going to be interesting. "Got it," I said, trying to sound more confident than I felt. "When are we heading out?"

"Soon as Emily gets here," Cody replied. He turned to leave, then paused, glancing back over his shoulder. "And, Cole... don't give me any reason to regret sending you both. Keep it professional."

I nodded again. "Sure thing, boss."

Cody left, and I took a deep breath, running a hand through my hair. Alright, this was fine. Just a day's work, nothing more. I was good with horses—no reason today would be any different. I busied myself with prepping the truck, checking the tires and making sure the trailer was hooked up right. The last thing I wanted was to make a fool of myself by missing something obvious.

By the time I had everything ready, Emily showed up, looking a little more awake than she had yesterday. She gave me a small nod, her eyes flicking over the truck and trailer. "Morning," she said, her voice cautious but not unfriendly.

"Morning," I replied, trying to sound casual. "Cody tell you about the plan?"

"Yeah," she said, glancing around. "Guess it's gonna be a long day."

"Guess so," I agreed. I could feel the awkwardness settling in between us, like we were both waiting for the other to make the first move. "You wanna drive, or should I?"

She hesitated, then shrugged. "You can drive. I'll ride shotgun."

"Alright," I said, hopping up into the driver's seat. Emily climbed in beside me, and I started up the truck. The engine rumbled to life, and we pulled out of the ranch, heading down the highway that led to the Lambert place.

The silence between us was thick, but not exactly uncomfortable. Just... tense. Like we were both trying to figure out how to navigate this new territory we found ourselves in.

I cleared my throat, glancing over at her. "So... any idea what kind of stock we're picking up?" I asked, trying to break the ice.

Emily shook her head. "Not really. Just heard they're a mix of colts and fillies. Probably just been pulled off the range. Could be a handful."

"Did he tell you what he got them for?"

She shrugged. "Probably no more than he told you, but if I had to guess, I'd say Cody got them cheap with the thought of training and selling them. Which means *we'll* be training them."

I nodded, keeping my eyes on the road. "Yeah, that's what I figured. Should be fun."

"Fun," she repeated, a hint of a smile tugging at her lips. "That's one word for it."

I chuckled, feeling some of the tension ease out of my shoulders. Maybe this wouldn't be so bad after all. "Well, at least it'll keep things interesting," I said, trying to sound upbeat. "Better than mucking stalls all day, right?"

She laughed softly, a sound that surprised me. "I guess you've got a point there," she agreed. "Besides, working with the real fresh ones, getting them settled in and helping their confidence grow... well, that's some of the most fun, if you ask me."

I glanced over at her—the way her curly blonde hair caught a halo of morning light filtering in through the truck window—and I had to flex my fingers on the steering wheel, because they suddenly shot through with that same kind of nervous ache that got me just before I went into the show ring. "Yeah," I said quietly. "Know what you mean."

We drove on in silence for a few more minutes, the sun climbing higher in the sky, warming the cab of the truck. I could feel myself relaxing a little, getting used to the idea of spending the day with Emily. Maybe this was a good thing—a chance to prove that I wasn't just some hothead who couldn't work with others. Maybe even a chance to show her that we could get along, maybe even work well together.

When we finally pulled up to the Lambert place, I cut the engine and glanced over at her. "Alright, let's see what we're dealing with," I said, feeling a mix of anticipation and nerves.

Emily nodded, her expression serious but not unfriendly. "Let's do it," she agreed, and we both hopped out of the truck.

Emily

The horses were in a small corral, shifting around restlessly. I could tell right away that these two-year-olds hadn't seen much handling. Pretty typical of ranch-raised colts. They tossed their heads and pranced nervously, eyeing us like we were the boogeymen coming to drag them away. I sighed, glancing at Cole, who was already looking serious, his eyes scanning the horses, probably figuring out which ones would give us trouble.

"Morning!" The rancher, an older man with a weathered face and a baseball cap pulled low over his eyes, called out as he walked up to us. "These are the ones Cody bought. Should be a good bunch—just need a bit of work."

Cole nodded. "Thanks for holding them for us," he said, polite but direct. "Let's get 'em loaded up."

The rancher tipped his hat back, surveying the horses. "They're a bit fresh," he warned, almost like it was an afterthought. "You sure you don't want me to give you a hand?"

Cole shook his head. "We got it," he said. "Better they get used to us now anyway."

I nodded in agreement, my eyes on a tall colt that kept pawing at the ground, snorting. This was going to be a job.

We moved slowly, taking our time, coaxing each horse toward the trailer. Most of them went up with a little encouragement, a few nudges and clicks of the tongue. But then we got to the jittery one, a colt with a nervous eye that kept sidestepping every time we got near him. He wasn't having any of it.

"Come on, now," the rancher muttered, getting impatient. He moved in quickly, trying to push the colt up the ramp with a firm hand. "Just gotta get him in there," he said. "Don't let him think he's got a choice."

Cole stepped forward, his hand out. "Hold on a second," he said calmly. "Let's give him a minute."

The rancher looked like he wanted to argue, but Cole had that tone in his voice that brooked no argument. I watched as Cole moved to the side of the colt, his hands steady, his posture relaxed. He didn't rush or push. He just let the colt sniff around, figure out the ramp, get used to the idea.

"Easy, now," Cole murmured, keeping his voice low and steady. The colt's ears flicked back and forth, still nervous but not panicking. Cole gave him a little more time, just standing there, quiet and calm.

And then, almost like he decided on his own, the colt took a tentative step forward, then another. Within a few moments, he was up the ramp and into the trailer, no fuss, no fight.

"Good job, boy," Cole said, giving the colt a gentle pat on the shoulder through the trailer slats. I was impressed—again. He had this way of reading horses, knowing just when to push and when to hold back. I could see it now, why Cody trusted him so much with the young stock.

The rancher grumbled something under his breath but didn't argue, and we got the rest of the colts loaded without much trouble. And before I knew it, we had the door closed, and Lambert was tipping his hat and wishing us luck with this bunch.

Back in the truck, Cole started up the engine, and we pulled away from the Lambert place, the trailer rattling behind us. The silence settled in the cab again, a little less heavy this time. I watched him from the corner of my eye, noticing the way he kept glancing in the side mirror, checking on the horses sticking their noses through the upper slats of the stock trailer. I glanced over at Cole, trying to find a way to start a conversation.

I wasn't sure what to say. After the clinic yesterday and our talk last night, I felt like I was starting to see a different side of him. Maybe he wasn't just a stubborn know-it-all who drove me crazy. Maybe there was more to him. But how did you go from "I'm impressed with your horse skills" to "Tell me your life story"?

"So..." I finally said, clearing my throat. "I guess we'll be packing up the show horses in a few days to head to that show in California. Supposed be a big one."

Cole nodded, his eyes on the road. "Yeah, we'll need to get them prepped. Should be a good show. Hopefully, we come back with a few blue ribbons."

I smiled, feeling a bit more at ease. "You think Cody's gonna want to start these two-year-olds right away, or wait until we're back?"

Cole glanced at me, his expression thoughtful. "Hard to say," he replied. "Could go either way. These colts are pretty green. Might be better to let them settle for a bit, but you know Cody—he might just want to get a jump on things."

I nodded, keeping my eyes on the road ahead. "Yeah, that sounds like him. Always thinking two steps ahead."

He gave a small chuckle. "Yeah. Keeps us on our toes, though."

I smiled at that, the tension in the cab easing a little. "I guess we're in for a busy few weeks, either way," I said. "I hope those horses from the clinic yesterday hold up alright while we're gone. Some of those folks are gonna need more help."

"Yeah," Cole agreed. "But they've got a good start. The rest will come with time and practice."

Cole glanced over at me, a small smile playing on his lips. "You did pretty good with them today. Kept your cool."

I felt a little warmth spread through me at the compliment. "Thanks. You too," I said. "That colt back there, the jittery one... you handled him well. Saved us from a potential wreck."

He gave a modest shrug. "Just gave him a little space to figure things out. Sometimes that's all they need."

I nodded, falling silent for a moment. I could feel the conversation starting to settle back into that comfortable rhythm we'd found yesterday, and I didn't want it to slip away. I wanted to know more, to dig a little deeper. But how did I get there?

"So…" I ventured again, choosing my words carefully, "I heard a rumor that Trent's seeing someone. Cassie Southerland, right?"

Cole groaned, rolling his eyes. "Yeah, Cassie," he said, his voice dripping with exasperation. "Only met her a couple of times, but she didn't exactly impress me."

I chuckled, glad to see him open up a bit more. "What's wrong with her?"

He shrugged, one hand on the wheel. "I dunno. Just… not my type, I guess. But hey, she's Trent's problem."

"Sounds like you're not too thrilled about it."

He sighed. "It's not that, exactly. I just… I don't see it lasting, you know? She's all into… I dunno, fancy dinners and expensive clothes. Trent's never been about that stuff. Doesn't seem like a good fit, but… whatever. Not my call."

I laughed. "Fair enough. Family's always complicated, right?"

He gave a small snort of agreement. "Ain't that the truth."

There was a brief silence, and I could tell he was trying to figure out how to keep the conversation going. He glanced at me, a little awkward, then asked, "At least you don't have to worry about your brother bringing home a weirdo. It's just you and your mom, right?"

I blinked, a little caught off guard. "Oh, uh… no, actually," I said. "I have a sister, Lauren. She moved to San Diego right after high school. Wanted to be closer to our dad."

Cole looked surprised. "Didn't know that."

I shrugged. "Not too shocking. She's a few years older than we are, and she wasn't much on the ranching scene even when she did live in town."

"You two close?"

"As close as you can be by phone. She was threatening to come see me at the show, so I'm hoping she makes good on that, but San Diego is a long way from Tulare, and she gets real busy at work. I'm not holding my breath."

"So... she lives near your dad, right? They must be pretty tight."

I hesitated, my smile tightening a bit. "Sure. That."

He raised an eyebrow, catching on to my hesitation. "Oh, there's more to that story," he guessed, a hint of teasing in his voice.

I shook my head but couldn't help the small laugh that slipped out. "It's not a big deal. She mostly wanted to get out on her own, make a name for herself, and Dad let her live with him for free for a couple of years until she got her feet under her. She's a social media manager for some big corporation now. Not exactly something you can do in a small town like ours."

Cole nodded, seeming to understand. "Sounds like she's doing alright for herself. Must be nice, living out there near the coast."

"Yeah," I replied, my tone more subdued. "She likes it, I think. But there's been some tension with Dad lately, mostly over his girlfriend. It's... complicated."

Cole nodded again, his eyes focused on the road. "Sounds like fun," he said with a dry chuckle. "Funny how families are, huh? Everyone's got their own mess to deal with."

"Yeah," I agreed softly. "But I guess that's what makes it interesting, right?"

He glanced over at me, a small smile tugging at his lips. "Interesting. That's one word for it."

The truck rattled along, and the silence between us didn't feel as heavy as it used to. We were making small talk, sure, but it was different now—more open, less forced. I wasn't exactly sure where to take the conversation next, but I found myself wanting to know more. Not just about his family, but about *him*.

"So... what about you?" I ventured, glancing over at him. "Any big plans for the future?"

Cole raised an eyebrow, giving me a sideways look. "Big plans?" he repeated, almost like the concept was foreign to him. He scratched his jaw, thinking it over. "I dunno. I'm just trying to figure things out, I guess. See where this training gig goes. Cody's giving me a good shot, and I want to make the most of it."

I nodded, feeling a flicker of curiosity. "Before you started working for Cody, did you ever think about doing something else? I mean, besides ranch work?"

He hesitated, his fingers tapping lightly on the steering wheel. "Sometimes," he admitted. "And more lately, of course. Especially with everything going on at home... Already told you that, though. There's plenty of work rebuilding around here since the fires. Could make a decent living."

I frowned a little at that. "I was wondering if you were actually serious last night or if it was just the heat of the moment. You'd leave the ranch? Just like that?"

Cole shrugged, his expression thoughtful. "Not saying I *want* to. But sometimes... you gotta do what you gotta do, y'know?"

I nodded, feeling a twinge of sympathy for him. I could see how much the weight of his family's problems was dragging him down. He was clearly under a lot of pressure, and I hadn't really seen that before. "Makes sense," I said softly. "But I don't remember ever seeing you so dug into anything before. It'd be a shame if you gave that up."

He tipped his head toward me. "What does that mean? You're talking about before I came to work for Cody?"

"Yeah, like in high school. You graduated, what... a year ahead of me?"

He rubbed his ear in thought. "Shoot, I guess. Something like that, but I almost didn't."

I laughed a little. "What is that supposed to mean?"

"Means Mrs Wallis almost didn't give me my diploma. Had to pull a few Saturdays at school to get my math and English grades up enough to pass."

"So, what you're saying is that you barely escaped being in my class after all?"

"Pretty much, but Mom would've had my hide, so I knuckled down. Bet you pulled straight A's, didn't you?"

"No. My GPA was only a 3.85."

He rolled his eyes so hard he almost jerked the steering wheel. "Seriously?"

"Well, I was busy," I said defensively. "I showed dairy goats and horses and worked for my mom and—"

"Hey, hey, I was kidding! Sheesh. You really pulled those kinds of grades with all that going on?"

I shrugged. "I don't like failing." But then I swallowed when his face changed color. Geez, what a snob I sounded like. "It was Meryl, really. My 4-H leader," I said quickly. "She would basically put us in time out if we didn't have the grades to compete."

Cole chuckled softly. "Yeah, I sort of remember you hanging out with that 4-H crew. Always with Kate and that whole bunch."

"Guilty," I admitted with a laugh. "And you were always with the rodeo guys. The whole 'too cool for school' thing you had going on."

He grinned, glancing over at me. "Too cool for school? Really?"

I shrugged, teasing him a little. "That's what it looked like from where I stood. All of you swaggering around in those cowboy hats and boots, thinking you ran the place."

He laughed, a real one this time. "Yeah, well, I'm sure it wasn't quite as glamorous as it looked. We were mostly just trying to make it through."

I smiled, thinking back on those days. "You guys had some fun, though. I remember hearing about the time you—wait, was it you and Tyler Miller—snuck a goat into the gym during prom?"

Cole's eyes widened, and then he let out a groan, shaking his head. "Oh man, *that* night." He laughed, rubbing a hand over his face. "Yeah, that was us. Tyler's idea, but I didn't stop him. Thought it'd be funny to let the goat loose in the middle of the dance floor."

I snorted, unable to stop the grin spreading across my face. "That was legendary. Everyone said it walked right through the middle of all the kids in their tuxes and gowns."

Cole winced, but he was smiling too. "Yeah, the principal wasn't exactly thrilled with us. I'm pretty sure I was banned from all school events for the rest of the year."

"I bet," I said, still laughing. "I wasn't there that year, but I heard about it from Kate. The pictures were all over Facebook."

"Man, that was a mess," Cole said, still grinning. "But honestly? Worth it."

"I can't believe you got away with half the stuff you did."

Cole shrugged, looking a little more relaxed now. "Guess I just figured high school was the time to push boundaries, y'know?"

I nodded. "Yeah, I get that. Though I wasn't exactly causing trouble like you guys were."

He looked over at me, one eyebrow raised. "Really? Not even a little?"

I smirked. "I was mostly focused on my horses. Trying to prove myself in the show ring. Didn't leave much time for shenanigans."

Cole shook his head, mock-serious. "You missed out."

"Did I, though?" I teased. "I don't know if I would've survived one of your pranks."

"Nah, you would've been fine," he said with a grin. "Besides, you were always serious, even back then. You probably would've kept us in line."

I smiled at that, feeling a warmth spread through me that I hadn't expected. It was easy talking to Cole like this. Like we were just two old friends sharing memories instead of the rivals we'd always been. And for the first time, I wasn't thinking of him as just the stubborn guy who always got in my way. There was more to him—there always had been, I just hadn't taken the time to see it.

Chapter Thirteen

Cole

The next morning, I showed up at the barn with a knot in my stomach that had nothing to do with being tired. Yesterday had gone... well, weirdly. I couldn't stop thinking about the long drive home with Emily, the way we'd talked like old friends, swapping high school memories like we hadn't spent years competing against each other. And that phone call the night before—her checking in, actually caring about what was going on with my family—that had thrown me for a loop. I wasn't used to her being so... understanding.

But that was yesterday. Today, I had to get my head back in the game.

Cody was already there when I arrived, going over some paperwork in the office with Dusty Walker. I gave him a nod as I grabbed my gloves and hat from the tack room.

"We've got the two-year-olds to start today," he said, not looking up from the papers.

I paused, my hand on my hat. That wasn't a small task. These colts were fresh, hardly any real handling, and they'd need more than just a couple of good ground work sessions to make progress. But Cody was pushing us lately, wanting more and expecting us to handle whatever got thrown our way.

"Emily's already got a few of them caught out back," he added, finally glancing up at me. "I'll be there in a bit to check on things. Just get them moving and see what they're ready for."

I nodded, pulling my hat down over my eyes. "Got it."

Out back, I found Emily by the round pen, holding a training flag in one hand and adjusting the halter on one of the colts with the other. She glanced up as I walked over, her eyes flickering with a mix of concentration and something else—hesitation, maybe. There was a quiet tension in the air, like neither of us really knew how to handle whatever was shifting between us.

"Morning," I said, grabbing the lead rope of one of the colts tied to the fence.

"Morning," she replied, her voice softer than usual.

I tried not to think too much about it and focused on the work ahead. We had a long day with these colts, and Cody was expecting us to get them thinking. Day one was about groundwork—getting these colts to start responding, learning to trust us, and figuring out what we were asking.

For a while, we worked in silence, both of us moving the horses around the pen, using the flag to help guide them and teach them to respond to pressure and release. I could see Emily out of the corner of my eye, steady and calm, like always. The colt she was working with moved easily, responding to the slightest cues. She had a knack for this—no denying that.

I circled my colt again, watching his movements, waiting for the right moment to ease off the pressure. The colt hesitated, one ear flicking back toward me, and I saw his muscles tense. I slowed my hand, giving him a second, and then he moved forward, a little more relaxed.

That's what this was all about—reading the horse, giving them space to figure things out. I could feel the tension building in the colt beneath the surface—his muscles tight, his ears swiveling back and forth. Something was off, but I couldn't quite put my finger on it. He circled around the pen again, his pace picking up, each step getting a little faster, a little more frantic.

I kept my hand light on the rope, trying to ease him back down. "Easy, now," I murmured under my breath. But before I knew it, the colt tossed his head, jumping sideways like he'd been stung, his hooves pounding harder than I liked. I gave him some slack, hoping he'd settle if I just stayed calm.

Across the pen, I heard Emily call out, "You might want to pull him up tighter. He's getting space to act up."

I clenched my jaw. That was the last thing I needed right now—Emily micromanaging from the sidelines. "He just spooked himself," I said, pulling the rope gently, trying to bring him back to me. "He'll be fine."

But I could still feel her watching me, and it made my grip tighten on the lead. The colt was blowing hard now, his nostrils flaring, his hooves scuffing the dirt as he tried to back up again.

"Maybe just push him forward a little, get his feet moving," Emily suggested, her tone careful but edging toward insistent. "You let him get sticky, and he'll blow."

I bit back a retort. "No, he needs to stand. He's blowing up because he's too worked up. Just give him a second."

Emily frowned but didn't say anything else. I could tell she thought I was wrong, but I'd done this before. The colt just needed space.

For a few tense moments, we were both quiet. I focused on the horse, loosening the rope just enough for him to figure things out. His eyes were still wide, his breathing heavy, but after another minute, I saw the change. His head dropped a little, and his feet stopped dancing. Slowly, he calmed down, the tension leaking out of his body.

I exhaled too, relieved we hadn't had a real wreck. "See?" I said, trying to keep my voice steady. "Just needed a minute."

Emily was still watching me, her mouth set in a thin line. "I just think if you'd encouraged him a bit, you could've gotten him moving forward instead of letting him hang back and stew. The sulky ones will eventually blow up if you let them."

I turned toward her, my eyes narrowing slightly. "And I think if I'd done that, he would've bolted. He needed time to think, not more pressure."

There was a moment of silence, the air thick between us. I could tell she wasn't convinced, but I wasn't about to back down. "Not every horse needs to be pushed."

Emily didn't respond right away, but I saw the way her jaw tightened. "I'm not saying push him," she said finally. "But sometimes they need a direction, so they don't get stuck and cause a real wreck. Cody always says you need forward motion so you don't create a time bomb."

I shook my head, focusing back on the colt. "He's right, usually. This one wasn't ready for that yet."

We worked the horses in tense silence for a little longer, neither of us saying much. I could feel Emily's eyes on me every now and then, and I didn't look her way. The last thing I wanted was to make this worse, but I wasn't about to let her second-guess me. I knew what I was doing.

Eventually, Cody showed up, his usual easy stride betraying none of the pressure he always put on us. He leaned on the fence, watching for a moment, then gave a short nod.

"How're they looking?" he asked, keeping his eyes on the colts.

"They're green, but they'll come around," Emily said, brushing her hand over the colt's neck.

Cody gave another slow nod. "Good. Show me how that bay colt handles stuff around his flanks. He looks ready for a little more, and I need to know what kinds of minds we're dealing with. Evan might put some of these to work on the ranch if they're any good."

I swallowed, knowing exactly what that meant. Cody liked the look of this one, and this was a test for me as much as the colt. I focused on my colt, keeping my signals calm and clear, waiting for him to respond.

It was slow work, like trying to communicate with a kid who only half-understood what you were saying. But progress was happening—step by step. I started gently brushing him all over with the training flag, getting him used to the sensation of it touching different parts of his body. Ears, legs, belly—places that would make any green horse flinch if they weren't ready.

At first, the colt was doing fine. He'd dance around a little, but he was taking it in stride. I worked the flag slowly over his back, letting him feel it slide along his flanks, then up to his shoulders. His ears flicked back and forth, and he snorted, but nothing too dramatic. We were starting to get somewhere.

Then, out of nowhere, something spooked him. Maybe it was the flag brushing against his belly, maybe a sound behind us—I couldn't tell. But all at once, his eyes went wide, and he tossed his head, backing up hard, his hooves slipping in the dirt.

"Whoa, easy," I murmured, loosening the rope a little, trying to give him space without letting him run. He wasn't having it. His whole body tensed, like a spring about to snap, and I could see the whites of his eyes. His legs went stiff, and he started backing up faster, nearly tripping over himself.

"Back off!" Cody's voice rang out from the fence. "Don't crowd him."

I held my ground, letting the rope slacken, giving the colt a second to figure it out. His chest heaved, nostrils flaring as he sidestepped, trying to decide if he wanted to bolt or settle. I kept my movements calm, keeping the flag lowered now, just waiting him out. The colt blinked a few times, still rattled, but eventually, he stopped moving, breathing harder than before but standing still.

"Good," Cody said, his tone more approving now. "Let him stand a minute, then ease him back into it. Let him think."

I exhaled, rubbing the back of my neck. The colt's ears were twitching, listening to me, and I gave him a second to calm down before I stepped closer, gently brushing the flag against his shoulder again. This time, he didn't flinch as much, and I could feel his muscles relaxing under my hand.

Emily had been watching the whole thing from across the pen, her eyes scanning every movement. I didn't look her way. I knew she'd been waiting for me to mess up, but now I'd got the colt back to calm, and I wasn't about to let anything else go wrong.

Finally, after what felt like hours, Cody said to call it a day with that colt. "Good work. Keep it up."

I wasn't sure if that was meant as praise or just Cody's way of saying we hadn't screwed up too bad. Either way, I'd take it.

As we turned the colts out and started filling the hay bunk in their corral, I glanced over at Emily. She was working quietly, her movements efficient as always, but I could tell she had something on her mind. There was a moment of silence before she finally spoke.

"Hey, uh..." she started, pausing as if she was picking her words carefully. "You were right about that colt."

I blinked. She wasn't the type to hand out compliments lightly, and that was two or three now. "Thanks," I muttered, not sure what else to say.

She nodded, but I could tell there was something else, something hovering between us. I grabbed my gear, getting ready to head out, when I hesitated. There was a knot of tension in my chest, the kind that I couldn't just shake off, and I didn't want to leave things weird between us.

I cleared my throat, feeling awkward as heck. "Listen, about earlier," I started, not meeting her eyes. "I didn't mean to jump in and criticize like that. I guess I just—" I paused, searching for the right words. "Look, I'm sorry if I was out of line."

Emily blinked, obviously not expecting that. "Oh," she said softly. "It's okay. We're both just trying to do what's best for the horses."

I shifted uncomfortably, then, in a sudden impulse, I added, "Can I, uh, buy you dinner or something? You know, as a peace offering?"

She looked up, eyebrows raised. "Dinner?"

I scratched the back of my neck, feeling like an idiot. "Yeah. You don't have to or anything, just thought—well, I... I'm tired of fighting all the time."

For a second, I thought she was going to turn me down, but then she gave a small smile. "Sure," she said, her voice light. "I could eat."

I nodded, feeling the tension ease just a bit. "Alright. Let's get these guys put away, and we can head out."

And just like that, the awkwardness between us started to fade. We finished up our work in silence, but it wasn't the tense kind of quiet we used to have. It was... different. Easier.

Maybe we were finally figuring each other out.

Emily

The bell above the door gave a little jingle as we stepped inside the Tavern. I glanced around, my eyes adjusting to the dimmer light. The place was packed, as usual, with folks we knew scattered at the booths and tables, chatting, laughing, eating. A couple of ranchers we'd worked with before gave us a nod from across the room. I waved back automatically, but my nerves were starting to get the better of me.

I didn't know why it felt weird to be here with Cole. It wasn't like this was a date or anything. We were just grabbing burgers after a long day. But as the hostess pointed us to a table for two near the front window, it hit me. To anyone watching, it sure *looked* like a date.

I glanced at Cole out of the corner of my eye as he sat down across from me, looking pretty relaxed. He leaned back in his chair, his eyes scanning the menu. It was strange to see him so at ease, especially after the tension we'd had all day. Here, away from the ranch, he was... well, different. Looser. He smiled more easily, like the weight he carried around wasn't as heavy.

I couldn't help but smile a little, too. Maybe it wouldn't be the worst thing in the world if people assumed we were on a date. Not that it was. Of course, it wasn't.

The waitress came by, dropped off a couple of laminated menus, and we ordered drinks—iced tea for me, cola for Cole. The place smelled like fried food and peanuts, the scent mixing with the sound of boots scuffing on the wooden floor, peanuts cracking underfoot, and the distant twang of country music playing on the jukebox.

I looked around as a few more familiar faces caught my eye—neighbors, old high school classmates. One of the local 4-H parents waved from across the room, and I waved back, feeling a little self-conscious under the attention. I could already imagine the whispers. I half-expected someone to come up and start grilling us, but thankfully, they just kept their distance.

"So," I said, eager to break the silence that was settling over us, "think any of those colts will work out on the ranch?"

Cole lifted his shoulder, his mouth quirking up at the corner. "Yeah, if that's what the boss wants. Couple of them had their hair on fire when we got started, but I think even those will settle in sooner or later."

"They'll come around. The chestnut you were working with—the one with the bald face had a good mind on him, once he figured out he didn't have to fight every little thing. Luke Walker sure liked him."

Cole was sipping from his straw, but he dropped it and shot me a weird look. "When?"

I laughed. "You didn't see him? He was staring at you guys for like fifteen minutes. Came over to check the colts and unless I miss my guess, he'll be aiming to make that one his next ranch horse, once you get him going under saddle."

"Huh." Cole nodded, taking another sip of his cola. "He'll be solid once he settles. I just hope Cody gives us time with them before we have to pack up for the show."

"I doubt it. Today was more about checking out what they'd just bought. The real work starts after we get back because Cody said we'll be washing the trailers and trucks tomorrow. Get everything ready for California."

Cole made a face, groaning. "Yeah, and I'll probably end up driving one of the rigs all by myself. I always draw the short straw."

I laughed, shaking my head. "You don't have to do it alone. I can drive for a while. You can ride shotgun, get some sleep."

He grinned at me, that teasing spark lighting his eyes. "Careful offering that. I might snore."

I laughed again, the tension I'd been holding onto loosening up. "I think I can handle it," I said, trying to think of something else to say to this version of Cole—a version that didn't have his usual edge of sarcasm or frustration.

We settled into easier conversation after that, talking about the up-coming show and the competition we'd probably face in California. It was nice. Comfortable, even. But just as we were finishing our burgers, Cole's phone rang. I glanced up, and I saw his whole face change.

He pulled the phone from his pocket, checked the screen, and cursed under his breath. "It's Gage. I gotta take this."

I nodded, watching him as he slid out of the booth and stepped outside, the door jingling again behind him. The Tavern was small, and even from inside, I could see him through the glass doors. His body was tense, his free hand running through his hair as he spoke. His voice was low, but I could catch the frustration in the way his shoulders hunched. Whatever his brother was saying, it wasn't good.

After a few minutes of watching Cole pace outside, I could hear him say, "Fine, I'll be home soon," as he turned back toward the door. His expression was tight when he came back inside, and I quickly looked away, pretending I hadn't seen or heard anything.

He didn't sit back down. "I'm sorry, Emily," he said, rubbing the back of his neck. "I gotta go. Something's come up."

I shrugged, trying to keep my voice light. "No big deal. I drove my own car, so I can leave whenever I'm ready."

Cole's mouth tightened, and he looked uncomfortable. "I—uh, sorry," he said again, though I wasn't exactly sure what he was apologizing for. He fished his wallet out of his back pocket, tossed some cash on the table for our meals, and without another word, turned toward the door.

I watched him go, the bell jingling again as the door swung shut behind him. Whatever was going on with his family, it was serious. And judging by the look on his face, it wasn't going away anytime soon.

Chapter Fourteen

Cole

By the time I pulled up to the house, the sun had dipped low, casting long shadows across the barn. My jaw was still clenched from the call with Gage, my stomach in knots. The second I got out of the truck, I could see Mom's silhouette moving around in the barn, but I didn't head her way. Not yet. There was a different kind of storm brewing inside the house, and I had a feeling it was about to hit.

I pushed through the front door, and the first thing I saw was Trent sitting on the couch with Cassie. Great. Why *she* was here for this, I had no idea. Wasn't like she had the first clue about ranching, anyway, but she sure liked giggling whenever Trent looked at her.

Gage was standing by the fireplace, arms crossed, looking like he'd been waiting for a fight. Chase was at the kitchen table, staring at a stack of papers with the same look he got when we were trying to calculate if the hay we had in storage was going to last through the winter.

I rubbed the back of my neck, feeling the heat rise. "What's going on?" I asked, my voice sharper than I meant it to be. "Why does this feel like an ambush?"

Chase looked up at me, sighing heavily. "Sit down, Cole. We need to talk."

I didn't sit. The tension in the room was thick, and I wasn't about to just roll over and wait to see what was coming. "Talk about what?" I asked, narrowing my eyes. "You couldn't wait for me to get home before having this little meeting?"

Gage's voice cut in, sharp as ever. "We've been trying to figure things out, Cole. We're running out of time."

My stomach tightened. "What are you talking about? What's this all about?"

Chase shifted in his chair, glancing at Gage, then back at me. Finally, he sighed again and leaned forward, his elbows on the table. "We've been talking about selling the ranch."

I felt like the wind had been knocked out of me. "What?" I asked, my voice barely a whisper. "Selling the ranch? Since when?"

Gage straightened, his jaw tight. "Since we started running out of options, Cole. We've been meeting with the bank, looking over the finances, trying to figure out how to keep this place running. But it's not looking good."

I shook my head, trying to wrap my brain around what they were saying. "And you're just now telling me this?"

"We didn't want to drag you into it unless we had to," Chase said quietly, looking almost apologetic. "You've been busy working at Walker Ranch, and we didn't want to pull you away unless it got serious."

"Well, it sounds pretty bleeding serious to me now!" I snapped. "You've been talking about selling everything, and I'm just finding out?"

Gage was on me in a heartbeat, his voice rising. "You haven't been here, Cole. You've been off at that fancy Walker Ranch, working their horses, while we've been trying to keep this place afloat. You don't need Ridgeview anymore."

The heat rushed to my face. "*What?* You think I *want* to be working over there instead of here? You think I don't want to be part of this?"

"You sure aren't acting like it," Gage shot back. "You left. And now, when it comes to making the hard decisions, you wanna swoop in and pretend you're all in? This ranch ain't a part-time gig, Cole."

I took a step forward, my fists clenched at my sides. "There wasn't a place for me! That's why I left. You think I didn't try? I've been busting my tail trying to make something of myself because there wasn't room here. You didn't *need* me."

Chase stood up, putting himself between us, his voice disgustingly calm. "Let's cool it. Look, Cole, we understand why you took the job. You did what you had to do. I get it. But we've been working on this for months, trying to figure out what's best. And the truth is, this ranch is sinking, man. We're running out of options."

"And Gage thinks the best option is to sell?" I asked, my voice shaking with anger. "Just like that?"

Gage let out a frustrated sigh. "We're hanging on by a thread, Cole. You know that. If we don't sell now, the ranch could be worth a whole lot less later. I'm trying to protect what Dad left us. What *Mom* has been trying to hang on to."

My eyes flicked over to Trent, who hadn't said a word yet. Cassie was sitting beside him, quiet but watching everything with those blank eyes that were smeared with too much makeup. "And how long have you all been talking about this?" I demanded. "This didn't just happen overnight. What does Mom think?"

A silence fell over the room. Gage and Chase exchanged glances, and finally, Chase sighed. "We haven't told Mom yet. We didn't want to worry her until we had a plan. She's been holding on to this place for *us*, Cole. Not for herself. We don't want her to feel like she failed."

"Failed?" I shot back, the words coming out harsher than I meant. "She's not the one failing. You're the ones giving up. You're handing over everything she and Dad worked their whole lives to build. And you didn't even have the guts to tell her? You were gonna make this decision for her?"

"That's not fair, Cole," Trent finally spoke up, his voice tight. "We called you here tonight to have this conversation. You're acting like we've been plotting behind your back."

I glared at him, shaking my head. "It sure feels like it. Seems like everyone's already made up their minds." I glanced pointedly at Cassie, who was looking at the floor, avoiding my eyes. "And why does *she* know about this before I do?"

Trent's face flushed red. He stood up from the couch, his jaw clenched. "Leave Cassie out of this."

"Oh, it's too late for that," I snapped back. "You dragged her into this family meeting, and she's not even family. I'm standing here wondering how long you've all been planning this without me."

"You're out of line," Trent said through gritted teeth, his fists clenched. "She's here for me, okay? You don't get to pick and choose who's part of the conversation."

"I know when my opinion isn't wanted," I growled, pulling my hat off and dusting it on my jeans. "You've made it pretty clear what's going on here."

"Because we don't have any other options," Gage said, his voice rising again. "We're drowning, Cole. The cattle aren't enough, the grazing rights are getting cut, and we're running out of time."

I could feel my blood boiling. This wasn't just about the ranch. This was about everything we were supposed to be holding on to.

Everything Mom and Dad had built. Everything I thought we were fighting for.

"I can't believe this," I muttered, shaking my head. "You've already decided, haven't you?"

"We haven't decided anything yet," Chase said, trying to calm me down. "But we need to be realistic. If we don't do something now, the ranch could be worth nothing in a few years."

I turned to leave, my heart pounding. "I need time to think."

"Cole!" Gage's voice stopped me in my tracks. "We need an answer. Mr. Mason is coming tomorrow to talk about listing the property, and we have to make a decision."

I glanced back at him, my voice cold. "If you want an answer, you'll have to wait. I'm working late tomorrow, and leaving for California first thing Wednesday morning."

Without waiting for a response, I stormed out of the house, slamming the door behind me.

Emily
Tulare, California

The air was thick with dust and anticipation as I worked Copper in slow circles, loosening up his muscles before his cutting class. The sound of hooves pounding the dirt, the hum of the crowd, and the distant calls of horses all blended together in the background. I kept my focus on Copper's movements, feeling the steady rhythm of his stride beneath me. But every so often, my eyes drifted across the warm-up pen to where Cole was loping Lynx, his posture stiff and his face unreadable.

It was like a switch had flipped, and we were back to where we'd started—barely speaking, barely acknowledging each other. Since the night at the tavern, when his brother called and he left in a hurry, Cole had gone cold again. It was subtle, but it was there. The easy banter we'd started to build was gone, replaced with this awkward distance. I'd tried to offer my help when we packed the trailers for the trip, even suggesting I could drive part of the way. He gave me a look like he was really considering it for a second, then shook his head and gruffly said he didn't need any help.

Now, a couple of days later, here we were. I sighed and pulled Copper up to a halt, letting him stand for a moment in the center of the ring. My eyes followed Cole as he worked Lynx through slow, precise footwork. They moved in perfect sync, his hands light on the reins as Lynx responded to every subtle shift in his body. It was like watching an intricate dance, but instead of appreciating the moment, I felt a pang of frustration. Something was off with him, and I couldn't figure out what.

Then I noticed something else. Cole had drifted into the wrong section of the warm-up pen, lost in his own world, oblivious to the other riders. There was an unspoken rule in these rings—lopers to the outside, slow workers in the middle—and Cole had somehow forgotten it. One of the riders, an older man on a chestnut, rode by and snapped at him.

"Watch where you're going!"

Cole blinked and looked up, his face dazed like he'd just been jolted back to reality. The hollowness in his eyes made my stomach drop.

Without thinking, I snapped back at the guy. "He wasn't in your way! Get over it!"

The man shot me a glare but rode off without another word. A moment later, Cole guided Lynx over to where I was standing, his expression clouded.

"You didn't have to do that," he said quietly, his voice rough. "I was in the wrong."

I shrugged, trying to keep it light. "You know I've got your back, right? We're on the same team here."

A faint smile tugged at his lips, but it didn't reach his eyes. He looked... worn down. Defeated, even. It wasn't like Cole. Not the Cole I knew, even the cranky, cocky one.

"You okay?" I asked, keeping my voice low. "You haven't been yourself since that phone call the other night."

Cole shook his head, brushing it off. "It's nothing."

"Doesn't seem like nothing. I want to help if I can. You know, be a friend."

He glanced over at me, and for a moment, the other Cole surfaced—a crooked grin tugging at his lips, that familiar spark flashing in his eyes. My heart did a weird flip in my chest as he said, "If you want to help, just cheer me on. Me and Lynx are up next in the draw."

I grinned back, trying to shake off the tension between us. "I'll be rooting for you."

With a nod, he turned Lynx and headed toward the gate to wait for their cutting class. I watched him go, my smile fading a little as I thought about everything he wasn't saying. Whatever was going on, it was bigger than just nerves before a show. And the way his smile hadn't quite reached his eyes... it was starting to bother me more than I wanted to admit.

I rode Copper toward the rail where we could watch, and hopefully stay out of the way. Cole and Lynx were already heading into the arena, the low hum of the crowd filling the air. I halted Copper and leaned forward on the saddle horn, watching as Cole settled Lynx into the herd. The filly moved like a shadow, her ears pricked and her muscles rippling under the saddle, ready to strike.

I wasn't the only one watching. Cody eased Rust up beside me, the thickly muscled roan snorting as Cody shifted in the saddle. He didn't say a word, but I knew him well enough by now to catch the slight hitch in his breath. He was watching Cole with the kind of intensity that only came when something was on the line. I glanced at Cody out of the corner of my eye. He had to know something was off with Cole, too. Maybe he was hoping, like I was, that whatever was eating at him wouldn't mess up his ride.

My attention snapped back to the arena as Cole eased Lynx deeper into the herd. The whole arena seemed to hold its breath as he picked his cow. I watched the play of his hands, so light on the reins, and I felt a small twist of envy. Lynx was something else, the way she slithered low to the ground, reading the cow's every move before it even made one. Copper was talented, sure, but he didn't have Lynx's raw instincts. That filly was bred for this, and watching Cole work her, it was clear they were in sync today.

For the first time in days, it looked like Cole was breathing again. He wasn't tense or over-correcting. He was just sitting deep in the saddle, trusting Lynx to do her thing. There was a brief moment when the cow he'd cut turned away quicker than expected. Lynx started to dive after it, her head low and muscles coiled to strike, but Cole picked her up smoothly and directed her to a different cow. It was seamless, a move that might've thrown off a less experienced rider. But Cole handled it like it was nothing.

The crowd let out a cheer as the run ended. The score flashed on the board: 71.5.

I blinked in surprise, my eyes going wide as I turned to Cody. He pounded his fist lightly on the saddle horn, a rare grin of satisfaction on his face.

"Is that the best score Lynx has ever posted?" I asked.

Cody nodded, his eyes still on Cole as he exited the arena. "Sure is."

Without another word, Cody urged Rust forward, heading toward Cole, leaving me to sit there for a moment, absorbing what had just happened. Cole walked out of the arena looking different. It was like he'd finally shaken off the darkness that had been hanging over him for days. His face looked fresher, lighter, and for the first time in a long while, I saw him smile. A real smile. His eyes lit up, and there it was—a cute dimple in his left cheek that I'd somehow never noticed before.

He looked over at me, and our eyes met. He smiled wider, that dimple deepening, and I had to remind myself to breathe. I gave him a thumbs-up, feeling warmth bloom in my chest. He stepped off Lynx, loosened her cinch, and called out to me across the arena.

"Good luck!"

I blinked, surprised for a second. It was the first time he'd ever wished me luck. I felt my own lips twitch into a grin as I nudged Copper forward, the warmth from his words carrying me toward the arena.

Maybe things were changing after all.

Chapter Fifteen

Cole

The cool evening air settled around me as I leaned back against the barn, the stone behind me finally losing its heat from the long day in the sun. Lynx had done well—better than I'd expected, even if she didn't blow them all away. Third in cutting, beating out Copper by half a point. She hadn't held up as well in the reining or boxing, though, coming in eighth overall. Emily and Copper won the points total for the day, but for the first time, I wasn't resentful about it. She certainly worked hard for it.

I let my head rest back on the cool stone, tapping it lightly against the wall, eyes closed, and I could feel the moment the sun dipped below the almond trees, pulling the last bit of heat with it. The stillness that followed was almost startling. A few cows mooed in the distance, but beyond that and the hum of the freeway, it was quiet.

That was a welcome change.

But with the quiet came the thoughts I'd been pushing away all day. I was going to have to face my brothers when I got back home. I couldn't shake the question that gnawed at me—had they already told Mom? My gut twisted at the thought of how she'd take it. Leaving the ranch, the place she and Dad had poured their hearts into, would break her. Forty years of memories, of raising us, of watching Dad work the land. Every horse she'd rehabilitated, every animal she'd loved—it was all tied up in that ranch.

What would she do if it was sold? What would any of us do?

The crack of a soda can startled me out of my thoughts. I opened my eyes to see Emily standing in front of me, holding out a Coke with a quiet smile.

"Thought you could use this," she said, and I gave her a tired grin, taking the can.

"Thanks," I said, taking a sip as she slid down the wall beside me, her back resting against the cool stone. She opened another Coke for herself and tapped her can lightly against mine.

We sat there for a minute, just letting the quiet settle around us. She sipped her drink, her eyes scanning the horizon.

"Congrats on winning today," I said, breaking the silence.

Emily shrugged, glancing away like it wasn't a big deal. "Thanks," she muttered, though I could see a small smile tugging at her lips. "You and Lynx beat us in cutting, though."

I studied her face for a moment—the light dusting of freckles across her cheeks, the way her clear blue eyes caught the last bits of sunlight. There was something honest in her smile, something that made me feel lighter just being around her.

Taking a deep breath, I asked slowly, "Can I ask you something?"

She blinked, then nodded. "Sure."

"Why are you doing this?" I asked, watching her closely. "What's your end goal?"

Emily frowned a little, looking down at her soda as she thought. After a moment, she took a drink and leaned back against the wall, her gaze distant. "I guess... I always dreamed of riding horses," she said softly. "When I got hired at Walker Ranch, it was because one of the hands, Danny, broke his arm, and Blake... I don't know, I guess he liked me. I thought that was my big break—and it was, but not in the way I expected."

I nodded, staying quiet as she spoke, my curiosity growing.

"After Danny healed, Morgan offered me a chance at White Pines. I worked with the therapy horses for a while, and I loved it, but... I didn't have the passion for it the way Kate does," she admitted. "Then, Cody said he was looking for a training assistant and offered the job to me. From that first day, it just fit. It felt like... like I found my calling. I've been dreaming ever since of building a real partnership with a horse, something like you see in the movies. It's all I want—to get better, to keep learning."

I realized I'd been holding my breath as she spoke, and I grunted softly, taking another drink of my Coke, staring out over the almond orchard. "So?" Emily asked after a moment.

I blinked. "So, what?"

"Well, it's your turn," she said, her smile playful but expectant.

I scrunched my face up, not really sure how to explain. "I just... I just want to do something worthwhile."

Emily raised an eyebrow. "There are people who'd say training show horses isn't exactly the most useful profession."

I grinned. "I beg to differ." She laughed softly, and I took another drink, glancing at her. "Tell me, what did you learn at White Pines?"

Emily frowned, thinking for a moment. "I learned that horses connect with people in a way nothing else can. They heal, they inspire."

"That's what I'm saying. It's not just therapy programs where horses make a difference. Look at the people at the clinic last week. They were all at different stages in their lives, but the one thing they had in common was how much they loved working with their horses.

We get to be a part of that. We help make better horses and better riders."

Emily turned her gaze to me, her smile softer now. "That's one of the most beautiful descriptions of a horse trainer's job I've ever heard."

I shrugged, trying to act casual, but her words warmed me more than I'd admit. We sat there for a moment, sipping our Cokes, the quiet of the evening settling around us like a soft blanket. The last rays of sun were gone now, leaving a pale glow over the almond orchard. I could feel Emily's presence beside me, steady and calm, like she wasn't in any hurry to leave. It was nice, just sitting here without needing to fill the silence with words.

"So," she said after a while, her voice soft. "What's really going on, Cole?"

I stiffened slightly, glancing at her sideways. "What do you mean?"

She gave me a look, the kind that said she wasn't buying my act. "You've been off these past few days. It's like... I don't know, you're here, but you're not really here. And it's not just about the show."

I exhaled sharply through my nose, my fingers tapping the side of my soda can. "It's nothing," I muttered, staring straight ahead.

"Whatever it is, it is not nothing. Look, I'm not trying to pry or anything. But... you can talk to me, you know. I'm not gonna judge."

I swallowed hard, the words caught in my throat. Part of me wanted to brush it off, to make some joke and change the subject. But another part—one I didn't fully understand—was tired of carrying it alone. And for some reason, Emily felt like the one person I could trust to hear me out, without thinking I was weak or... whatever else.

I sighed, running a hand through my hair. "It's... the ranch," I admitted slowly, the words feeling heavy in my mouth. "My family's ranch. We've been having trouble—big trouble—for a while now."

Emily didn't say anything, just stayed quiet, listening, her blue eyes locked on mine.

"Gage—my oldest brother—he thinks we should sell. He's been talking to Chase and Trent about it, and... well, they think it might be the best option, too. Land's still not recovering from the fires, then the droughts, and now we're losing grazing rights because of this stupid spotted owl thing. It's like everything's working against us."

Emily blinked. "Sell the ranch? Your ranch?"

I nodded, feeling a lump form in my throat. "Yeah. It's been in our family for three generations, but... I don't know. Maybe they're right. I mean, it's been barely hanging on for years now. But I just... I can't get my head around the idea of letting it go. I don't even know what that would look like for us—for my mom. What she'd do."

Emily was quiet for a long moment. "That sounds... really hard. I didn't realize things were that bad."

I shrugged, feeling a little embarrassed that I'd let it all spill out like that. "Yeah, well... it's not exactly something I go around telling people."

"I get that," she said. "But you don't have to just roll over and do what they want, you know? I mean... it's *your* family's ranch, too. Your opinion matters."

I let out a bitter laugh. "I'm not sure they think it does. Gage has been running the place since Dad died. And Chase, well, he's the practical one. He looks at it like a business decision. I'm just... I'm the youngest. The one who's off working for some fancy ranch instead of helping out at home."

Emily frowned. "But that's not fair. You took the job with Walker Ranch because it was an opportunity. And you've been learning so much—doing so much. Doesn't that count for anything?"

I shrugged again. "I don't know. Maybe it doesn't matter. I'm thinking more and more maybe I should just take a construction job for a while, make some decent money, and help them out that way. Or... I don't know. I'm just tired of feeling like I'm stuck."

There was a long pause before Emily spoke again. "You're not stuck, Cole. You're just... in a hard place right now. And it's okay to feel that way."

I looked over at her, surprised by the conviction in her words. She wasn't pitying me. She wasn't telling me to just toughen up and deal with it. She was just... understanding.

And somehow, that made it easier to breathe.

"Thanks," I mumbled, glancing down at the soda can in my hand. "I mean... for listening. I didn't expect to spill all that on you."

She smiled, just a little. "Well, I've got your back, remember?"

I chuckled softly, nodding. "Yeah. I guess you do."

Emily

"Are you hungry?" I asked, the question slipping out before I had time to overthink it.

Cole glanced at me, his crooked grin appearing again. "Starving, actually."

I swallowed, nerves creeping up my spine. "I've got some chicken stir fry in my trailer. It's nothing fancy, just leftovers I brought from home, but... if you want?"

His grin widened a little. "I don't usually eat stir fry, but I'm game for trying it."

My heart stuttered. I hadn't expected him to say yes, and now I was realizing that I'd just invited him into my tiny trailer. But... I wanted to. I wanted to spend more time with him, to maybe see if that easy conversation we'd started could continue.

I stood up, brushing off my jeans. "Okay, then. Come on."

Cole got to his feet, following me as I led the way toward my trailer. My stomach was doing flips, and I tried to act casual, but... well, this was the second time now—not a date, but it wasn't exactly *not* a date either. And I had no idea what I was doing.

We reached "my" trailer, and I unlocked the door, stepping inside first. The space felt even smaller with Cole standing at the entrance, ducking his head slightly to avoid the ceiling. It was cozy in here, to say the least—barely enough room for the dinette, the tiny kitchen, and the cramped sleeping area tucked into the nose of the gooseneck. But it was my little hovel when we were on the road, and it felt like home.

Cole hesitated at the door, glancing around awkwardly before stepping inside. "This one is cleaner than the one Cody and I share," he said.

I laughed nervously, gesturing toward the little dinette. "You can sit down, if you want."

He nodded, taking his hat off and holding it in his hands for a second before squeezing himself into one of the seats. The table barely accommodated his broad shoulders, and I had to bite back a smile. He was so big in such a little space, and for some reason, that made my heart race even faster.

I stepped around him, pulling out the leftover stir fry from the mini fridge to pop it in the microwave. As I started warming it up, I watched Cole out of the corner of my eye. He was sitting there, fidgeting a little, looking like he wasn't sure what to do with himself. Then his gaze landed on the deck of cards I had sitting on the table.

He picked it up, flipping through the cards absentmindedly. "You play a lot of solitaire?"

I turned, leaning against the counter with a smug smile. "Poker, actually."

His eyebrows shot up, and he met my eye with a challenge. "Poker, huh? Well, I'm the reigning poker champ in the Langton family."

I raised an eyebrow, grinning as I set the stir fry aside. "Is that so? Well, consider yourself challenged."

He leaned forward, resting his forearms on the table and giving me that crooked grin that made my heart skip a beat. "Alright then, you're on."

I couldn't help but laugh, the tension easing a little as I grabbed the food and set it on the table between us. Maybe this wasn't so nerve-wracking after all. Maybe, just maybe, this could be... fun.

We shuffled the cards, and I gave Cole a playful smirk. "So, what are we betting?"

He leaned back in the dinette, casually popping a bite of stir fry into his mouth. "How about bragging rights?" he said, grinning. "I'm not about to let you take my title without a fight."

"Bragging rights it is," I said, dealing the cards with a flourish. "Prepare to lose."

Cole snorted, glancing at his hand. "We'll see about that."

We played a few hands, shuffling the cards and dealing out rounds, and it didn't take long before the teasing started.

"That's a terrible poker face you've got there," I said, glancing at Cole over the top of my cards, trying to hide my grin.

He snorted, raising an eyebrow. "You think? Maybe I'm just letting you think that."

"Yeah, sure," I teased, tossing down a pair of eights. "Bluff all you want, but it's not going to save you."

Cole narrowed his eyes, laying his cards down on the table. "A pair of kings, sorry. Looks like I'm the one with the better hand."

I groaned dramatically, picking up the cards to reshuffle. "Ugh, fine, I'll give you that one."

"Don't sound so disappointed," he said, leaning back in his seat with a cocky grin. "I'm just getting started."

I rolled my eyes, dealing out another hand. "Uh-huh. Let's see if you can keep that winning streak going, cowboy."

We kept playing, our banter flowing easily between bites of stir fry. Cole was grinning more, his shoulders relaxing, and I found myself laughing out loud, something I hadn't done with him in... well, ever. After another round, I laid down a flush, my grin wide as I saw Cole's eyes widen. "What was that you were saying about your winning streak?"

He threw his cards down in mock defeat. "Alright, alright, you got me. But don't get too cocky."

"Too late," I smirked, gathering up the cards. "You're losing your edge, Langton."

Cole shook his head, chuckling. "I'm just warming up. I could wipe the floor with you if I wanted."

"Uh-huh. We'll see about that."

With each hand, the conversation shifted from teasing to talking about the day—about the horses, the show, the plans we had for the next few days. The poker game became less about winning and more about just enjoying each other's company.

"Not bad, by the way," Cole said, gesturing toward his empty plate. "Didn't expect stir fry to be on the menu for a ranch girl."

I blushed, shrugging. "Thanks, but I can't take credit for it. My mom made it."

He nodded, looking impressed. "Well, tell her she's got skills."

I smiled, feeling a little warmth creep into my chest. Cole could be a tough nut to crack, but moments like this reminded me that he wasn't all rough edges. We kept playing, the stakes rising with each hand. He won a couple, I won a couple, and we dealt again.

"You're getting cocky, Langton," I teased, laying down my cards. "What's that saying about pride before a fall?"

He glanced at his cards and then back at me, that mischievous glint returning to his eyes. "You think you've got me, huh?"

"I know I've got you," I shot back, flipping my hand over to reveal a winning flush.

His eyes widened, and he stared at my cards in mock disbelief. "No way."

"Way," I said with a grin. "Looks like the poker champ has been dethroned."

Cole let out a low chuckle, shaking his head. "I let you win."

I crossed my arms, leaning back in my seat. "Sure you did."

"I did," he insisted, but the smile tugging at the corner of his lips told me otherwise.

I stood up, starting to clean up the cards and empty plates. "Well, either way, it looks like I'm the new champ."

Cole pushed back from the table, stretching his legs before standing. "Alright, alright, you got me this time," he said, holding his hands up in surrender. "But don't get too comfortable with that title."

"Noted," I teased, tossing the dishcloth aside.

He grabbed his hat from the counter, setting it on his head as he stood up. "Guess I'd better call it a night," he said, though he didn't seem in a hurry to leave.

I stood by the door, watching as Cole squeezed out of the small living quarters. As he stepped outside, the cool night air hit, and the stars were just beginning to twinkle in the darkening sky.

Cole turned to me, his hand resting on the doorframe. "Thanks for dinner."

"Thanks for the company," I replied, leaning against the door.

We stood there for a moment, the space between us charged with something unspoken. He shifted his weight, hesitating, and I suddenly felt my pulse quicken. Before I could second-guess myself, I leaned forward just slightly, closing the distance.

And then, as if we'd both been waiting for this, his lips brushed mine. It was soft, tentative at first, like he wasn't sure if he should—but then he kissed me a little firmer, and I felt myself melt into the warmth of it. My hand found the front of his shirt, holding on like I wasn't ready to let go, and for a moment, the world around us disappeared.

When we finally pulled back, his eyes stayed on mine, and I couldn't help but smile.

"Goodnight, Cole," I whispered, my voice barely above a breath.

"Goodnight, Emily," he replied, his lips still curved in that crooked grin as he stepped back.

I watched him walk away, my heart doing a little flip, and I touched my lips, still warm from the kiss.

What had just happened?

Chapter Sixteen

Cole

Morning hit early at the showgrounds, the kind of crisp air that wasn't quite cold, but hinted at the day heating up fast. We were already packed into the arena to watch Cody work Rust in his reining class, and even though my eyes were on the action, my mind wasn't. It kept wandering back to last night—to that kiss. I barely slept, just kept replaying it over and over. Felt good, yeah, but it was the kind of good that made everything else complicated.

I glanced sideways, catching Emily's silhouette in the morning light, her face shadowed under the brim of her hat. She was watching Cody, but there was a tightness around her mouth, like she wasn't as relaxed as she wanted to look. She hadn't said a word about the kiss, and neither had I. We'd been moving like clockwork this morning, loading gear, getting horses ready for the trip back, but neither of us addressed the elephant in the room.

Cody and Rust made their final slide, clean and sharp, and the crowd let out a light cheer. Cody tipped his hat in his usual modest way and rode over to the exit gate. Rust had placed third. Not a bad finish, but not the win Cody had been looking for to hang on to his season points lead. Still, he looked satisfied as he rode over to us, his eyes scanning the trailers.

"Let's get packed up," Cody said, his tone businesslike, even as he patted Rust's neck. "Long road ahead."

Emily and I nodded, turning back to the task at hand. It wasn't like we needed any more instructions—this was routine by now. Load the horses, double-check the tack, make sure everything was secure for the two-day drive back to Idaho.

I led Lynx up the trailer ramp, and she stepped on without a fuss, settling in with her hay bag. Good girl. I ran my hand down her neck, feeling her muscles twitch under my palm, then tied her off and made sure she had enough water in front of her for the trip. My mind kept wandering back to the kiss, though. Should I say something? Should I just let it hang there?

Should I be hoping for another one?

Emily worked on the other side of the trailer, moving quietly. I tried not to stare at her, but I couldn't help it. Something about the way she moved this morning—deliberate, almost careful—made me feel like maybe she was overthinking it, too.

We got the last of the gear loaded and made sure everything was secure. Cody was still busy talking to a few folks around the show-grounds, so Emily and I found ourselves standing around, the hum of the show grounds slowly dying down as other riders began packing up as well.

I rubbed the back of my neck, finally breaking the silence. "Looks like it's gonna be a long ride home."

Emily gave me a small smile, her fingers fidgeting with the lead rope she held. "Yeah, it always feels longer on the way back."

I nodded, feeling the awkwardness hang between us for a beat too long. Before I could think of what to say next, my phone buzzed in my pocket. I pulled it out, glancing at the screen—*Chase*.

"Hang on a sec," I muttered, turning away from Emily and hitting the call button. "Hey."

"Cole, we need to talk," Chase's voice came through, tense, and I immediately felt my stomach drop. "Where are you?"

"I'm still in California," I replied, glancing over at Emily, who was busying herself with loading the last of the grooming boxes, trying to look like she wasn't listening. "We're about to hit the road."

"Gage and Trent are pushing hard to make a decision," Chase said, his tone grim. "They met with the agent from Fish and Wildlife again this morning. Guy even brought his supervisor this time. The guy's holding firm on the restrictions."

I bit back a curse, tightening my grip on the phone. "Even after they showed him the land? They took him out again, right?"

"Yep. He's not budging. Said just because he didn't see any spotted owls doesn't mean they're not nesting nearby."

I felt the anger bubble up inside me, and I pinched the bridge of my nose. "What in blazes are we supposed to do, then?"

Chase sighed. "That's the thing, Cole. Gage... he's ready to sell. Trent's on the fence, but Gage is convinced it's the best move."

I kicked at a loose rock on the ground, watching it roll a few feet before coming to a stop. "I'll be back soon," I said quietly, my voice tight. "Just... hold them off until I get home."

"I'll try," Chase muttered. "But Gage is set on calling Mason soon. He wants this dealt with before it gets worse."

I hung up the phone and shoved it back into my pocket, my jaw clenched so hard it hurt. Emily had closed the tack room door and was watching me, concern in her eyes.

"Everything okay?" she asked softly.

I shook my head, trying to push down the frustration. "Just family stuff."

She didn't pry, just nodded like she understood more than I gave her credit for. Cody walked up a minute later, his usual easy stride looking bright and eager to hit the road. One of us, at least, was ready to get back to his family.

"Let's roll out," Cody said, glancing between us. He must've noticed the tension, but he didn't ask.

We got into the trucks, Emily hopping into the passenger seat of mine. I tried to focus on the road ahead, but my mind was still back home, with my brothers, and the ranch that felt like it was slipping through our fingers.

Emily

The first day of driving felt like it stretched on forever. California faded into the rearview mirror, replaced by the flat, sun-drenched stretch of desert as we neared Nevada. We'd driven most of the day in silence, the occasional hum of the radio filling the gaps when words didn't come. Cole was on edge, I could tell. Ever since that phone call earlier, something had shifted.

I didn't push, though. I'd learned to read him well enough by now—he wasn't the type to spill his guts unless he was ready. So I just stayed quiet, running the maps and radio when I was on Shotgun and taking my turn at driving when he was ready for a break.

By the time we pulled off the highway that evening, stopping at a rest area just across the Nevada border, we were both stiff and exhausted. The horses needed tending to, and there was a small diner down the road where Cody said we could grab dinner.

After we parked the trailers and got the horses settled, we all walked over to the diner. Cody called Morgan, like he always did in the evenings to chat about the day's events, then he put Nikki on speaker so we could all say hi to his daughter. I'd babysat her a couple of times, and she always squealed when she heard my voice.

Cole was quiet, though, his hands stuffed in his pockets under the table, his gaze distant.

Cody finally hung up with Morgan and stretched in the seat. As we waited for our food, he started talking about strategy for the next show, the things he wanted to do to dial the horses in better before then, but Cole wasn't really listening. His fingers drummed on the table, and every now and then, he'd glance at his phone, like he was waiting for something.

I couldn't take the silence any longer.

"Hey," I said softly, leaning forward a bit. "You okay?"

Cole blinked, pulled out of his thoughts. "Yeah, sorry. Just... you know."

I wanted to ask more, but something told me not to push. Instead, I just nodded, offering him a small smile. "Yeah."

He gave me a quick smile back, but it was weak at best. We finished dinner with little conversation, and as we walked back to the trailers, I found myself walking next to Cole, with Cody scooting on ahead saying he wanted to grab a shower before he crashed. The night air had cooled, and for a moment, we just walked in comfortable silence.

Cole walked me to the door of my trailer, like a gentleman, and I stopped and turned to him. "You sure you're alright?"

He shrugged, his eyes shadowed under the brim of his hat. "Yeah."

I studied him for a long moment, the tension still tugging at the corners of his mouth. I wanted to help, but I knew better than to push a stubborn cowboy. Instead, I did something I never would have expected to do.

"Do you want a hug?" The words just slipped out before I could stop them.

Cole blinked, clearly taken aback, but then his eyes softened, that guarded look fading a little. "Yeah," he said quietly. "Yeah, I think I do."

I stepped forward, sliding my arms around him and tucking my head under his jaw. At first, it was just a simple hug, his arms wrapping around me, warm and firm, but then something shifted. I felt his breath against my hair, the rise and fall of his chest as he pulled me closer. My heart started racing in my chest, and before I even realized what was happening, I tipped my chin up to look at him.

His eyes met mine, something intense flickering in their depths, and then he leaned down, his lips brushing mine in a kiss that was soft and careful at first. But the longer we stood there, the more it deepened, growing warmer, more... just *more*. My hands slid up to his shoulders, holding onto him as if letting go would bring the night crashing down around us.

The kiss lingered, a slow, steady heat building between us, until finally, we broke apart, breathless. My head was spinning, my heart thundering in my chest as I stared up at him, completely dazed.

"Cole," I murmured, my voice barely a whisper. "What is this? What... what are we doing?"

That crooked grin I was starting to love flashed across his face. "I don't know," he said, a soft chuckle escaping his lips. "But I really like it."

I felt myself smile, my heart doing a little flip. "I do, too."

He leaned down, kissing me again, but this time it was softer, slower. It was like we both knew there was something fragile between us, something that needed time to grow. When he pulled back, his eyes lingered on mine, searching, before he took a slow step back, his hand brushing mine one last time.

"Goodnight, Emily," he said quietly, his voice carrying that same warmth from the kiss.

"Goodnight," I whispered back, watching as he walked across the lot to his own trailer. I stood there for a moment longer, the cool air biting at my skin, but all I could feel was the heat of his kiss.

Cole

The drive back to Walker Ranch had been quiet, the radio humming low as the miles blurred by. Cody woke up with a headache—claimed he was getting sick—so Emily and I ended up driving the rigs. I kept replaying the moments from the show, her kisses still fresh in my mind, mixed with the heat of California sun and the thrill of the competition. But as the familiar landscape of Big River Valley rolled into view, the weight of reality crept back over me like a storm cloud.

We pulled into the gravel drive at Walker Ranch, the gate swinging wide for all the trailers to roll through. Dusty and Jess were already there, standing by the barn, waving as soon as they spotted us. Emily climbed out of the truck first, a smile lighting up her face as she rushed to greet them.

"Hey, y'all! You won't believe it—Copper and I won the whole dang thing!" she called out, her voice bright and full of pride.

Dusty grinned, tipping his hat back as he gave her a fist bump. "Well, look at you. I knew you had it in you, Em."

Jess looped her arm through Emily's, pulling her into a hug. "I want all the details—every second of it."

As they stood there, chatting and laughing, I stayed back by the trailer, watching them. Emily fit right in with Dusty and Jess, and the sight of it made something twist inside me. It wasn't just grudging admiration anymore—it was a pull, a warmth I hadn't felt in a long time. It scared me, but it thrilled me, too. There was something about the way she laughed, the way she lit up when she was talking to people she cared about... And the thought crept up, uninvited: *Could she ever be mine?*

That thought slammed into me hard, and I stiffened, shoving it aside. I couldn't afford to think like that. Not now.

Just as I was about to start unloading the trailer, I heard the sound of another rig pulling up. I turned to see Marshall and Kelli Walker stepping out of their shiny SUV—the one they'd just bought to drive the twins around because Marshall said Kelli's old Civic scared the daylights out of him... especially with the way she drives. Kelli, bubbly as ever, bounced over, her arms wide for a hug.

"Welcome back, y'all!" she squealed. "I heard you rocked that show, Emily!"

Emily turned, beaming as Kelli embraced her. "It was a good day, that's for sure!"

Kelli's enthusiasm was contagious, and she quickly pulled me into the conversation, too. But as soon as her eyes met mine, that storm cloud settled back over me. Her father, Mr. Mason, was the realtor my brothers wanted to call. The guy who could potentially take away everything I'd grown up with—our ranch, our home. I couldn't shake the connection.

Fortunately, Kelli seemed oblivious to my terse greeting—she was always really nice to me, and I tried to be friendly, but I just couldn't talk to her. She was going on about how we had to celebrate the next time we were all together, maybe with a barbecue at the main ranch house with some of Meryl's apple pie. I nodded along, half-listening, half-distracted, as the steam inside me built.

Eventually, the trailers were unloaded, and the tack put away. The sun was low on the horizon, casting long shadows across the yard as everyone started to disperse. I pulled my keys out of my pocket, ready to head home, when Emily walked over to me.

"Hey," she said brightly. "My mom's probably working late tonight. You wanna grab a burger before you head home?"

Her voice was gentle, hopeful. And for a second, I almost said yes. I could picture us sitting at that little diner, laughing over something stupid like we had before. But then reality slammed into me again.

What business did I have being with someone like *her*?

She had a whole world in front of her—so much promise, so much potential. She'd work hard and get anything she wanted, that much was clear. And me? I didn't even have a ranch anymore. I didn't have a horse to my name. I was just a broke cowboy who couldn't even fix his family's problems. What right did I have leading her on?

I shook my head, my voice coming out gruffer than I meant. "I don't think so."

Her face fell, just for a second, before she forced a smile. "Oh. Okay."

I hated the look in her eyes—like I'd just crushed some small piece of her. But I couldn't take it back. I didn't deserve her, and the last thing I wanted was for her to waste her time on someone like me.

"Sorry, Em," I muttered, guilt twisting in my gut. "I just... I got some stuff I need to figure out."

She nodded, but the hurt in her eyes didn't disappear. "Yeah. I get it."

Without another word, I turned and headed for my truck. Each step felt heavier than the last, like my boots were sinking into the dirt. The thought of Emily standing there, looking at me like that, twisted something deep in my chest. I hated that I'd put that look on her face, but I couldn't let myself believe I had any business being with her—not with everything falling apart the way it was.

Chapter Seventeen

Emily

When I opened the door to the apartment, the first thing that hit me wasn't the usual musty scent of secondhand goods from the shop below or the comforting warmth of home. It was the emptiness. A hollow, echoing sort of emptiness that made me freeze in the doorway.

I blinked, glancing around the living room. The shelves that were usually crammed full of knick-knacks and mismatched picture frames were bare. The cluttered coffee table, which normally had a stack of bills, a few old magazines, and one of Mom's half-finished projects on it, was cleared off. Even the old recliner Dad used to sit in—the one piece of furniture she'd saved from the house they shared—looked strangely out of place, like it had lost its purpose.

I stepped inside, my boots clunking against the old wood floor, and shut the door behind me. The sound echoed, bouncing off walls that seemed bigger somehow. Cleaner.

"Mom?" I called, setting my bag down by the couch, which now had exactly one throw pillow and nothing else.

"In here!" Her voice came from the kitchen, bright and chipper, like she was about to reveal a great surprise. I walked in, half-expecting to find everything back to normal in the kitchen, but no. It was just as stripped bare as the living room.

Mom was sitting at the dining table, her hair pulled back in a messy bun and a pen in her hand, paying bills. The stack of mail, usually a chaotic mess, was neatly organized into little piles. Even the old salt and pepper shakers were gone from the table. There was nothing on it except the bills and a single cup of tea.

She looked up at me with a smile, a proud sort of smile that tugged at the corners of her mouth. "I cleaned up," she said, nodding toward the space around us. "Like you said. You think it looks better now?"

I stared at her, unsure how to respond. It was *too* clean. Too empty. It didn't feel like home. The words were on the tip of my tongue, but I swallowed them back, feeling a sharp pang of guilt. I'd lashed out before I left for the show, snapping at her about the clutter, and now... this.

"Yeah," I said, my voice quiet. "It's... it's something."

Her smile faltered just a bit, and she put the pen down. "I know it's a lot," she said, gesturing toward the living room. "But I figured it might make things easier for you. Less... embarrassing. I didn't realize how much I'd let it pile up until you said something."

I opened my mouth to say something—anything—but nothing came out. Guilt twisted in my gut, knotting tighter with every word she spoke. This wasn't what I meant. I hadn't wanted her to strip the place down to bare bones. I just... I just needed space, and now the apartment felt like a stranger's home. Too clean, too cold.

"I went through a lot of stuff," she continued, her hands fidgeting with the edge of a bill. "Got all the stuff for the store moved downstairs, and got rid of things we didn't need. Donated some. Planning to sell a few of our things in the shop, too. Figured we could use the extra cash."

"Mom." I dropped my duffel bag off my shoulder. "Where is your fridge magnet collection? Your cuddly blankets from the sofa?"

"Oh, you know," she said with a wave, her voice a little too bright. "That stuff just gathers dust, and it's all old. It's a fresh look for the apartment, right?"

I forced a smile, nodding along like I agreed. "Yeah, sure. That makes sense."

But it didn't. Not really. The apartment felt hollow now, like someone had taken all the memories and stuffed them in a box somewhere. It wasn't clutter, it was... home. And I'd ruined it.

"I just thought you'd like it better this way," she said, her voice softer now, almost uncertain.

I swallowed hard, the guilt so heavy in my chest I could barely breathe. "Mom, I..." I started, but the words got caught in my throat. "I'm just tired from the show," I said, waving it off. "I think I'm gonna lie down for a bit."

"Oh, of course," she said quickly, nodding. "You've been working hard. Go ahead, sweetheart."

I gave her another strained smile and retreated to my room, the door closing with a soft click behind me. Once inside, I slumped against the wall, letting out a long, frustrated breath. What was I supposed to say? How was I supposed to apologize for this? I'd snapped about the clutter, and now... she'd gone and done all this because of me.

I ran a hand through my hair, pushing off the wall to flop down on my bed. The room was just as sparse as the rest of the apartment, the shelves cleared, my desk almost entirely empty except for my phone charger and a notebook. It felt... wrong.

Pulling my phone from my pocket, I scrolled through my messages and landed on Lauren's number. If anyone would know what to say, it was her.

You ever feel like you're the bad daughter? I typed, hitting send before I could rethink it.

A minute later, my phone buzzed.

Nope, but I don't live there, came Lauren's reply, followed by a winking emoji. *Why, what happened?*

I sighed, staring at the screen for a moment before typing back.

I made a comment about Mom's clutter, and now the place looks like a display home. I feel terrible.

She's just trying to please you, Lauren texted. *You know how she is. She probably thought she was doing something good for you.*

I bit my lip, staring at the empty walls of my room. *Yeah, but I didn't mean for her to get rid of everything. Now, it feels... wrong. Cold.*

You need to talk to her, Lauren typed back. *Explain that it's not about getting rid of everything, just finding a balance. She's probably feeling bad about it now, too.*

I groaned, tossing my phone onto the bed beside me. Lauren was right. I needed to have that conversation, but the words just wouldn't come. I'd hurt Mom enough already. What if I made it worse?

Another buzz from my phone.

You'll figure it out, Lauren added. *Just be honest. She'll understand.*

Thanks, I replied. *I'll try.*

Cole

I drove back home with my thoughts in a tailspin. The sky had turned from pale blue to a deep orange as the sun dipped lower, casting long shadows across the fields. The closer I got to the ranch, the heavier my chest felt, like the weight of everything I'd left behind was waiting for me at the front gate.

When I finally pulled into the driveway, I spotted Mom out by the barn, cleaning up around the yard. I parked the truck and stepped out, tugging my hat lower as I walked toward her. She didn't look up right away since she was busy stacking a pile of old fencing T-posts.

"Hey, Ma," I called as I got closer.

She glanced up, her face lighting up with a tired smile. "Cole! You're back."

"Yeah, just got in," I said, nodding. "How's everything?"

She wiped her hands on her jeans, brushing off bits of grime. "Oh, you know. Same as always. The boys are inside." She glanced toward the house, her smile faltering a little. "Dinner's about ready."

I nodded, feeling the unease settle in my gut. She didn't have to say anything else. I could tell something was off, and I had a feeling it had to do with Gage and Trent.

"I'll be in soon," I said. "Just gonna put my stuff away."

"Alright," she said. "Don't stay out too long. It's been a long day."

I nodded, heading toward the barn to drop off some of my gear. The whole way there, my mind was spinning. I wasn't ready for this conversation. I didn't want to face my brothers, especially not after everything that had been left hanging before I went to California.

After putting away my things, I headed into the house, bracing myself for whatever was waiting inside. Sure enough, Gage and Trent were at the dinner table, the tension thick enough to cut with a knife.

They glanced up as I walked in, and I could tell from the looks on their faces that this wasn't going to be an easy night.

"Hey," I muttered, taking a seat at the table.

"Hey," Gage replied, his voice clipped. He stabbed a fork into his plate of mashed potatoes, not looking up. Trent was quiet, which was never a good sign.

Mom bustled around the kitchen, bringing over a dish of roast chicken. "Here we go," she said too-brightly. "Everyone dig in."

The silence that followed was heavy, uncomfortable. I barely touched my food, my mind too wrapped up in the ranch and what was happening. I couldn't help but glance at Gage and Trent, both of them looking like they had something to say but weren't willing to start.

Finally, I set my fork down. "What's going on? You couldn't wait for me to get home before deciding to sell the ranch?"

The words hung in the air, thick with tension. Trent, leaning against the counter, shot Gage a wary look. Gage just crossed his arms, his jaw tight.

"It's not like that," Gage said. "But you haven't been here, Cole. We've been carrying the weight of this for months now, trying to keep things afloat while you've been—" He stopped, catching himself, but the damage was already done.

"While I've been what?" I demanded, stepping closer. "Working my tail off? Doing what I can to bring something back to this family?"

Gage rubbed his temples. "No one's saying you're not working hard. We get that. We all want to fight to keep the ranch. But if we don't sell soon, there won't be anything left to fight for."

"So you're giving up?" I spat, the anger rising in my throat. "Just like that?"

Trent pushed off the counter, stepping into the conversation for the first time. "It's not about giving up. It's about survival. Look around, Cole!"

"I get that things are bad," I growled. "But you didn't even talk to me before making your minds up. This is our family's land. Our legacy. You can't just—"

"You weren't here!" Gage interrupted, his voice hard. "We didn't keep you out of the loop on purpose. We've been trying to figure this out for months, and you're over there, training show horses like everything's fine. But it's not fine, Cole. We're drowning."

I felt like I'd been punched in the gut. "I told you, I was only—"

"We know, Cole," Trent broke in. "We know you've been building something for yourself. Maybe that's the right thing for you. But for the rest of us... staying here is killing us."

Gage nodded, his arms dropping to his sides. "Look, we're not saying you don't belong here. But the reality is, this ranch isn't enough for all of us anymore. Not like it was when Dad was around. Things have changed."

I stared at them, my mind spinning. Everything had been falling apart, and I'd been too focused on my own life to see it. I felt a surge of guilt, but it was quickly swallowed by the anger simmering in my chest.

"So, what?" I asked, my voice low. "We all just walk away? Pretend like this place doesn't matter?"

Gage shook his head, but he didn't say anything. Neither did Chase, and neither did Mom. I shook my head and threw my hands in the air. So... that was it?

But I also knew Gage wasn't wrong. The ranch was bleeding us dry.

Trent broke the silence. "We don't want to drag this out forever. We just... we don't want to lose everything we've worked for. And if we don't make a move soon, that's exactly what'll happen."

I could see the pain in Trent's eyes, the way his shoulders slumped like he was carrying the weight of the world. And Gage—he'd always been the strong one, the one who kept everything together after Dad died. But even he looked tired, like he was running out of fight.

"Mom?" I asked. "Are you okay with this?"

She was sitting in her usual chair, her hand twirling her water glass until it left little wet rings on the table, and she wasn't looking up. She just pursed her lips and sighed.

Chase, who had been quiet until now, finally spoke. His voice was steady, but there was an edge of sadness in it. "Mom's not the one making the decision, Cole. We are. And we have to think about what's best for her, too. She doesn't need the stress of trying to keep the ranch going. She deserves to... to take a break once in a while!"

My chest tightened, and I realized how little I'd been around to see what was happening to her. I thought about the way she smiled at me when I visited—how tired her eyes looked even when she tried to pretend everything was okay.

"And what's your plan then?" I asked, trying to hold it together. "Where does that leave us?"

Trent looked away, his mouth pulling into a grim line. "That's the thing, Cole. We don't know."

I opened my mouth to argue, to fight back—but I didn't know what to say. They had a point. I'd been ignoring the warning signs, thinking that working for Cody, learning a trade for myself, would somehow fix everything. But this was bigger than me. Bigger than any of us.

"Mom," I sighed. "Really... is this what you want to do?"

Mom shifted in her chair, leaning back until she looked me in the eye. "I love this place," Mom said, her voice trembling slightly. "But it's not worth losing my sons over. I've been holding on for you all, but if it's time to let go... then we'll let go."

I felt like the ground had been pulled out from under me. All this time, I'd been so angry, so sure that I had been left out of the decision-making. But Mom had known. She'd been carrying this burden right alongside my brothers, and I hadn't even noticed. I thought I had been protecting something—protecting *her*—but she'd been carrying the weight of the decision, waiting for us to come to terms with it.

Chase cleared his throat, his voice quieter now, but steady. "We all want to make the right call, Cole. But... maybe holding on too tight isn't the answer anymore."

I felt my hands clench into fists, but not out of anger. It was helplessness. The ranch had always been a constant, a cornerstone, but now it felt like it was slipping through my fingers.

"And what about Dad?" The question slipped out before I could stop it, my voice tight with something between frustration and loss. "What would he think about all this? Us selling off everything he built?"

Mom's face softened, the lines around her eyes deepening with sadness. "Your father worked his whole life for this ranch," she said, her voice low, almost reverent. "But I think if he were here, he'd care more about you boys than he ever did about the land. It was always about the family first."

I looked at my brothers—Gage's rigid jawline, Trent fidgeting with the cap in his hands, and Chase, steady as always, but with a weariness in his eyes I hadn't noticed before. They weren't trying to cut me out. They were trying to do what was right, and I had been blind to it.

But it didn't make it any easier.

I swallowed hard, my voice quieter now. "Okay," I said, my throat tight. "If selling is the best thing for us, then... I'm not going to stand in the way."

There was a pause—a stillness, as if the air itself had stopped moving. Gage's eyes met mine, his expression unreadable for a moment before he gave a short nod. Chase let out a quiet breath, relief etched across his face.

Mom didn't say anything right away. She just looked at me with those tired, understanding eyes and nodded too. I could see the sadness in her, the grief that came with letting go of the life we'd built here. But there was also a kind of peace—like she'd been waiting for this moment, waiting for us to come to terms with the inevitable.

"It's not what any of us wanted," I added. "But if we have to let it go, then... no point in us all fighting about it."

Gage stood up, his shoulders loosening for the first time in what felt like weeks. "Thank you, Cole."

Trent, still fidgeting with his cap, finally spoke up, his voice quieter than I'd ever heard it. "It'll be better this way. For all of us."

I nodded, feeling the sting of the truth in his words. Better... but not easier.

There was nothing left to say. I didn't need to take a walk to clear my head. The decision had been made. And no matter how much it hurt, we'd find a way to move forward.

As I turned to head out of the room, Mom's voice stopped me in my tracks.

"I'm proud of you, Cole," she said softly.

I paused, swallowing the lump in my throat. I couldn't bring myself to look back at her, not right now. But I nodded. "Yeah," I muttered. "I'll see you in the morning."

Chapter Eighteen

Emily

I was tightening the cinch on Copper the next morning when I spotted Cody striding toward me, his boots kicking up dust in the late morning sun.

"Emily, Cole, got a favor to ask," he said, stopping just short of where I stood. He glanced over at Cole, who was working with one of the two-year-olds a few yards away. "Either of you could do it, but I need someone to run up to White Pines and pick up Nikki. Morgan's short-handed today, and I've got a sponsor stopping by. Prefer to handle that conversation in person if I can."

I glanced at Cole, who was focusing on his horse, but I could see him pause for a second, like he was considering volunteering.

"I'll go," I offered, stepping forward quickly. Cody looked relieved.

"You sure? Kelli said she could watch her, but she just put Tuff and Lane down, and it's just easier if..."

"I got it. I don't mind. Be back soon."

Cole glanced over briefly, our eyes catching for a moment before he returned to his task. The tension between us was thick, like neither of us really knew what to say anymore. He had barely spoken to me since last night when I'd asked him to grab a burger, and he'd turned me down without much of an explanation. I didn't know what had shifted between us, but whatever it was, it left a hollow feeling in my chest. Part of me wanted to march over there and ask what his deal was, but the other part... the more cautious part, figured it was better to leave it alone for now.

Still, the silence felt wrong. He'd been so open, so vulnerable when we were on the road and at the show, and now it was like he'd shut down completely. I couldn't make sense of it.

I sighed and gave Copper a pat on the neck, more to settle my own nerves than anything. The truth was, I wasn't sure what I'd done wrong, and I didn't have the energy to figure it out right now. This errand felt like a good way to put some space between us, at least for a little while.

I waved at Cody as I passed, then headed to the truck, trying not to think too much about Cole or the fact that he hadn't even bothered to look my way again.

The drive to White Pines didn't take long. I parked near the barn and hopped out, taking in the familiar surroundings of the riding center. Horses grazed lazily in the pastures, and the smell of hay and leather filled the air. The sound of hooves clopping along the dirt paths brought back a flood of memories from when I'd worked here with Morgan.

I was only halfway to the barn when I spotted Kate working with a client, guiding them through a session on one of the therapy horses.

She waved me over with that big smile of hers. She was in the middle of a session with one of the therapy horses but was never too busy to stop and greet an old friend.

"Well, look who's back! Walker Ranch too much for you already?" she teased as I walked over, giving the horse she was working with a gentle pat on the neck.

I smiled, but it must not have been a great smile because Kate's teasing grin mellowed into something more serious. "What's up with you?" she asked, her eyes narrowing as she studied me.

I shook my head, waving off her concern. "Oh, nothing. Just came to pick up Nikki for Cody. He said Morgan's short-handed today."

"Boy, are we! But... what else is up?"

"What makes you think something is 'up'?"

"Oh, just that..." She pointed to my forehead. "That deep line right there. You're always focused and serious, but that looks different."

I shrugged. "Just been busy."

"Uh-huh." She wasn't buying it, her brow arched like she was waiting for me to spill the real reason I looked like I was on the verge of snapping. "C'mon, Em. You never could hide anything. What's going on?"

I sighed, leaning back against the side of the truck. "It's just been... a rough few days. Mom's been... I don't know, weird, ever since I got back. And Cole's acting all distant. I thought things were getting better between us, but now he's just shutting me out."

Kate gave me a long, thoughtful look, her fingers tracing lazy circles on the horse's shoulder. "You know, you can't solve everyone's problems all at once, right?"

I chuckled half-heartedly. "Yeah, but it feels like everything's falling apart. I'm trying to figure out how to fix things with Mom, and every time it seems like Cole and I..."

"Wait." She held up a finger and eyed me strangely. "You sound like this is more than workplace friction. I know you said you were getting along better, but... is this more than that?"

I swallowed. "I thought so."

She narrowed her eyes. "So, it is, or it isn't?"

I chewed my lip. "This last week or so, it's been... different. Really *good* different. But as soon as we got home last night, it was like he pulled the rug out from under me. I just want to fix it, make things make sense."

Kate shrugged, her tone matter-of-fact. "Maybe it's not about fixing things. Maybe you just gotta let it be messy for a while. Trust me, I know a thing or two about messes."

I smiled at her, knowing she wasn't just talking about horses or ranch life. Kate's life hadn't exactly been picture-perfect either, but she had a way of cutting through the nonsense and seeing things clearly.

"Thanks, Kate. I guess I just... I don't know, needed to get it out."

"Anytime, girl. You know that." She leaned closer, her voice softening. "Hey, you and I should grab a burger later. Sound good? We can talk it out properly then."

I nodded, feeling a bit of relief at the thought. "Actually, that sounds great. I'll need a break by then. This day's been... well, you get it."

Kate chuckled, giving me a quick nod before heading back to her session. "I always get it."

I gave her a wave and made my way back toward the truck, glancing over at the therapy office where Morgan would be with Nikki. For now, at least, I could push everything else to the back of my mind.

Cole

I was working with one of the colts in the arena when I saw Emily's car pull in. She stepped out, holding little Nikki, and I could see them walking toward the barn office where Cody was holed up, likely dealing with another one of his sponsors or going over the books with Dusty or something. Emily paused for a moment, pointing me out to Nikki, and the little girl waved enthusiastically in my direction.

I couldn't help but smile back, lifting my hand in return, though it was more for Nikki than Emily. But as I watched them disappear into the barn, a strange pang hit me. It was that quiet, sinking feeling I'd been getting more often lately, like something in my chest was starting to hollow out.

I wasn't going to have this—family, close ties, growing old on a ranch and raising kids like Cody had. Walker Ranch was bustling with life, always someone laughing, working, kids running around underfoot. And me? My ranch was being sold right out from under me. My brothers were talking about new lives, new jobs, and I hadn't even figured out where I stood.

I looked back at the colt I was saddling, running a hand down his neck. It was supposed to be enough—working horses, learning the craft, maybe even taking over a program like this someday. But today, it didn't feel like enough. Not even close.

A little while later, I spotted Cody coming out of the office, with Nikki on his shoulders, her little arms wrapped around his head as she giggled. He was taking her out to the truck, likely to drop her off with Kelli and Marshall. They'd raise their kids here, too—another generation at Walker Ranch.

I swallowed hard and turned my focus back to the colt, feeling the latigo in my hands, pulling it tighter, trying to push the thoughts from my head. But they stayed there, no matter how much I worked, gnawing at me from the inside out.

Just then, Emily came out to the arena. I noticed her walking up, a little tentative at first, like she wasn't sure how to approach me. I could feel her watching, waiting for me to look at her, maybe even give her a smile. But I couldn't. I didn't have it in me.

She leaned on the fence. "Need a hand with anything?"

I kept my eyes on the colt. "I've got it."

She didn't move, and I felt her waiting, lingering. Finally, I sighed and turned to face her. "What do you want, Emily?"

Her brow furrowed slightly, and she shifted on her feet. "I was just... hoping you'd talk to me. I thought we were talking, but you've been kind of distant today."

I grunted, tightening the cinch on the colt before swinging into the saddle. "Yeah, well... things are complicated."

She crossed her arms, leaning a little closer to the fence. "Does this have to do with your family?"

I kept my eyes on the horizon, feeling the weight of her question sinking in. After a moment, I nodded. "They're selling the ranch."

There it was. The words just hung there, heavy and real. I hadn't said them out loud until now, and it hit me harder than I thought it would.

Emily's face fell, her eyes widening in shock. "Just like that?"

I shrugged, gripping the reins tighter than I needed to. "They don't think we can keep it running anymore. Grazing rights, money issues... it's all stacking up against us." I paused, my jaw tightening. "I guess I've been the only one not ready to face it."

She took a step closer, her voice soft. "What does that mean for you?"

I shook my head, feeling the colt shift beneath me as I adjusted in the saddle. "I don't know."

I didn't want to talk about it anymore. It was too much, too soon. Before she could ask anything else, I urged the colt forward, feeling him move beneath me as I rode off into the arena. Behind me, I heard Emily sigh softly, and I knew she was watching me go.

But right now, I couldn't give her—or anyone else—what they were looking for.

Emily

The sound of the truck's engine hummed softly as I pulled into the parking lot of the little diner just off Main Street. The neon sign for burgers and fries flickered in the dusk, casting a warm glow over the gravel lot. I spotted Kate's car parked near the entrance and sighed in relief. After the day I'd had, I needed her humor more than I'd realized.

Sliding out of my car, I smoothed my shirt and headed toward the entrance. When I pushed open the door, the scent of fried food hit me like a comforting embrace. The low murmur of voices and the clatter of silverware filled the room. It was busy but not crowded, with people I recognized from town sprinkled around the booths.

Kate waved from a booth near the window, flashing me a grin as I walked over. She had her hair pulled back, with a few strands escaping and framing her face, her skin glowing in the warm diner light. "Took you long enough," she teased.

I rolled my eyes and slid into the seat across from her. "Sorry, had a lot of work."

Kate chuckled and flagged down the waitress. "Busy day with the horses?"

I sighed, rubbing my forehead. "You could say that."

The waitress approached with a friendly smile and handed us menus. I didn't really need to look. The diner always had the same options, but I pretended to study it for a second while Kate ordered a cheeseburger with extra pickles.

"I'll take the same," I added, giving the waitress a quick nod before she left.

Once she was gone, Kate leaned forward, resting her chin in her hand. "Alright, spill. You've got that look like you're holding back."

I fidgeted with the salt shaker in front of me, my fingers tracing the rim. "It's just been a lot, you know? With work, and then home stuff..."

"Home stuff?" Kate's brow shot up. "Oh, girl, what's going on? Last time we talked, you weren't exactly on great terms with your mom."

I sighed and leaned back in the booth, staring out the window for a moment. The streetlights flickered, and the faint sound of cars passing on the main road filled the silence between us. "Yeah... I snapped at her before we left for the show. About the clutter in the apartment."

Kate nodded slowly. "Right. The mess thing." She tilted her head. "Did she take it badly?"

I laughed, but it was humorless. "That's an understatement. When I got home, she'd basically stripped the place clean. It didn't even look like the same apartment. I know she did it because of what I said, but..." I shook my head. "It's just so weird now. Like, I'm not sure what to say to her anymore."

Kate leaned back, tapping her fingers thoughtfully on the edge of the table. "You know what? Your mom probably feels like she's stuck in a no-win situation. Like, if she keeps things the way they were, she's worried it's going to push you away even more. And if she changes too much, she's afraid she's doing the wrong thing."

I sighed, running a hand through my hair. "Yeah, I get that. I just didn't think she'd react like this—stripping the place down to nothing. It's like she's trying to fix something I didn't even mean to break."

Kate nodded slowly. "You know, I hear things at work... I'm not as good as Morgan, mind, but I've picked up some things. Sometimes people go overboard when they don't know how else to handle things."

"Hah. Good counseling." I slumped back in my seat. "I just wanted things to feel a little less... chaotic at home. But now I feel like I've just made everything worse."

Kate's eyes softened, and she reached across the table, squeezing my hand briefly. "Well, you've got to give yourself a little credit. I know you didn't mean to hurt her. Maybe you two just need to talk, like actually talk. Not about the clutter or any of that, but about everything else."

I gave her a small smile. "Yeah, you're probably right."

"Of course, I'm right," she teased, winking. "I'm always right."

I chuckled, feeling the weight lift slightly from my shoulders. "Okay, Miss Always Right. What's new with you?"

Kate's grin widened, her whole face lighting up. "Oh, not much. You know, same old. Walter's been helping me with the car again."

"Still giving you trouble?"

She rolled her eyes. "Like you wouldn't believe. But Walter's con-vinced it's got another fifty thousand miles in it." She paused, her tone shifting to something more serious. "My dad's been on my case about the car though—says I need to ditch it and get a 'real job' so I can afford something better."

I frowned, knowing how much that got under her skin. "But you love working at White Pines. And you're good at it."

"Yeah, well, tell that to him. He's still pushing for me to go into something 'respectable,' like banking or real estate. Because, you know, those are super fulfilling." She gave a sarcastic laugh.

I snorted. "Real estate? Seriously?"

"Yup. Because apparently, helping people with horses isn't impor-tant enough." She shrugged, but I could see the frustration simmering beneath the surface.

The waitress brought our food over then, sliding the plates in front of us. I took a bite of my burger, savoring the comfort of it, but my mind was still on Kate's struggle with her dad. She always tried to play it cool, but I knew how much it bothered her that he didn't support her dream.

"Well, I think what you do is important," I said after a few mo-ments.

She grinned through a mouthful of fries. "Thanks, Em. That means a lot."

We ate in companionable silence for a bit, the clatter of plates and laughter from other booths filling the air around us. After a while, Kate leaned back in her seat, wiping her hands with a napkin.

"So," she said, giving me a pointed look. "How's everything going with Cole?"

I almost choked on my fries, setting them down as my face heated up. "What? Cole? What do you mean?"

Kate gave me a knowing smile, wagging her eyebrows. "Oh, come on. Don't play dumb with me. I saw the way you two were acting last time I stopped by the ranch. Something's going on."

I sighed, glancing down at my plate. "It's... complicated."

"Isn't it always?" she quipped, sipping her soda. "So, what's the deal?"

"Well," I started, hesitating for a moment. "There's been... something between us. Like... when we were on the road." I cleared my throat.

"Oooh." Kate slurped loudly from her straw, her eyes wide. "Spill it."

I sighed. "Fine. He kissed me. A couple of times, and... it wasn't all him."

She gasped, her hand flying to her mouth. "No! Get out. Cole Langton, the prankster, chip-on-his-shoulder, the guy who's always mad that you're better than him? *That* guy?"

I shifted uncomfortably in my seat. "I'm not better than he is."

"Tell that to him. Everyone can see it. He hates that you always beat him. Between you and me, I'm not shocked that he secretly likes you, but I bet I'm the only one."

"I'm not so sure he does like me." I frowned and stabbed my straw through a hole in the middle of an ice cube melting in my soda. "I was just there, you know? Someone he could talk to."

"Trust me, girl, he didn't kiss you because you were 'there'. People talk, and those Langton boys are about the pickiest dudes around."

I bit my lip, playing with the straw in my drink. "Yeah, but... after that, he shut me out. We haven't talked like we did since the show. It's like we're back to square one."

Kate rolled her eyes. "Typical. That's a guy who's scared, Em. Trust me, when they start pulling back after something like that, it's because they don't know what to do with their feelings. Especially guys like Cole—tough on the outside, but a total mess inside."

I shook my head, staring at the condensation on my glass. "Maybe. But he's got a lot going on with his family. They're... well, it sounds kind of like my problems, only... ranch-sized."

Kate's eyes softened. "Yikes. That's rough. I mean, no wonder he's all over the place."

"Exactly," I said, exasperated. "So how do I even help him? How can I be there for him, even if it's only as a friend, when he's barely letting me in?"

Kate leaned forward, her face serious for a moment, which wasn't like her. "Listen, you've gotta give him time, but you also have to be real with him. You can't just let him shut you out forever. Guys like Cole? They need someone to push back a little. Let him know you're there, but don't let him walk all over you."

I chuckled dryly. "Yeah, like that's ever been my problem."

Kate snorted, shaking her head. "True. But seriously, he wouldn't have kissed you if you were just 'there.' You're under his skin. I bet he's figuring out how to deal with that, but don't give up. Let him come to you, but don't be afraid to nudge him if he doesn't."

I nodded slowly, thinking about the way Cole had looked at me after the show, the way his smile had started to reach his eyes for the first time. Maybe Kate was right. Maybe Cole was just scared. But how long was I willing to wait for him to figure things out?

I sighed, feeling the weight of everything—my mom, Cole, work. It was all swirling together, and I didn't know how to make sense of any of it.

Kate gave me a sympathetic smile. "Hey, no pressure. Just... play it cool. You're good at that."

I grinned, the tension easing a little. "Yeah, cool. That's me."

Kate laughed, flicking a fry in my direction. "Right. But seriously, just take it one step at a time. If Cole's worth it, he'll figure it out. And if he doesn't, well, you've got better things ahead."

I smiled, feeling a little lighter. Maybe Kate was right.

Chapter Nineteen

Cole

The air was thick with the smell of fresh hay and the faint dust kicked up by hooves as Lynx moved under me, her muscles coiled tight and ready to spring. We weren't working live cattle today—just the practice flag, that stupid mechanical thing swaying back and forth on its line like a lazy cat. Lynx was all business, her ears flicking toward the flag, and she was eager. Too eager. Her energy wasn't the problem though; it was mine.

I was tense, my body fighting her rhythm instead of flowing with it, like I had something to prove. My hands tightened on the reins as I guided her through another quick turn, but it didn't feel right. Nothing felt right today.

"Keep her shoulder up," Cody called from the side, leaning against the gate, his tone even but threaded with that patience that could either calm you down or make you want to bite back. "Stand her up straight, and stop dropping your own shoulder. You're throwing her off."

I gritted my teeth, keeping my eyes locked on the flag as it swayed again. She was fine. I was fine. I didn't need the extra comments right now, not with my head so full of everything else. Lynx wasn't the problem.

"Cole," Cody's voice came again, sharper now, like he could sense my frustration building. "You're pushing her too hard. Let her think. Give her a minute."

I shifted in the saddle, rolling my shoulders back. "She's doing what she needs to," I snapped back, sharper than I intended. "We're just trying to get through it."

"Yeah, but you're dropping your shoulder in every turn," Cody pointed out. "She's reading off you, and you're sending her the wrong message. Sit up and keep your hands quiet."

I could feel my jaw tightening, that familiar frustration creeping up my spine. "She's fine, Cody. I just need to get this done today."

Cody's eyes narrowed, his patience thinning. "You're fighting her, Cole. Let her work. Stop getting in her way."

The words hit me like a slap. I knew he was right, but the tension that had been sitting in my chest for days now wouldn't let me admit it. Instead, I snapped. "I'm not fighting her! I'm doing it right!"

Cody straightened from where he was leaning against the fence, his eyes hardening in that way that said he wasn't here to argue. "Cole, I'm telling you, back off. You keep pushing like that, and she's gonna shut down on you."

I pulled Lynx to a stop, my chest rising and falling in uneven breaths as the frustration swirled. It wasn't about the horse or the flag anymore. It was everything—Gage, the ranch, the whole blasted mess back home. I didn't want to hear Cody's corrections, not today.

"Fine," I muttered, unclenching my fists from the reins. "We're done."

Cody just stared at me, his eyes cool but questioning, like he was trying to figure out what had snapped in me today. I could feel Emily watching from the far side of the pen, her horse standing still as she waited, probably wondering why I was on edge.

Without another word, I slid off Lynx, pulling the latigo loose, trying to steady my breathing. I already regretted snapping like that, but I couldn't take it back. Cody didn't say anything for a beat, just studied me with that calm, piercing look he always had when he was deciding if a fight was worth picking.

"You need to leave whatever's going on at home out of the work here," he said, his voice cool but firm. "Get back on and go do some circle drills."

I sucked in a breath, the tension in my shoulders winding even tighter. I wanted to argue, to push back. But I didn't. He was right. He was always right. I just couldn't let it go—this thing inside me that had me wound tighter than Lynx herself.

Without another word, I tugged my cinch tight again and swung back on. Lynx softened the instant I stepped on, her ears spinning—listening—and it made me feel worse. I wasn't being fair to her. Or to Cody. But every time I thought I had a handle on things, something would bring it all crashing down again.

For the next hour, we worked in silence. Cody stayed by the gate, his eyes on everything, though he didn't say much else. I kept my head down, focused on Lynx, trying to block out everything except her movements. It was easier that way—just me and the horse.

But when we finally finished, and Cody called it a day, the weight of everything came back. I led Lynx out of the arena, my boots heavy in the dirt. Cody didn't say anything as I walked past him, but I could feel his eyes on my back, waiting for me to cool off.

I wasn't mad at him. Not really. But the pressure from home, the decision to sell... it was eating at me from the inside out. And I didn't know how much longer I could keep it from spilling over into everything else.

Emily

I had just finished cooling down Copper when I spotted Luke and Evan Walker working calves in the chute. Luke was sorting fresh calves into the squeeze every few minutes while Evan was running vaccines, his expression calm but focused as always.

Copper gave a tired snort, so I patted his neck one last time before turning him out into his paddock for some down time. I was about to head over to check on the feed schedule when Luke glanced my way and waved me over.

"Hey, Em!" Luke called. "You busy, or you got time to help us out?"

I wasn't technically on cattle duty, but I could spare a few minutes. "What's going on?" I asked as I walked up to them.

Evan pointed to a little makeshift table where he'd set his supplies. "I'm almost out of vaccine. Thought I had more. Can you fetch another one from the fridge in the barn?"

"Yeah, sure thing." I jogged back to the barn and grabbed a bottle of vaccine. I was back just a minute later, but the guys both had their hands full, so I stopped to wait. Luke was pushing the next calf into the squeeze, holding it steady while Evan filled a syringe.

Luke shot me a grin. "Thanks, Em. I told him we'd run out before the job was done, but think this old cuss would listen?"

I handed the bottle to Evan, and he took it with a nod. "I'd rather have too many calves than too few," he muttered, concentrating on drawing the liquid into the syringe. "

Luke chuckled, giving the calf a pat. "Yeah, hard to market steers you don't have. Hey, speaking of that, Evan, how'd it go at the sale yesterday?"

Evan glanced at Luke, his voice low but casual. "Fine. Ran into Gage Langton."

Luke gave a grunt, adjusting the rope as the next calf settled into place. "Really? I passed him this morning on the highway. Waved at him, but he didn't even see me. Looked like he had a lot on his mind."

"Seemed like it yesterday, too," Evan said, filling another syringe. "He's selling off some of his breeding stock."

Luke's hands paused mid-movement. "Breeding stock? You serious?"

Evan nodded, frowning as he lined up the needle. "Didn't want to talk much about it, but he had a good number of cows going through the sale. Gage isn't the type to part with good cattle unless he has no other option."

My heart did a little flip, and I kept my eyes down, focusing on the calf I was leading. Luke tightened the rope around the chute post and stood up, dusting his hands on his jeans. "Selling off breeding stock... that's a bad sign."

Evan made a low noise of agreement, shaking his head. "Makes you wonder how deep in they are. You don't sell the future of your herd unless you're in trouble."

Luke scratched his chin, his eyes narrowing. "Yeah, Gage ain't the kind to make rash decisions, but if he's offloading his best... Well, it's none of my business, really. Just thought it was odd."

I bit the inside of my cheek, not wanting to make eye contact with either of them. They were talking about the Langtons like the sale was just business, but for me, it hit a little closer to home. I'd overheard enough from Cole to know what was really going on.

"You don't think they'll sell the whole place, do you?" Luke asked, his voice lower now, almost thoughtful.

Evan shrugged, tying off the syringe and checking the next dose. "Hard to say. But if they're selling stock, the ranch could be next."

Luke's jaw tightened, and he sighed. "A ranch like that... hard to imagine the valley without the Langtons in it."

I swallowed the tightness in my throat, trying to keep myself busy with the calves, but the weight of their conversation pressed heavy on my mind. I didn't want to think about it, didn't want to picture Cole's family without their ranch, but the reality was staring me right in the face.

Evan nodded in agreement. "Yeah, well... times are tough for everybody. Ain't just the Langtons feeling the squeeze."

Luke stood up, stretching his back. "Ain't that the truth? Anyway, we'll see what happens. Hope Gage can turn things around."

I kept quiet, helping guide the last calf into place. Luke didn't seem to notice my silence as he turned back to Evan, talking about the next steps in their routine. But the knot in my stomach was tightening. I was standing there, listening to them talk about the Langtons, knowing what I did about the ranch, and I couldn't say a word. Not to Luke, not to Evan, not even to Cody.

"What do you think, Emily?" Luke's voice broke through my thoughts. "You hear anything from Cole about what's happening over there?"

I shook my head quickly. "No, I haven't really talked to him much lately. He's been busy with the colts, and we've been focused on getting ready for these shows." I hated lying, but it wasn't my place to tell anyone what was happening.

Evan nodded, though his expression still held that air of suspicion. "Well, just thought it was odd. You don't see a ranch like the Langtons' offloading stock like that unless they're makin' some serious changes."

Yeah. They were making some changes. The Langtons were in deeper trouble than anyone realized, and I had a sinking feeling that things were only going to get worse.

I had just finished cleaning up the remnants of dinner, and the apartment was quiet. Mom was still downstairs working in the shop, and I had been flipping channels. The apartment felt emptier than usual, and I couldn't quite shake the sense of loneliness creeping in.

A knock at the door almost made me drop the remote control. It was late—too late for anyone to just stop by casually. My heart skipped a beat, and I got up from the couch, wiping my hands on my jeans before opening the door.

It was Cole.

"Hey," he said, his voice low, his hat in his hand. He looked tired, his face shadowed under the dim hallway light, but his eyes were intense, searching mine. "Got a minute?"

I blinked, caught off guard. "Yeah, sure. Come on in."

I stepped back, motioning him inside. He hesitated for a second before stepping through the door, glancing around like he was taking in every detail of the small apartment. I gestured to the couch. "Sit down if you want. Do you... want anything? Water? Coffee?"

He shook his head, rubbing the back of his neck. "No, I'm good. Thanks."

I sat down across from him, squeezing my hands between my knees. Something was wrong—his whole posture screamed that this wasn't just a casual visit. He looked like he hadn't slept in days, his shoulders slumped, and his eyes ringed with dark circles.

"I, uh..." He paused, fiddling with his hat. "I'm sorry for just showing up like this, but I needed to talk."

I folded my legs up under myself and grabbed the lone throw pillow Mom had left on the couch. This seemed like a conversation worth getting comfortable for. "It's okay. What's going on?"

For a moment, he just stared at his hands, his fingers tracing the brim of his hat. Then he sighed, lifting his gaze to meet mine. "It's the ranch," he said, his voice rough. "I can't... I don't know what to do, Em. We're selling it."

I felt the breath leave my lungs. I knew it was coming—he'd hinted at it before, but hearing it out loud, from him... it made it real.

"Cole..." I started, but he shook his head, cutting me off.

"No, listen. I know I haven't been handling things right. I've been avoiding you, avoiding everyone, because I'm just trying to figure out where I fit in all this. My family's falling apart, and I can't fix it. I can't stop them from selling the ranch, and I feel like I'm losing everything." His voice cracked slightly, and he looked away, swallowing hard. "I've never felt this lost before."

My heart twisted as I listened to him, the vulnerability in his voice hitting me harder than I expected. Cole was always so sure of himself, so in control—even when we butted heads, he'd never shown me this side of him before. I didn't know what to say, so I just reached out, placing a hand on his arm.

"I'm so sorry. I can't imagine what you're going through."

He glanced at me, his eyes full of gratitude, but also something else—something deeper, something I hadn't seen before. He let out a shaky breath, leaning back against the couch.

"I don't know what to do," he admitted. "The ranch is the only thing I've ever known. And now... it's slipping away."

I squeezed his arm gently. "Maybe this isn't the end," I said softly. "Maybe it's... it's a chance to try something new." Even as I said it, the phrase sounded trite and lame. Worthless. But I couldn't think of what else to say.

He gave me a small, bitter smile. "Yeah, maybe. But right now, it feels like everything's just... ending."

We sat in silence for a while, the weight of his words settling between us. I wanted to say something to make it better, to help him, but I didn't have the answers. All I could do was be here for him, let him know he wasn't alone.

"Thanks for listening, Em. I didn't mean to dump all this on you."

"You're not dumping anything. I'm glad you came to me."

He looked down at his hands again, his fingers still toying with the brim of his hat. "I didn't know who else to talk to."

I smiled at him, trying to offer some comfort, even though I knew I couldn't fix the situation. He smiled back, a small, genuine smile that made something inside me flutter.

"Hey," I said, "Are you hungry? I've got some leftovers if you want to stay for a bit."

He raised an eyebrow, his smile widening a fraction. "Leftovers?"

I grinned. "Chicken stir fry. Again."

He chuckled, shaking his head. "I'm game. Better than going home right now."

I stood up and made my way to the kitchen. It felt good to have something to do, even if it was just reheating the same chicken stir fry from last night.

As the microwave hummed, I turned to find him leaning back into the couch, his hat resting on his knee. His eyes were closed, but I could tell his mind was still racing. He looked so... *tired*, but not just physically. It was deeper, like the exhaustion came from somewhere inside him.

The microwave beeped, snapping me out of my thoughts. I grabbed the plates and brought them over to the coffee table. "Here you go. Gourmet stir fry, courtesy of the microwave," I said with a half-smile.

He opened his eyes and sat up, taking the plate from me. "Thanks, Em. You're a lifesaver."

We ate in comfortable silence for a few minutes, both of us too wrapped up in our own thoughts to talk much at first. I poked at my stir fry with my fork, glancing at Cole from the corner of my eye. He was chewing slowly, staring down at his plate, clearly lost in thought.

"So..." I finally said, breaking the quiet, "... have you thought any more about what you're gonna do? You know, after... everything with the ranch?"

He sighed, running a hand through his hair, his gaze dropping back to his plate. "I've been thinking about it, yeah. I just... I don't know. I can find a job, but my mom? The rest of my family? I don't know what comes next."

I frowned, leaning forward a little. "You're not thinking about leaving town completely, are you?"

He looked up at me, his eyes serious. "Honestly? I don't know. Part of me feels like I should stay and help my family figure things out. But I might need to move on. I don't want to, but..." His voice trailed off, and he shrugged. "I don't know what's best right now."

I studied his face, feeling the weight of his uncertainty. "It's hard when everything you've ever known feels like it's slipping away."

Cole nodded slowly, not saying anything for a moment. Then he cleared his throat, sitting up a little straighter. "What about you? What's next for you, Emily? You've got this great thing going with Cody, training horses and all. You ever think about what's down the road?"

I hesitated. "Honestly? I haven't thought too far ahead."

He stirred his noodles with his fork and raised a brow. "Liar."

I cracked a grin. "Well, okay. I guess... I sort of had this fantasy that someday I could make a name for myself, like Cody did." I shrugged. "Maybe go learn under some more trainers for a while, get some gig out of Texas or something. But, well... gotta have some luck for that."

He studied me, smiling slightly. "You'll get it. If anyone does, you will."

I shook my head. "Nah, I just..."

"Cody put you on his best horse, didn't he? He didn't do that because you ain't got what it takes."

I swallowed, my fork stilling on my plate. "Cody didn't... That's what you think?"

Cole shrugged. "Sure. Why wouldn't I? Copper's the next 'big' horse for the ranch. He wins everything. You got a shot at the year-end title."

I looked up. "Cole, Copper is a really nice horse, but..."

He snorted. "You're so modest, Em. 'Nice?' He's a whole lot more than that."

I thinned my lips. "Yeah. Yeah, he is." I wanted to say more—the truth, and what Cody had told me when we started Copper and Lynx under saddle. But I just sighed and took another bite.

We finished eating, and as I stood up to clear the plates, Cole watched me quietly, his gaze lingering for a moment before he spoke again. "Thanks for the dinner, Em."

I turned back to him, holding the plates in my hands, and smiled. "I'm glad you came. Anytime you need to talk, or... just need stir fry, you know where to find me."

He chuckled, shaking his head. "Might take you up on that."

I smiled back, and... boy, I wanted to do a lot more than that. I wanted to say something, do something to put things back like they were a few days ago.

But before I could say anything else, Cole leaned in, closing the small space between us, and pressed his lips to mine. It wasn't rushed or uncertain this time—just soft, lingering, and full of something I couldn't quite describe. My hands moved up to his shoulders, steadying myself as he kissed me, and for a moment, everything felt... right.

When we finally pulled apart, he rested his forehead against mine, his eyes still closed. "I should probably head out," he said quietly, though neither of us moved.

"Yeah," I whispered back, my voice soft. "You probably should."

But he didn't move right away, and neither did I. The silence between us was comfortable now, like we didn't need to say anything more. Eventually, Cole sat back, offering me a crooked smile, and brushed a strand of hair away from my face. "I really appreciate dinner," he said, his voice lighter, more at ease. "Even if it was stir fry again."

I laughed softly, giving him a playful nudge. "Anytime."

He stood up, grabbing his hat and settling it on his head, his smile lingering as he made his way to the door. As he opened it, he paused, turning back one last time. "Goodnight, Emily."

"Goodnight, Cole."

Chapter Twenty

Cole

The air was still cool in the barn as I made my way down the aisle, the early morning sun just starting to peek through the windows. The familiar smell of hay and leather wrapped around me, but today, it felt suffocating. I could hear Lynx shifting in her stall, her hooves stirring the shavings as she waited for me.

I paused for a moment, staring at the worn lead rope in my hands. Yesterday had been a mess. Cody didn't deserve the attitude I threw at him, and Lynx certainly didn't deserve the way I'd pushed her. I knew better than to let my head get in the way of my hands. Today, I had to get it right.

Cody was already there, standing by the tack room with his arms crossed. His expression was as steady as ever, but I could sense the strain behind his eyes—he'd been patient with me, too patient. I swallowed the knot in my throat as I headed toward Lynx's stall, trying to gather my thoughts.

"Morning," Cody said, his voice even, but I could hear the edge to it.

I nodded back, unhooking the stall door and stepping inside with Lynx. She pricked her ears at me, already keyed up, ready to move. Her muscles twitched under my hand as I stroked her neck, feeling her energy buzzing beneath the surface. She wasn't the problem. I was.

I grabbed the saddle from the rack and settled it on her back, my fingers fumbling with the cinch for a moment longer than usual. I had to say something. I owed him an apology, but the words didn't come easy.

"I... uh, I'm sorry about yesterday," I said, my voice rougher than I intended. "I shouldn't have snapped at you."

Cody didn't say anything for a beat. When I finally looked up, I saw him watching me closely, his brow furrowed in thought. Finally, he nodded slowly. "I've been where you are, Cole," he said, his voice low and calm. "When things are rough at home, it's easy to let it bleed into your work, especially when you're working with animals. But if you want to be a horseman—if you want to make it in this business—you have to learn how to compartmentalize."

I nodded, tightening the cinch on Lynx, keeping my eyes on her to avoid Cody's gaze. He wasn't wrong, and I knew it. "I'll do better," I muttered, adjusting the bridle as I slipped it over Lynx's head.

Cody walked over, resting a hand on the stall door. "It's not about doing better, Cole. It's about being present. Lynx doesn't care about what's going on in your life. She just needs you to be here, right now, working with her."

I exhaled slowly, giving Lynx a quick pat as I led her out of the stall. She was calm, but her eyes were sharp, ready to get going. I clipped the lead rope and walked her toward the arena, where we'd start the day's work. Cody followed me, his boots crunching lightly against the gravel.

When we reached the practice area, I swung into the saddle, settling in. Lynx shifted under my hand, eager to get moving, and I gave her a quick pat on the neck.

"You ready to work her?" Cody asked, his voice a little lighter now.

"Yeah," I said, stepping toward the practice flag, ready to put yesterday behind me.

We worked Lynx quietly at first, warming her up with some slow movements. Her hooves made soft thuds against the dirt, and I focused on keeping my own body loose, trying to listen to her as much as she was listening to me.

After a little warmup, we started working Lynx on the practice flag. Her eyes were locked on the movement, every muscle in her body tuned into the rhythm of the flag as it zigzagged across the arena. Cody watched from the fence, his arms crossed, silently assessing.

"Keep her shoulder up," Cody called from his spot by the fence. "Stand her up straight—don't drop *your* shoulder, Cole."

I gritted my teeth but kept my focus on Lynx. He was right. I had a habit of anticipating the turns, of dropping my own shoulder before she even moved. I could feel Lynx hesitate, waiting for my cues, but I wasn't giving them clearly enough. She needed me to be in sync with her, not ahead of her.

"Let her come to you," Cody added. "Don't rush her."

I loosened my grip on the reins, letting her figure out the turn on her own. As she moved, I felt a subtle shift in her rhythm, like she was finally settling into the work. Her body moved fluidly, and I matched her pace, keeping my movements soft, deliberate. She followed the flag smoothly, and for the first time in days, I felt a sense of calm settle over me.

"That's better," Cody called out, his voice approving. "Now you're working with her."

I nodded, a small sense of satisfaction blooming in my chest. Lynx responded to my every cue, her body light and nimble beneath me. She was going to be something special—I knew it. But it wouldn't come without patience and focus, two things I had been sorely lacking lately.

"Back her a step before the next turn," Cody suggested. "That's right. Feel how she's starting to draw? That's the muscle memory she needs, right there."

I felt a small flicker of pride as Lynx moved beneath me, her body loose and responsive. It wasn't perfect, but it was progress. She wasn't fighting me anymore. She was waiting for my cues, trusting me to guide her. But a cutting horse didn't have time to always be waiting on their rider—she had to manage herself, but be willing to listen when necessary. I loosened the reins a little more, giving her the freedom to move without over-correcting.

We worked for a while, the steady rhythm of the flag and Lynx's hooves the only sounds in the arena. My body relaxed into the motions, and for the first time in days, I felt like I was back in control. Lynx was a heck of a horse, and I owed it to her to be the rider she needed.

When we finished the session, I pulled Lynx to a stop and dismounted, wiping the sweat from my brow. Cody walked over, his usual easy stride back now that the tension between us had eased.

"You're getting there," he said, clapping me on the shoulder. "Just keep that focus. Lynx is gonna be something special if you let her."

I nodded, leading Lynx back toward the barn. "Thanks, Cody. I appreciate it."

Cody gave me a nod and turned toward the office. "Get her cooled down. We've got a busy day ahead."

I watched him walk away, feeling a sense of relief wash over me. The weight that had been sitting on my chest since yesterday had lifted, and for the first time in a while, I felt like I was on the right path. Lynx nudged my shoulder, and I smiled, giving her neck a pat.

"Let's go, girl," I muttered, leading her back to the barn to untack.

As I walked back, I couldn't help but feel like I was starting to get my feet under me again. But the ranch... my family... that was a whole different mess waiting for me to figure out. One thing at a time.

Emily

I was mucking out Copper's stall when I heard the faint buzz of a conversation coming from the barn aisle. Luke's voice filtered in, and I could tell from the sound of it that he was on the phone. I didn't pay much attention at first, keeping my head down as I worked, but as he stepped closer, the conversation caught my ear.

"Yeah, I know," Luke muttered, glancing down at his watch. "But I've got to run out and help Evan fix the sprinkler line. That thing busted again, and I'm already late." There was a pause, and he sighed. "I'll figure something out. Just hang tight, okay?"

He turned the corner into the barn, his phone still pressed to his ear as he scanned the stalls. His eyes landed on me, and I gave him a small wave, though he barely acknowledged it, too preoccupied with whatever crisis was unfolding on the other end of the line.

"Alright, Audrey. I'll figure it out. Love you." He hung up with a frustrated huff, running a hand through his hair as he shoved the phone into his pocket.

"Everything okay?" I asked, leaning on the stall door.

Luke groaned, shaking his head. "Lizzy was supposed to go up to White Pines to help with the youth camp Morgan's running today. Audrey's stuck with some last-minute stuff at work, and Evan just called me about the hay sprinkler. I don't know how I'm supposed to be in two places at once."

I wiped the back of my hand across my forehead, thinking it over. Lizzy was always a handful, but she was good with kids, and I knew Morgan could use the extra help. "I could take her," I offered, trying to keep my tone casual. "I was planning to head up there later anyway. I don't mind swinging by and picking her up."

Luke's face lit up with relief. "Really? You sure?"

"Yeah, no problem," I said, waving off his concern. "It'll give me a chance to catch up with Kate, too. And Lizzy's always fun."

Luke chuckled, shaking his head. "You're braver than me. That kid's got more sass than the whole ranch combined."

I grinned. "I can handle her."

He pulled out his phone again, quickly tapping out a message. "I'll let Audrey know you're taking her. Thanks, Emily. You're saving me a world of stress."

"Anytime," I said, watching as he headed out, his pace quick as he jogged toward his truck.

I finished up Copper's stall and tidied up the rest of the barn before grabbing my keys and heading toward Lizzy's place. I had a feeling this would be an interesting drive.

Lizzy was already waiting on the porch when I pulled up to Luke and Audrey's ranch house, her backpack slung over one shoulder and a mischievous grin plastered across her face.

"Aunt Audrey says you're taking me to White Pines," she said, hopping down the steps. "Guess I'm your problem now."

I laughed, leaning out the window as I unlocked the passenger door. "Hop in, troublemaker."

She flopped into the seat, tossing her bag in the back as she clicked her seatbelt. "Don't worry, I'll go easy on you."

"Gee, thanks," I said, pulling out of the driveway and heading toward White Pines.

For a few minutes, the drive was quiet, save for the hum of the tires and the soft country music playing on the radio. Lizzy was tapping her fingers on her knees, staring out the window like she was plotting something. She probably was.

"So," I said after a while, glancing at her. "You excited to help out with the camp today?"

Lizzy shrugged, her lips twitching into a smirk. "Yeah, I guess. It's mostly little kids, though. They're cute and all, but I'm not much of a babysitter."

I chuckled, shaking my head. "That's what youth camps are all about. Herding kids around like cattle."

Lizzy snorted. "I can handle cattle, no problem. It's the kids that get me."

"Well, you've got the attitude for it," I teased, giving her a sideways glance. "Maybe they'll straighten up after they see who's in charge."

She puffed out her chest, grinning. "Darn right, they will. I'll whip 'em into shape."

The rest of the drive went by quickly, Lizzy keeping up a steady stream of commentary on the various antics happening at her school.

She had a way of turning the most mundane details into something entertaining, and I found myself chuckling more than I expected to.

"You know, you were right," I said, glancing over at her. "About not having to go back to school after you got suspended right before summer break."

Lizzy grinned, clearly pleased with herself. "Told ya. Didn't even have to step foot back in that place."

I raised an eyebrow. "You seem pretty proud of yourself for getting suspended."

She snorted, rolling her eyes. "Well, it's not like I did anything *that* bad. That kid deserved it."

"I'm sure your aunt didn't see it that way."

Lizzy groaned, her mood shifting instantly. "Don't remind me. She didn't let me off that easy. I still had to do all my stupid assignments and send them to school with Dustin's mom. How's that even fair? If you're suspended, shouldn't that mean no schoolwork?"

I laughed, shaking my head. "Not when Audrey Walker's in charge. You know she's never going to let you slack off, suspension or not."

Lizzy huffed, crossing her arms. "I was so mad. I had to sit there doing homework while Dustin was outside goofing off on his bike. If that's not cruel and unusual punishment, I don't know what is."

I grinned at her exaggerated tone. "Well, I'm sure you learned your lesson."

"Yeah, yeah," Lizzy mumbled, kicking her feet up on the dashboard. "Lesson learned. Never get caught again."

I shook my head. "You're lucky you're charming, Lizzy."

"Darn right I am," she quipped with a smirk. "How else would I survive in this family? Luke says I get it from him."

"I'm not sure that's how it..." I shook my head. "You know, never mind, we're here. Ooh, looks like a full parking lot today."

As I parked the truck, Lizzy jumped out before I could even turn off the engine. "I'm free!" she hollered, running toward the barn with her arms stretched out like she was escaping prison.

"Try not to terrorize the kids too much!" I called after her, laughing as I grabbed her backpack from the backseat. She just waved me off and disappeared into the barn.

I slung the bag over my shoulder and headed inside, my eyes scanning the familiar space. Morgan was already busy, organizing a group of young campers by the stalls. She waved when she saw me, her smile as bright and welcoming as ever.

"Hey, Emily! Thanks for bringing Lizzy," she said, quickly guiding one of the campers to a horse before making her way over to me. "She's going to be a big help today."

I handed over Lizzy's bag. "Just make sure she doesn't lead a revolt."

Morgan chuckled. "I'll keep her in line. She's actually really good with the kids. Helps them feel comfortable."

"That's good to hear," I said, glancing around. "I'll get out of your hair, then."

Before I could turn to leave, I spotted Kate leaning against the fence outside, chatting with one of the younger volunteers. She waved when she saw me, her wide smile immediately making me feel at ease.

"Hey, stranger!" Kate called as I approached. "What brings you up here?"

"Luke needed someone to drop Lizzy off," I said, gesturing toward the barn. "He had to run off to fix a busted sprinkler line."

Kate raised an eyebrow, looking impressed. "You volunteered to drive Lizzy all the way up here? You're braver than I thought."

"It wasn't that bad. She kept me entertained, at least."

Kate grinned, leaning against the fence. "Well, at least you're still sane after that. So, how's Mr. Langton treating you lately?"

I shifted uncomfortably, pushing a piece of hay with my boot. "It's... been good. Complicated, but good."

"Complicated?" Kate raised an eyebrow, her expression amused. "Last time we talked, you mentioned the guy kissed you. That's a pretty solid development in my book."

I sighed, shrugging a little. "Yeah, that happened. But there's just... a lot going on with him right now. I'm not sure where we stand. It feels like something, but at the same time, I don't know."

Kate gave me a long, knowing look. "Uh-huh. Sounds like classic Cole—gets close, then pulls back 'cause he doesn't know what to do with his feelings. So, what's the deal? He's not ghosting you, is he?"

"No, nothing like that," I said quickly, shaking my head. "He's just... dealing with a lot right now. Family stuff." I bit my lip, not wanting to say too much. It wasn't my place to share what was happening with the ranch.

"So... he's not shutting you out?"

I shook my head. "Kind of the opposite. I think it's more that he's overwhelmed."

Kate nodded, her eyes softening with understanding. "Yeah, family can do that. I get it. But what about the two of you? You kissed, and I'm guessing... more than once?

I swallowed.

"More than twice?"

I took a deep breath and let it out with a shrug and a smile.

"Well, okay—now what? You're clearly into each other. I don't blame you, either, by the way. Those Langton boys..." She fanned herself and grinned.

"I don't know, Kate. It's not that simple. There's something there, but with everything happening... it's hard to know where we stand."

Kate raised an eyebrow. "So, have you guys talked about it?"

I shook my head. "Not really. I mean, we've shared some... moments, but I don't think either of us knows what this is yet."

She studied me for a moment before nudging my arm. "Well, at least it's something. You could've kissed, and he could've run for the hills, but he's still around. You're obviously important to him."

I smiled faintly. "Uh, Kate, we work together. We sort of have to see each other every day."

Kate leaned in closer, her voice dropping conspiratorially. "Well, I'm rooting for you. But, speaking of Langton boys... does Cole ever talk about Chase?"

I blinked at the sudden change in topic, narrowing my eyes at her. "Chase? Not really. Why?"

Kate shrugged, trying to act casual, but there was a flicker of something more in her expression. "Oh, no reason. I just... ran into him in the feed store the other day. He seemed... interesting."

"Interesting?" I smirked, folding my arms. "Kate, are you crushing on Chase Langton?"

She blushed, waving her hands defensively. "No! I mean... maybe. I just thought he was cute. Quiet. Mysterious, you know?"

I laughed, shaking my head. "He's definitely quiet. I'm not sure about mysterious."

Kate rolled her eyes. "Whatever. I'm just saying... I think he's got potential."

"Well, if you like cowboys who barely talk and always have their heads in the clouds, Chase is definitely your guy."

Kate sighed. "Yeah, well, quiet's fine by me. Maybe I'll get lucky, and he'll notice me one day."

I chuckled. "I'll keep an eye out for you, don't worry."

Kate gave me a playful wink before glancing toward the barn. "Well, I'd better get back to work. Try to keep Lizzy from burning the place down."

"Good luck with that," I said, waving her off as I headed back to the car.

Chapter Twenty-One

Cole

I ran my hand down Lynx's neck, feeling the slick coat of her muscle as I brought her into her stall for the evening. My mind kept wandering, especially with everything waiting for me back at Ridgeview.

I could hear Emily moving quietly a few stalls down, working with Copper. I hadn't talked much to her today, not since that kiss last night. Every time I saw her today, a part of me wanted to say something—anything—but the weight of the ranch, the family... it pulled me back every time.

I brushed Lynx down, trying to focus, but I couldn't stop thinking about how the conversation at home was going to go tonight. The sale papers. The logistics. The fact that my brothers and I were actually talking about where we'd move Mom after Ridgeview was gone.

I sighed and shook my head, hanging the brush back on the stall door.

"Hey," Emily's voice cut through the barn. She was walking toward me, her hat low over her eyes. "You heading out?"

I nodded, resting my arms on Lynx's back. "Yeah, I think I've done enough for today." I tried to sound casual, but I could feel my words coming out heavier than I intended.

Emily's smile wavered, and she tipped her head a little, studying me. "Everything okay?"

I wanted to say yes. I wanted to tell her that I was fine, that things were normal. But I couldn't lie. "I'm heading back to Ridgeview," I admitted. "We've got some... family stuff to work through."

Emily's face softened, and she nodded slowly, like she understood without me having to say more. "Do you want to... I don't know, grab a bite to eat before you go?" Her voice was hopeful, but there was a small, cautious edge to it. Like she was offering me an out, a chance to escape.

I thought about it. Really thought about it. Being with Emily, even for just an hour, sounded like exactly what I needed. Something normal, something comforting. But I knew that if I stayed, if I delayed this any longer, it would only make things worse.

"I wish I could," I said, my voice catching. "But I need to go home tonight. We've got to figure out what to do with the place."

Emily nodded again, but I could see the disappointment flicker in her eyes. "I get it," she said softly, tucking a ringlet of hair behind her ear. "Family comes first."

There was a long pause, and I almost wanted to take it back. To tell her that I'd stay, that I'd come to dinner and forget about everything for a while. But I couldn't.

Instead, I took a step closer, hesitating for a second before reaching out and gently cupping her cheek. "I'll see you tomorrow," I said, my voice low.

Her cheek rounded under my fingertips, and her smile warmed. "Goodnight, Cole."

I gave her a nod, turned, and walked out of the barn.

I pulled up to the house at Ridgeview Ranch and killed the engine.
The sun had just dipped below the hills, casting the place in a dusky
shadow. I sat there for a second, staring at the familiar outline of the
barn and the house, my chest tightening.

This might be the beginning of the lasts.

The last time I come home. The last dinner all together around the
old table. The last autumn gather, the last time I saw smoke curling
out of that chimney as I rolled into the driveway.

I shook the thought away, grabbing my hat and heading inside. The
house was quiet, the old screen door squeaking as I walked in. The
smell of Mom's cooking still lingered in the air, but tonight it didn't
bring the usual sense of comfort.

In the living room, Gage, Trent, and Chase were all sitting around
the table, papers scattered everywhere. Financial reports, real estate
offers, tax estimates—they'd been here all evening, and I'd missed most
of it.

Mom sat at the head of the table, her hands folded in her lap. She
looked tired. Maybe more tired than I'd ever seen her.

Gage was the first to notice me. "About time," he muttered, though
there wasn't any bite in his tone. He just sounded worn out.

I gave him a nod and pulled up a chair. "Sorry I'm late. I got held
up at Walker Ranch."

Trent pushed some papers toward me. "We're going over the offers."

"What? Offers already?"

"Yeah. Lowballs, all of 'em."

I scanned the paperwork. There were three offers, and, like Trent said, all pathetic.

"Where does that leave us?" I asked, the words heavier than I intended.

Gage sighed, rubbing a hand over his face. "It leaves us with a decision. Do we sell the whole thing and walk away, or do we try to keep some of it?"

Chase spoke up. "We've been talking about maybe selling off part of the land instead of the whole ranch. But the problem is we've already sold off too much stock to keep it running. We'd need to rebuild from the ground up."

I glanced at Mom, who hadn't said much yet. "And what do you think, Mom? Does this give us enough to start over somewhere? And where could we even go?"

She looked up at me, a sigh creasing her face. "I wish I knew. I saw Morgan Haskins this morning, and she said they're planning to put a trailer on the property for some live-in ranch help, and they're looking for the right person. I might... Oh, I don't know. I'm not sure if they want an old lady for a ranch hand."

"That's not a viable plan. Not long-term. So, where does that leave us?" I repeated, my voice softer this time.

Trent leaned back in his chair, staring at the ceiling. "It leaves us with a choice. We sell now at these prices, or we go further into debt waiting for a better offer."

"And how likely is that?"

Gage sighed, his voice tight. "Not very."

Chase spoke up again. "What if we sold off some of the land to raise the capital and rebuild?"

Mom shook her head gently. "It's too late for that, honey. We've sold too many cows to keep even a small operation going."

I felt my stomach drop. The reality of it all hit me square in the chest. "So that's it? We sell Ridgeview for a fraction of what it's worth, and we're done?"

Mom reached over, taking my hand in hers. "It's not the end of us, Cole. No matter what happens to the ranch, we're still a family."

I nodded, swallowing hard. But I couldn't shake the feeling that something important was slipping through my fingers, something I couldn't get back.

And I didn't have a plan.

I was untacking Lynx, the late afternoon sun beating down on the barn roof when Cody walked over, looking at me and Emily with that knowing smile he'd been throwing our way a lot lately.

"Hey, you two." Cody leaned on the fence, wiping the sweat from his brow. "How 'bout you go fetch a fresh batch of cows from the back pasture? They're due for rotation. Good way to cool out your horses after today."

I nodded, glancing over at Emily, who was already smiling. Her cheeks were flushed from the heat, but she looked up at Cody like she knew exactly what he was getting at. "Sounds good," she said, wiping Copper's neck. "I'll grab the gate."

Cody tipped his hat, that grin still tugging at the corners of his mouth. "Alright then. Have fun, you two."

As he walked off, I felt a small flicker of something warm in my chest. It wasn't lost on me that Cody had been giving us these little "errands" more often. And to be honest, I didn't mind. Not one bit.

I cinched up Lynx's saddle again, leading her out of the barn toward the gate where Emily was already swinging up into her saddle. Copper was pawing at the dirt, ready to go. I swung onto Lynx's back and gave Emily a smile, maybe the first real one all day.

"Ready?" I asked.

She nodded, grinning back. "Lead the way."

We headed out toward the back pasture, the swish of long grass brushing against the horse's legs. For a few minutes, neither of us said anything, just enjoying the quiet rhythm of the ride. The fields stretched out in front of us, the tall pines that ringed the perimeter swaying in the breeze. It felt good to be out here, away from the barns, just the two of us and our horses.

Eventually, Emily broke the silence. "Cody's been giving us a lot of these 'jobs' lately, huh?"

I chuckled. "Yeah, I noticed. Think he's trying to tell us something?"

She laughed, shaking her head. "I don't know. Maybe he just likes having someone else deal with the cows for a change."

"Or maybe he's just happy we're getting along," I said, half-joking.

Emily's eyes sparkled as she shot me a sideways glance. "Well, he's not the only one. I like this better."

I grinned at that, feeling the tension I'd been carrying all day start to melt away. "Me too."

As we reached the stretched wire gate to the pasture, I hopped off Lynx and walked over to open it. Emily waited, watching as I led Lynx through first, then waved her in with Copper. Once the gate was shut behind us, we started moving through the field, scanning for the herd.

It didn't take long to spot them grazing near a stand of trees, their dark shapes easy to make out against the golden grass.

After we'd rounded up the cows and started herding them toward the gate, I glanced over at Emily. She was focused on the cattle, her eyes scanning the herd like she was reading each animal's mood. Her ease on a horse never failed to impress me. We hadn't said much since we left the barn, and though the silence wasn't uncomfortable, I felt like talking. Anything to ease the heaviness I'd been carrying.

As if she somehow sensed that, Emily glanced over at me. "You know," she said, her voice breaking the quiet. "Maybe thinking about the good times could help. You know, with everything changing on the ranch."

I gave her a sideways look. "What do you mean?"

She shrugged, keeping Copper in line with the herd. "I don't know. Whenever things were tough for me growing up, like when my parents split, I used to think about all the good memories I had—family vacations, holidays. It made me feel better, even when things weren't great. Might be worth trying."

I nodded, considering what she said as we continued moving the cows. "Yeah, we had some good times, I guess. My brothers and I, we were always up to something."

"Like what? I know you probably got in trouble plenty, but I always figured Gage and Chase were pretty straight-and-narrow."

I couldn't help but grin a little. "You'd be surprised. Gage and I were always at each other's throats. Typical older brother stuff, you know? He'd give me a hard time, and I'd always try to one-up him."

Emily smiled, her eyes lighting up with interest. "Like what?"

I scratched my chin, thinking back. "Well, one time, when we were supposed to be building a new fence line, Gage dared me to ride this wild colt we had in the barn. Said I wouldn't last five minutes."

Her eyes widened. "And? Did you?"

I chuckled. "I lasted about three. Thing bucked me right into the fence. Gage thought it was hilarious, and of course, I had to act like I wasn't hurt. But man, I couldn't move my shoulder for days."

She laughed, shaking her head. "That sounds about right for you. Never one to back down from a challenge."

"Yeah, well, I didn't always win, but I couldn't let him see me quit." I paused, remembering the look on Gage's face when I got back up. It was the same one he had when he offered to sell the ranch.

"Alright, I've got one for you," she said. "What's the weirdest thing you've ever seen on the ranch?"

"Weirdest thing? Oh, man. That's a tough one."

"Come on," she coaxed, her grin widening. "I know you've seen some crazy stuff."

I thought for a second, then smirked. "Alright, how about this? A few years back, we had a stray pig show up out of nowhere. No idea where it came from, but this thing was huge. It wandered onto the property like it owned the place."

Emily's eyes widened. "A pig? What did you do with it?"

"Well, we tried to corral it, but that didn't go so well. Turns out, pigs are fast when they want to be." I laughed, remembering the sight of Gage and Trent running after the thing, their hats flying off. "We finally got it penned up, but it took all day. Mom wanted to keep it, but Dad said no way. He called around, and turns out, it belonged to a neighbor. The whole thing was ridiculous."

Emily was laughing now, her eyes crinkling with amusement. "I can just picture you guys chasing a pig around all day. That's amazing."

"It wasn't amazing at the time," I said, shaking my head. "But yeah, looking back, it's pretty funny."

We both laughed, and for the first time in what felt like days, I felt a weight lift off my shoulders. This—riding, talking, just being out here with Emily—it was good. It was easy.

"And Chase?" Emily asked, nudging Copper a little closer. "He's the quiet one, right?"

I nodded. "Yeah, Chase was different. Didn't say much, but when he did, you'd better listen. He was always the thinker. If Trent and I were busy trying to prove who was tougher, Chase was already three steps ahead, thinking of how to fix whatever we were about to break."

Emily laughed. "Sounds like a good balance."

"It was." I sighed, feeling a tug in my chest as I thought about it. "He's the one who taught me to work with the horses. Showed me how to get inside their heads instead of just muscling them into doing what I wanted. I owe him a lot."

She was quiet for a minute, letting that sink in. "Do you think about those times much? The good stuff, I mean?"

I shrugged. "Not as much as I should, I guess. Lately, all I can think about is how much we've messed things up."

Emily shook her head. "You haven't messed anything up, Cole. Your family's been through a lot, and yeah, things are changing, but that doesn't erase everything you've built together. Maybe remembering the good times could help you see that."

I thought about that, my eyes drifting out over the fields. The sun was low now, casting a warm orange glow over the cows as they ambled along. She had a point. I'd been so focused on the problems that I'd forgotten all the things that had made the ranch home in the first place.

"Maybe you're right," I said softly. "We did have some great times. Even when we fought, it was always because we cared about the same thing."

Emily smiled at me, and for the first time in a while, I felt like I could breathe a little easier. Maybe there was a way to hold onto those memories, even if everything else was changing.

We rode on in silence for a few minutes, the steady rhythm of the cows moving ahead of us. After a while, I glanced over at her again, feeling lighter than I had all day.

"Thanks for reminding me," I said, my voice a little softer than usual.

She gave me a small, understanding smile. "Anytime."

Chapter Twenty-Two

Cole

I stepped out of the barn, wiping the sweat off my forehead with the back of my hand. The day had been long, filled with endless chores and the kind of tired that sank deep into my bones. The weight of everything—work, family, the ranch—felt heavier with each passing day. Lynx had worked well today, though, giving me a few moments of satisfaction while we were in the arena. But now I was home, and as I walked across the yard toward the house, the exhaustion set back in. Not the kind that came from work, but from thinking too much. From knowing what was waiting inside.

My brothers were all still here, Gage and Trent over by the truck with its hood up, arguing about the state of the old engine. I could hear their voices rising, and I didn't need to get closer to know what the fight was about. It wasn't just the truck. It was everything.

"Could've told you that was a waste of money," Trent grumbled, tossing a wrench into the bed of the truck.

Gage shot him a glare, his jaw tight. "Yeah? And what's your big idea, Trent? You wanna start fixing things up around here?"

Trent scoffed, shaking his head. "No point fixing it now."

I stayed back for a second, trying to gather myself before I walked into the middle of it. The last thing I needed was to get dragged into another fight. Gage and Trent had been at each other's throats for days. Maybe it was just the stress of knowing the ranch was slipping away, or maybe it was because they both knew that once it was gone, there wouldn't be much holding them together anymore.

Finally, I sighed and walked over, knowing there was no avoiding it. "What's going on?"

Trent snorted. "Nothing. Just another day in paradise."

Gage wiped his hands on a rag, his expression dark as he turned toward me. "Got a call from the buyer."

That made me stop in my tracks. "The buyer?"

He nodded, tossing the rag onto the hood of the truck. "Yeah. They're getting the land reports from the county. Checking on water rights, looking into what it would take to get permits for tearing down the ranch house and putting up some kind of guest ranch."

The words hit me like a punch to the gut. I knew it was coming—I'd known for a while now—but hearing it out loud made it real. "Tearing down the house?"

Gage met my eyes, his face set hard. "They wanna make the place look like one of those luxury ranches. You know, with cabins and pools. That's what they're after."

I felt my stomach turn, the thought of watching our home get bulldozed down, replaced by something that didn't belong here. "And you're thinking about taking the offer?"

Gage ran a hand over his face, looking more tired than I'd ever seen him. "It's not what I want, Cole. Not even that great of an offer, but they're serious, and they have cash. They're ready to buy as soon as they get the green light from the county."

"Yeah, but..." I swallowed hard, my chest tightening. "They're low-balling us."

"I know," Gage snapped, his frustration boiling over. "But we don't have the luxury of holding out for something better. We're out of options."

I could feel my blood starting to heat up, the frustration building inside me. "Out of options? We're just gonna let them bulldoze the place? Everything Dad built—everything we've worked for—gone just like that?"

Trent, who had been quiet until now, spoke up, his voice sharp. "You think we haven't thought about that? We're not happy about it either, but we're broke, Cole. What else are we supposed to do?"

I opened my mouth to argue, but no words came out. I didn't have a solution. I didn't have some grand plan that would save the ranch. Gage was right—there was no money left, no stock to rebuild with. The ranch wasn't just slipping away anymore. It was already gone.

Gage sighed, his anger ebbing away as he looked at me. "I don't like it any more than you do, Cole. But we gotta face the facts. If we don't sell now, we're gonna lose the place for nothing."

I shook my head, feeling like the ground was slipping out from under me. "I don't know, Gage. It just feels wrong."

Gage met my eyes, his voice quieter now. "It is wrong. But we can't rebuild without money, and there's no money coming in."

I swallowed hard, my hands clenching into fists. I wanted to fight him on it. I wanted to tell him there had to be another way. But deep down, I knew he was right. The ranch wasn't going to save itself, and we didn't have the resources to keep fighting.

"So what now?" I asked, my voice hollow.

Gage sighed again, looking down at the ground. "We wait for the county to get back to the buyer, I guess. Once they do, we'll have to all go in and sign the paperwork. And Cole, I need you on board with this. Dad put all our names on the mortgage."

I stared at him. For the first time, I felt the full force of what we were losing. It wasn't just the land or the house. It was our history, our legacy. And there was nothing I could do to stop it.

"I'll talk to Mom," I muttered, turning away before the others could see the anger and pain on my face. "She deserves to know."

Gage nodded. "She already does."

I didn't look back as I walked toward the house, my thoughts a tangled mess of frustration and grief. All I knew was that the ranch—the life we'd known—was going to be even less than a memory.

Emily

I pulled into the lot and parked my car in front of the resale shop. The sun had just dipped below the horizon, casting everything in a dim, orange glow. Normally, I'd head straight upstairs, throw my boots off, and sink into the couch. But tonight, as I sat there staring at the dashboard, I realized something was tugging at me. I'd told Cole maybe he was missing the good by dwelling on the bad, and... well, maybe I was doing the same thing.

It had been days since I'd had a real conversation with Mom. Since we'd actually talked without tension hanging between us. After everything I'd said about the clutter and the way I'd stormed out, I still hadn't made things right. I'd been avoiding it, if I was being honest with myself.

As I glanced over the dashboard at the resale shop, I noticed the light was still on. Mom was in there late, working—again. Even though I knew how much that place meant to her, how it had helped keep a roof over our heads all these years, I'd been so wrapped up in my own frustration that I hadn't even tried to help. And the truth was, the only way I was going to make things better between us wasn't by hiding upstairs, pretending everything was okay.

No, I needed to make an effort. I needed to step into *her* world for once.

With a deep breath, I unbuckled my seatbelt, slid out of the truck, and walked toward the shop. The glass door swung open with a little jingle of the bell, and there she was—Mom, bent over a table, sorting through a pile of clothes that had just been cleaned. Her glasses were perched on the edge of her nose, and she was humming softly, lost in her work.

I stood there for a moment, just watching her. She looked peaceful, content in the way she organized everything. It was something I'd never quite understood before—why she loved this shop so much, why she spent so much time down here. But now, seeing her like this, I started to get it. This was her space. Her way of making things right in a world that didn't always make sense.

"Hey, Mom," I said softly, stepping further into the shop.

She looked up, surprised, her hands freezing over a blouse she was folding. "Emily! I didn't hear you come in."

"Yeah, I just got home." I paused, glancing at the pile of clothes she was working through. "Do you need any help? I've got some time if you want an extra pair of hands."

For a second, she just blinked at me like she couldn't quite believe I'd offered. Then, slowly, a small smile tugged at the corners of her lips. "Sure, honey. I could always use some help with this batch."

I moved closer to the table, picking up a shirt from the pile and starting to fold it. We worked in silence for a few minutes, the sound of fabric rustling and the occasional squeak of the shop's old door filling the quiet. It was a peaceful kind of silence, though—different from the tension that had been hanging between us since I'd snapped at her.

As I hung a jacket on a hanger, I glanced over at her. "You've been working hard down here," I said, trying to ease into a conversation. "I didn't realize you were still getting so much new stuff in."

Mom chuckled, adjusting her glasses. "Oh, you know me. I can't help myself when I see a good deal. And it keeps me busy. Gives me something to focus on."

"Yeah," I said, nodding. "I get that."

We fell into another comfortable silence as I helped her hang a few more pieces. The space between us felt less strained now, and I could feel the weight of our earlier argument starting to lift.

"You know," I said after a while, trying to find the right words, "I'm sorry I've been... distant lately. And for snapping at you about the apartment. That wasn't fair."

Mom was slow to respond. "I know you didn't mean it the way it came out. I just..." She hesitated, her voice growing quieter. "I guess I've been worried that I'm embarrassing you. With the shop, the clutter... everything."

Hearing her say it out loud made my heart ache. "You're not an embarrassment, Mom," I said, my voice firm. "This shop... it's important. I see that now. I should've seen it sooner."

She gave me a small, sad smile, her hands stilling over the pile of clothes. "I just want to make sure you're proud of me. I know things haven't always been easy for us, but I've always done my best."

Tears pricked at the corners of my eyes, and I quickly blinked them away. "I *am* proud of you, Mom. You've done more for me than I can ever repay, and I didn't realize how much this place means to you. I'm sorry if I ever made you feel like I wasn't proud."

She reached out, her hand squeezing mine gently. "We're okay, Em. I'm just glad we're talking again."

I nodded, swallowing the lump in my throat. "Yeah, me too."

For the next hour, we worked side by side, folding clothes, hanging up new stock, and chatting lightly about the usual things—weather, how busy the shop was, what I had planned for the weekend since we didn't have a show. I was starting to feel more comfortable, the tension between us gradually easing as we got back into a familiar rhythm.

As I smoothed a blouse and put it on a hanger, something caught my eye—a really nice leather jacket that I hadn't seen before. It stood out against the rest of the secondhand clothes on the rack.

"Hey, where'd you get this?" I asked, lifting it off the rack to examine it closer. The leather was soft, like it hadn't even been worn.

Mom looked up from her stack of sweaters. "Oh, that came from an estate sale last weekend. A woman was moving to Florida and didn't need her winter clothes anymore. Can you imagine? Moving to a place where it never snows?" She chuckled and shook her head. "Anyway, I snagged a bunch of stuff like that. Real high quality."

I smiled back, putting the jacket in its place. "You always seem to find the best deals."

She shrugged, but I could see the pride in her eyes. "I've got an eye for it. Keeps the shop fresh, you know?"

I nodded, glancing around at all the neatly displayed clothes. "Yeah, it does. You're really good at this, Mom."

She blushed a little, then looked back down at her pile of clothes. "Well, I try. Helps that I enjoy it."

We kept working for a few minutes in silence, and then, as we were folding the last of the shirts, Mom glanced at me with a sly smile. "Speaking of trying... how's work going? Is that golden boy ready for his next big show?"

I smiled and nodded. "Yeah, we've been busy getting ready. This is the big one—Vegas—it's coming up in a couple of weeks."

She raised an eyebrow, her smile widening. "And how's that nice Langton boy you work with? What was his name again? Cole?"

I nearly dropped the shirt I was folding. "Uh... yeah, Cole," I said, feeling my cheeks heat up. "He's... doing great. Better than great."

Mom chuckled softly. "Better, huh? You didn't use to say such nice things about him."

I fumbled with the shirt, trying to smooth it out and avoid her gaze. "Yeah, well... things have changed. We've had to work together a lot more, and I guess we've figured out how to... you know, get along."

She leaned on the table, giving me a knowing look. "Mm-hmm. And is that all? Just getting along?"

I bit my lip, feeling a little embarrassed. "Well, maybe more than just that. He's... we've gotten closer."

Mom's smile softened, her teasing tone giving way to something warmer. "He seems like a nice young man. I'm glad to hear you're getting along."

I nodded, not trusting myself to say much more. My mom didn't know the half of it—how Cole and I had gone from bickering to something else entirely, something that I couldn't quite put into words yet. But it felt good to hear her say that. It felt good to know she approved, even if she didn't know all the details.

We finished hanging the last of the clothes, and I stepped back, feeling lighter than I had in days. It wasn't just about the shop—it was about reconnecting with her, about seeing things from her side for once. And even though there was still a lot left unsaid between us, I knew we were on the right path.

Mom put the last hanger on the rack and turned to me with a tired but contented smile. "Thanks for helping out tonight, Em. I know you've got a lot going on."

I smiled back, feeling a warmth spread through my chest. "Anytime, Mom. Anytime."

Chapter Twenty-Three

Emily

I tugged Copper's reins, leading him into the arena. His ears flicked forward, picking up on the quiet signals of the ranch coming to life around us, and I could feel the subtle tension in his body. I gave his neck a quick pat as we approached the center of the ring, my mind already ticking through the exercises we needed to work on.

Cody was already waiting by the fence, leaning casually against the post, his sharp eyes following every movement. He gave me a nod as I approached, his expression unreadable as usual. I'd gotten used to that look—it meant he was watching closely, calculating, but holding back until he saw what I'd bring to the table today.

"You ready to get some work in?" Cody asked, pushing off the fence and adjusting his hat.

I swung up into the saddle, settling in as Copper shifted beneath me. We had put in so much time and effort, but today, I could feel that extra bit of nervous energy humming through his muscles.

"Take your time," Cody added, watching me carefully. "Let's start slow and get him thinking."

"Got it."

Copper seemed to pick up on my energy, flicking his ears forward as I gave him the signal. We moved together easily now, almost like breathing. I could feel the tension in his body, but it wasn't the jittery kind—it was the good kind, the kind that let me know he was eager to work.

"Let's see a few turns and spins," Cody called, stepping back from the fence. "Take your time, though. Focus on keeping him collected. I want cadence and smoothness more than speed."

I nodded, squeezing gently with my legs to guide Copper into a slow trot, feeling for his rhythm. His body felt like an extension of mine, and we moved fluidly through the motions, spinning tight, controlled turns, every step landing where I wanted it.

Cody watched for a while, his eyes narrowing slightly as Copper and I worked through our exercises. "Not bad," he finally said, his voice thoughtful. "He's steady, but don't let him fall into a pattern. Keep him fresh."

I adjusted my grip on the reins, focusing on keeping Copper alert as we moved through a series of figure eights, bending and keeping his ribs on the arc. He was listening, responding quickly to my cues, and I couldn't help but feel a swell of pride at how far we'd come.

After a few more minutes, Cody called out, "Alright, bring him in."

I rode over, halting Copper in front of Cody, who was already giving me that measured look again. He glanced at Copper, then back at me. "He's solid, Emily. You've done a great job with him."

I smiled, feeling the warmth of his words settle over me. Coming from Cody, that meant a lot.

"But," he continued, his tone softening, "we've talked about this before. You're doing everything right, but you need to be prepared for the fact that Copper's gonna start leveling off. His talent's got a ceiling. You know that."

His words hit me hard, sinking in deeper than I expected. It wasn't the first time Cody had said something like this. He'd been honest with me from the start, and I knew Copper wasn't destined to be a superstar, but hearing it again stung a little. I guess I'd been hoping we'd find some miracles along the way, but Copper was still the same horse he had been six months ago. No miracles, just the magic of a smart horse with a lot of try.

"I know," I said quietly, stroking Copper's mane. "He's not the most talented, but he's got heart. He's steady."

Cody nodded. "That's why he's gonna be valuable. Not every horse *should* be dynamite. He's consistent and pretty and sound, with a terrific mind, and for a lot of people, that's more important than a flashy performance. There's always a market for horses like him—ones that folks can trust. That's why Blake and I made the call to campaign him, get his name out there. But in the competition world, especially as we get later in the season and horses like Lynx start catching up, you're gonna see other horses start to pull ahead."

I swallowed, trying to push down the disappointment creeping up in my chest. "So... what are you saying? I should stop pushing him so hard?"

Cody shook his head. "No, not at all. Keep working with him, keep developing him. He's gonna be a great asset. But I just want you to be ready, mentally, for when things get tougher in the show ring. Some of the horses you'll go up against are gonna have a higher ceiling. That's not a reflection on you or Copper—it's just the way it is."

I nodded, appreciating his honesty. It wasn't like I hadn't known this was coming, but still, the reality of it made my chest tighten. Copper wasn't flashy like Lynx, but he was my partner, and we'd built something together. I had to be okay with the fact that his strength was in his consistency, not his ability to blow everyone away in the show ring.

Cody stepped forward, resting a hand on Copper's neck. "You're doing everything right, Em. And this isn't about winning Vegas—it's about making you the best trainer you can be. That's my goal."

His words hit me in a way I didn't expect. It wasn't just about Copper or the show—it was about me. About how much I'd grown as a trainer since I started working at Walker Ranch. Cody wasn't pushing me to make Copper something he wasn't; he was pushing me to be the best I could be, no matter what horse I had under me.

I took a deep breath, nodding. "I get it. And I'm not giving up on him."

Cody smiled, a rare expression from him. "Good. I don't expect you to."

We stood there for a moment, the early morning sun casting long shadows across the arena. Over at the gate, Cole was just leading Lynx in for their work, and I gave him a nod and a smile.

"Let's wrap it up for today," Cody said, stepping back. "We've got a long road ahead, but you're on the right track."

I nodded, giving Copper a final pat before dismounting I felt a strange mix of emotions—pride, determination, and a hint of sadness. Maybe Copper wasn't going to be a Vegas champion, but that wasn't the point. The point was to keep growing, to keep learning, and to make the most of the partnership we had.

And I wasn't done yet.

Cole

I swung up into the saddle, taking a deep breath as I settled onto Lynx's back. She shifted under me, eager, like she was already anticipating the work ahead. I tried to relax into the saddle, but the tension I'd been carrying all day didn't ease. Cody stood by the fence, his arms crossed, watching me with that hooded expression of his.

"Alright, let's see what you two have today," Cody called, his tone easy, but I could hear the edge of expectation beneath it.

I nodded, nudging Lynx into a walk. Her steps were light, but my hands felt stiff on the reins. We started the first few maneuvers, and I could tell right away that I wasn't completely in sync with her. My mind was too tangled up with everything—my family, the ranch, everything I couldn't seem to fix. Lynx flicked her ears back, sensing my distraction, and I cursed under my breath.

"Easy," Cody said, his voice cutting through my thoughts. "You're thinking too much."

I gritted my teeth and exhaled, trying to loosen the tension in my body. He was right, of course. I needed to stop thinking and just ride. Lynx had more than enough skill to carry us both through if I'd just get out of her way.

We circled the arena a couple more times, and finally, something clicked. Lynx responded to the subtle shift in my weight, and we slipped into that familiar rhythm. I gave her more rein, and she surged forward, quick and precise. Her hooves moved smoothly beneath us, her body low and snaky as she glided into the turns.

As we worked through the exercises, I could feel her power, the sheer athleticism that made her different from any other horse I'd ever ridden. She was sharp, her movements crisp, her focus locked in on the job. We pushed through another series of stops and turns, and Lynx responded perfectly, dancing beneath me like she was born for this.

Cody was nodding, watching us closely. "There it is," he muttered to himself, loud enough for me to hear. "That's what I've been waiting for."

I loosened the reins slightly, letting Lynx relax as we finished the run. Her chest was heaving, but she was steady, her ears still pricked forward, tuned into me like we were two parts of the same machine. I couldn't help but feel a flicker of pride in my chest. She wasn't just good—she was something special. And it wasn't just me who could see it anymore.

Cody walked up as I brought Lynx to a halt, patting her neck. "She's got it, Cole. But remember, don't get too caught up in what she can do. Focus on staying calm. You don't need to overdo it."

I nodded, wiping the sweat from my brow, still catching my breath from the intensity of the run. "I know. It's just... it's hard not to push when she's feeling this good."

Cody chuckled softly, shaking his head. "Yeah, that's the challenge, isn't it? You've got a horse with raw talent like Lynx, and it's tempting to let her show it all at once. But you've got to be smart. Keep her energy focused, make her wait for you. A horse like this will give you everything, but if you take too much too fast, she'll burn out before you hit the top."

I listened, letting his words sink in. He was right. Lynx was hitting all the right marks, but I couldn't let myself get carried away. There was still a long road ahead, and if I didn't play it right, I could ruin everything we'd worked for.

"I get it," I said after a beat, running a hand down Lynx's neck. "I'll keep it in check."

Cody gave me a knowing smile, like he could tell I was finally starting to understand. "Good. Just remember, it's not about the flash. It's about consistency. You build that up, and by the time you're at the top, nobody will be able to touch you."

I nodded, feeling the truth of his words settle deep inside me. Consistency. Patience. That's what separated the best from the rest.

As Cody turned to walk back to the gate, I caught sight of movement near the fence. Blake Walker was standing there, leaning casually against one of the posts, his arms crossed over his chest, watching us. My heart sank a little, that old familiar weight of nerves creeping back up my spine.

Blake wasn't just any rancher. He was the driving force behind the entire Walker Ranch horse program, the reason Cody had a string of show horses to train in the first place. And here he was, watching me work his best horse. Well, *I* thought she was his best, anyway. I swallowed hard, suddenly feeling like I was being judged all over again.

Blake didn't say anything right away, just gave me a slow, thoughtful grin as he uncrossed his arms and walked toward me. "You did well out there," he said quietly.

I swallowed, feeling a rush of relief, but also a fresh wave of anxiety. "Thanks," I managed to say.

Blake nodded, glancing over at Lynx. "She's shaping up to be a fine horse. Good hands on her."

I shifted, trying to gauge his tone, but Blake was as hard to read as ever. "Appreciate that," I said, rubbing Lynx's neck.

Blake's grin widened a little. "When you're done here, how about you put her up and come up to the house? I've got coffee on. We can talk."

I blinked, surprised. Blake had never asked me to come up for coffee before. I glanced at Cody, who gave me a little nod, like this was just a normal thing. But it didn't feel normal. My stomach twisted with nerves, and I forced myself to nod back.

"Uh, sure," I said, clearing my throat. "I'll be up after I get her settled."

Blake gave a short nod, then turned and headed back toward the house, leaving me standing there with my thoughts racing. I looked down at Lynx, still catching her breath, and wondered what kind of conversation I was walking into.

One thing was certain—it wasn't going to be an ordinary cup of coffee.

The sun was already high in the sky by the time I made my way up to the Walker ranch house. It stood tall and quiet, an old, stately home that had been a part of the valley longer than I'd been alive. I took a deep breath before knocking on the door, my nerves on edge after Blake's invitation.

I wasn't sure what to expect. Blake was a good guy—respected and easygoing, but private. It wasn't every day he called someone up for a sit-down.

The door opened, and Meryl, Blake's wife, greeted me with a warm smile. "Good morning, Cole. Come on in."

"Morning, Mrs. Walker," I replied, tipping my hat politely. I stepped inside, the smell of something savory hitting me right away. My stomach grumbled in response, and I realized I hadn't eaten anything since early that morning.

Meryl noticed, her smile widening. "You look like you could use some food. Come on into the kitchen. I've got a late breakfast going."

"Thank you," I said, following her into the spacious kitchen. The house had that old ranch charm—wood beams, big windows letting in the sunlight, and a long dining table that could seat the entire Walker clan and then some.

Blake was already sitting at the table, a cup of coffee in front of him. He gave me a nod as I entered. "Cole."

"Blake," I said, trying not to sound too nervous.

Meryl set a plate of scrambled eggs, bacon, and toast down in front of me. "Eat up. I've got to tend to the chickens, but you boys enjoy."

I thanked her again, feeling a little more at ease as I sat down across from Blake. He motioned for me to help myself to the food, so I picked up my fork and started eating, my appetite suddenly back in full force.

Blake didn't say much at first, just sipped his coffee and let me eat. Once I'd made a decent dent in the plate, he finally broke the silence. "I heard Ridgeview's for sale."

The words hit me like a punch, but I kept my expression neutral, glancing up at him. "Yeah, looks like it."

Blake nodded, his face thoughtful. "I've seen the signs. You've sold off a lot of cattle, haven't been buying hay. Gage has been keeping things quiet, but you can't hide that big For Sale sign."

I swallowed the bite of toast in my mouth, feeling the weight of his words settle on me. I wasn't expecting sympathy from Blake, but that's what it sounded like. "Yeah. Things... haven't been good."

Blake leaned back in his chair, his eyes steady on mine. "I'm sorry to hear that. What's been going on?"

I hesitated, not sure how much I wanted to get into it. But Blake's steady gaze made it clear he wasn't judging—he was just listening. And for some reason, that was enough to get me talking.

"We've got this offer on the ranch," I started, setting my fork down and rubbing my palms on my jeans. "It's from some company looking to build a guest ranch. Tear down the barns, build new ones, renovate the house for tourists. Gage is thinking about taking it because, honestly, we're drowning. The Fish and Wildlife restrictions cut into our grazing land, and we've already sold most of the breeding stock."

"What restrictions?"

I swallowed. "Spotted Owl."

Blake groaned. "They pull that old trick pony out every time they don't really know what's going on. You sure?"

I shrugged. "They sent an inspector out and everything. Twice."

Blake's fingers drummed on the table. "Was it Ben Watson?"

"I don't know. You'd have to ask Gage. But it doesn't matter, because they won't change their minds. Our grazing rights are gone and nothing we can do about it."

"There's always something you can do. You may not like whatever it is, but there's always something."

"Yeah." I swallowed a mouthful of scrambled eggs. "I can go get a job. I've been..." I cleared my throat and sighed. "I guess I've been putting it off, but I gotta tell Cody."

Blake nodded, his face still calm. "You'd quit now? Right before the big show?"

I looked down at my hands, feeling my gut twist. "I don't want to. I mean, Lynx is really coming on strong, and Cody's been pushing me to get ready for Vegas. But..." I shook my head, hating how small my voice sounded. "My family needs help now. We need money now. I can't keep chasing a dream while they're about to lose everything."

Blake leaned forward, resting his arms on the table. "You thinking about getting another job? Something outside the ranch?"

I nodded, feeling a flush of embarrassment creep up my neck. "I might have to. Construction or something. There's work out there, and it pays. I can't sit around hoping things turn around while my brothers are selling the ranch from under us."

Blake raised an eyebrow, a small grin tugging at the corner of his mouth. "Am I not paying you enough to train horses?"

I blinked, realizing with a jolt that Blake Walker was technically my boss. "No! No, you're paying me plenty, I mean—" I stopped, rubbing the back of my neck. "I just meant... you know how it is. Starting out in this business, you don't make much until you get established."

Blake chuckled softly, but his expression grew serious again. "I get it. Every trainer starts out like a starving artist. But it sounds like you don't have time to wait on that dream."

"I don't. My family's gotta figure out a new place to live. I don't have the luxury of waiting."

Blake was quiet for a long moment, his eyes thoughtful. Then he sighed, pushing his coffee cup aside. "I sure hate to see you give up on this, Cole. You've got talent. But I understand the situation you're in. Ranchers have to have each other's backs."

I glanced up, surprised by his tone. "What do you mean?"

Blake leaned back in his chair, crossing his arms. "I've got a buddy who runs a construction crew. He's always looking for good hands. If you're serious about this, I could put in a good word for you."

I felt a wave of nausea roll through me at the thought, but I forced myself to nod. "I... I'd appreciate that. I'm not sure I've got a choice."

Blake studied me for a moment like he was trying to gauge just how serious I was. Then he nodded. "Alright. I'll give Mike Lundbergh a call. But think about it, Cole. Don't make any rash decisions. You've got a future here, too. Maybe it's not as bad as you think."

I swallowed hard, my throat tight. I wanted to believe him, but the truth was, I wasn't sure how much longer I could hold on to this dream. Not when my family needed me.

"Thanks, Blake," I said quietly, standing up to leave. "I appreciate it."

Blake gave me a firm nod. "Get back to work, Cole. You've still got horses to train."

I smiled weakly and tipped my hat, then walked out of the ranch house, my mind spinning. As I walked back toward the barn, a thought kept tugging at the back of my mind—*Emily*. Lately, every time I was around her, I felt this pull, something deeper than just attraction. But the truth was, I didn't have much to offer her.

She was talented, ambitious, and had a future that seemed to stretch ahead of her. What did I have? A ranch on the verge of being sold, a family hanging by a thread, and a job that barely paid the bills.

Emily deserved more than that—more than me. The idea of trying to build something real with her, while everything around me felt so uncertain, was like setting myself up for failure. I couldn't help but wonder if I was fooling myself, thinking I could be part of something bigger, when all I'd ever known was scraping by.

I hadn't told anyone, not even myself, what I was really feeling. But as much as I tried to push it down, it was getting harder to ignore.

Sure, we'd been getting closer lately, and it felt good—natural, even—but every time I thought about what came next, my stomach twisted. What could I possibly give her?

The truth was, Emily was the real talent between the two of us. She had Copper dialed in like nobody else could. She just did the work, never worrying about what anyone thought, and she'd earned the respect of everyone at Walker Ranch. People noticed her, talked about her. Good grief, even I couldn't stop thinking about her.

And here I was, scrambling just to figure out my next move.

I swallowed hard, feeling a knot form in my chest. What kind of future did I have with Emily if I couldn't even figure out my own life? Maybe I was fooling myself thinking I could be part of something bigger. Maybe I was just dragging her into my mess.

Emily deserved someone who had their life together, someone who could offer her more than I ever could. She was strong, capable, and she had dreams bigger than this town. She was going places, and what was I doing? Thinking about working construction, leaving behind the thing I loved just to pay the bills.

But that was the reality, wasn't it? I had to face it—sooner or later, I needed to step up and do what was right for my family. If that meant giving up on the show horses and taking a job swinging a hammer, then maybe that's what it would take. I'd been fooling myself, thinking I could balance it all.

And with Emily... I wasn't sure I could give her what she deserved. Maybe I never would.

I clenched the lead rope a little tighter, my steps slowing as we reached the barn. Blake's offer hung in the back of my mind. Construction. Manual labor. A paycheck. It wasn't glamorous, and it wasn't what I wanted, but it was practical. And at the end of the day, maybe that's all I could offer—to be practical, to keep my family afloat.

But with Emily...

I took a deep breath, closing my eyes for a second. I had to stop pretending like I could have it all. Emily, the horses, my family's ranch... something had to give.

Chapter Twenty-Four

Cole

The sun beat down hard as I stepped onto the construction site, the sound of hammers and saws filling the air. A half-framed house stood in the middle of the lot, beams rising up against the blue sky like a skeleton waiting to be fleshed out. Workers were scattered everywhere, hauling wood, framing walls, shouting instructions. The place buzzed with a kind of energy that felt miles away from the calm rhythm of working horses.

I spotted the foreman, Mike Lundbergh, near a pile of lumber, and made my way over. He looked tough, built like a guy who'd spent his life working with his hands. He gave me a firm handshake, his grip almost bruising. "You Cole Langton?" he asked, though he already knew the answer.

"Yeah. Nice to meet you."

Mike grunted and gave the house behind him a nod. "We've got deadlines to hit. You any good with a hammer?"

"Grew up building barns and fences. I can handle it."

"Good," he said, crossing his arms over his chest. "I need someone who's reliable. Full-time. You got that?"

"Right, sir. I'm on it." I hesitated, feeling a twinge of doubt creep in. "It's just that, uh... I've got a prior commitment at Walker Ranch. I was supposed to go to a big show in a few weeks—Vegas. It's important."

Mike raised an eyebrow, his face hardening. "Vegas, huh? What are you, some kinda rodeo star?"

"Not rodeo, no. I train cutting horses. We leave next Wednesday, and I got practice—"

"Whatever it is, it's not full-time here. Look, I don't need part-timers. This is all or nothing. I can't be shuffling crew and having other guys waitin' around because one guy takes off whenever he feels like."

"I'm only talking about a couple of weeks, sir. I don't want to leave the Walkers high and dry."

"Then why are you here now? You shoulda waited til this was all settled."

I caught my breath. "I... I can't wait, sir."

"Then Monday it is. Otherwise, you're wastin' my time." His words hit like a punch to the gut.

I swallowed hard, feeling the weight of it all pressing down. "I get that, but I've worked for months to prepare for this show. After it's over, I'll be full-time. I just need a few weeks."

Mike shook his head, crossing his arms tighter across his chest. "Not how it works. You either show up Monday, seven sharp, or I'll find someone else who can."

I stared at him, my mind spinning. I needed this job—needed the money to help my family. But walking away from Vegas? Walking away from everything I'd worked for with Lynx? It felt like tearing a piece of my soul out.

But I didn't have a choice.

"I'll take the job," I said, my voice sounding hollow, even to myself.

Mike slapped me on the shoulder, satisfied. "Good. See you Monday. And don't be late."

Emily

The barn was quiet, just the sound of Copper's breathing as I ran a brush down his side. The familiar rhythm of grooming always calmed me down, but today, my thoughts were everywhere—drifting back to the show, to the way things had felt unsettled between Cole and me lately.

I was finishing up when I heard footsteps behind me. I turned and saw Cole walking toward me, his shoulders slumped, his hat pulled low over his face. Something was off—he looked weighed down, like the world was resting on his back.

"Hey," I called softly, giving Copper a final pat before stepping out of the stall. "Everything okay?"

Cole stopped a few feet away, his hands stuffed in his pockets. For a moment, he didn't say anything, just stared at the ground. Finally, he muttered, "I took the construction job."

The words hung in the air like a punch I didn't see coming. I blinked, the brush slipping from my hand as I stared at him. "You what?"

He let out a breath, his gaze still fixed on the ground. "Blake hooked me up and I had the interview today. They want me full-time, starting Monday. No more waiting around for the show in Vegas."

My heart sank. "So... you're not going?"

He shook his head, looking like the decision was eating him up inside. "I can't. My family... they need the money. I can't keep pretending like this dream of mine is more important than what's going on back home."

I took a step closer, my chest tightening. "But Cole... you've worked so hard for this. You've put everything into Lynx."

"I know," he said, his voice rough. "But what choice do I have? We need every penny we can get. This isn't about what I want anymore."

I stood there, feeling the weight of his decision sinking in. He was walking away from everything we'd worked for, everything we'd dreamed of. "But this is your dream," I whispered, almost more to myself than to him. "You're just... giving it up?"

His jaw tightened as he finally looked at me, guilt flashing in his eyes. "I don't have a choice, Emily."

I could see the pain behind his words, the way this decision was tearing him apart. And yet, he was still walking away. From the show. From Lynx. Maybe from me, too.

He looked down at his boots, shaking his head. "I'm sorry. I wish things were different."

I swallowed the lump in my throat, trying to find something—anything—to say that would make him change his mind. But nothing came. I couldn't change his situation. I couldn't fix this for him.

"I understand," I said softly, even though my heart was breaking.

Cole nodded, his face hard with resolve. "Thanks, Em." He swallowed, looking away. "I gotta go talk to Cody now."

Without another word, he turned and walked away, leaving me standing alone in the barn, my mind spinning with everything that had just happened. He was doing what he thought was right, but it felt like he was tearing apart everything we'd been building. I watched him go, my hands trembling as I picked up the brush again, trying to focus on anything but the pain gnawing at my chest.

Cole

The air was thick with the scent of horses and hay as I stood outside Lynx's stall, running my hand over the smooth grain of the wood. She poked her head out, nudging me for a treat, her ears pricked forward like she was ready for another day of work. But there wouldn't be any more days like that—not for a while.

I gave her a pat, my chest tightening as I thought about the decision I'd made. Construction work. It was what my family needed, but it felt like I was turning my back on something more. On a future I'd started to build for myself.

I grabbed a brush from the tack box, trying to keep my hands busy while my thoughts spun. Lynx shifted under my touch, sensing something wasn't right. She always did. She was a smart horse, maybe the smartest I'd ever worked with. The thought of leaving her behind made my stomach twist.

"You're really going through with it?"

Emily's voice cut through the silence, and I turned to find her leaning on the barn door, her eyes heavy with something I couldn't quite name. Disappointment, maybe. Sadness. I didn't blame her.

I nodded, focusing on the brush in my hand. "Yeah. I start Monday."

She stepped inside, her arms crossed, but not in a defensive way. "I get it, Cole," she said softly. "Your family's in a rough spot. But there's got to be something else you can do than just walking away."

I let out a breath, hanging the brush on the stall door before turning to face her. "It's not like I'm giving up," I said, trying to make her understand. "I'm trying to help my family."

She walked a little closer, her gaze steady. "And what about you? What about all the work you've put in? Lynx is ready for Vegas, and you know it. You're ready."

I ran a hand through my hair, frustration bubbling up again. "I'm not saying it's what I want, but I don't have the luxury of thinking about that right now. My brothers are counting on me."

Emily frowned, her voice turning firmer. "You're not being selfish by thinking about what you want. It doesn't have to be one or the other—family or your dream."

I shook my head, glancing at Lynx, who was chewing lazily on a piece of hay. "It feels like it does. There's no middle ground here. I need to make money, real money. Framing houses is the only job offer I've got that'll do that."

She stepped even closer now, her voice barely above a whisper. "Cole, you're one of the best riders I've ever seen. You belong in Vegas with Lynx. Why not find another way to help your family without giving up everything you've worked for?"

I looked at her then, really looked at her, and the concern in her eyes cut right through me. It was like she saw the part of me I was trying to bury, the part that wanted so badly to say, "Yeah, I belong in Vegas." But how could I say that when everything else was falling apart?

"I don't know if there is another way. Maybe this is it."

She reached out, her hand brushing my arm, and I felt something inside me start to unravel. "Maybe it's not," she said softly. "Maybe you just haven't looked hard enough yet."

I blinked, her words sinking in, but before I could respond, she pulled her hand back and gave me a small, encouraging smile. "Just... think about it, okay?"

I didn't answer. I couldn't. Not without saying something I'd regret. Instead, I gave Lynx a final pat and hung the brush back on the hook. "You'll do fine in Vegas," I said, my voice rough. "You and Copper... you're gonna kill it. And you're gonna show Lynx, too. Better 'n I could've."

She scoffed. "Do you really think riding Lynx is more important to me than you going to Vegas?"

I crossed my arms, staring at the ground, trying to make sense of why she was pushing so hard. "I don't get it, Em. Why does it matter so much? You've got this in the bag. You and Copper—you're the ones everyone's watching. Lynx and I... we're not winning anything."

I could feel her eyes on me, sharp and almost angry. "You really don't see it, do you?"

I frowned, looking up at her. "See what?"

"It's not about me," she said, her voice tightening. "It's about you and Lynx. You're the ones Cody's been banking on for Vegas, not me."

Her words hit me like a punch to the gut. I blinked, confused. "What? That doesn't make sense. Copper's been winning all season."

Emily shook her head, frustration clear on her face. "Yeah, Copper's been consistent, but that's not enough. He's not the champion you think he is. He's good, but... there's a limit. Cody knew that from the start. *I* knew that from the start. Lynx is the athlete, and you can't tell me you haven't always known that."

My mind raced, trying to catch up. "But you're ahead of me in points."

"For now," she said, her voice softening. "But Lynx is just getting started. You and her... you've barely scratched the surface of what she can do. Cody's been waiting for this. Lynx is peaking, Cole. *She's* the one who can take Vegas."

I opened my mouth to argue, but her words stopped me cold. I'd been so wrapped up in everything—my family, the ranch, trying to just keep my head above water—that I hadn't even seen it. Lynx... she was different. And Emily, she believed in her. In *me*.

"You really think that?" I asked, my voice coming out rougher than I meant.

Her eyes softened, but there was no doubt in her voice. "Yes, I do. And you should, too."

I stood there, stunned, the truth of what she was saying finally sinking in. Lynx wasn't Copper, and I wasn't just filling in space behind Emily. I had something real, something worth fighting for, and for the first time in a long while, I felt the weight of it settle on me. She was right.

But even with that realization, there was still the part of me that wondered if I was ready to take that leap. I wanted to believe it, wanted to see what Emily saw in me—but with everything else going on, it felt like too much.

"I don't know, Em..." I started, but she cut me off.

"You do know, Cole. You're just scared to admit it."

She wasn't wrong. I swallowed hard, the truth of it too big to ignore. "Yeah... maybe I am."

Emily looked down, and I could see the frustration building in her eyes, but she didn't argue with me. Maybe she understood more than I realized.

"Thanks," I murmured. "For what it's worth, Em... thanks for everything."

We stood there for a moment, the weight of everything unsaid hanging between us. Then I turned and walked out of the barn, leaving Lynx, leaving Emily, and feeling like I was leaving a part of myself behind, too.

Emily

After Cole left the barn, I stood there, feeling the silence settle like a thick blanket over the space he'd occupied just moments before. It was hard to watch him walk away. Harder still knowing he felt like he had no choice. But the truth was, he did have a choice. He was just too scared to take it.

I shook my head and tried to focus, turning my attention back to Copper. He was tied just outside the tack room, his ears flicking toward me as I approached. "Looks like it's just you and me," I said quietly, running a hand down his neck.

I saddled him up, trying to push the conversation with Cole out of my mind, but it stuck like a burr in my thoughts. The way he looked when he talked about his family—the anxiety he carried—made my heart ache. It felt like he was walking away from a lot more than just the horses.

I didn't want to lose him, but I couldn't make him stay if he didn't want to.

I mounted up and nudged Copper into a trot, the familiar rhythm of his hooves on the dirt helping to settle the chaos in my head. We started working on some patterns, weaving through the cones Cody had set up in the arena earlier for a cornering drill. Copper was steady as always, responding to my cues like he could read my mind.

But today, it felt different. The focus wasn't there, not like it usually was. My mind kept drifting back to Cole, to the way things felt like they were slipping between us. It wasn't fair—not to him, not to me—but life wasn't fair, was it?

I brought Copper to a stop, taking a deep breath and patting his neck. "We've got work to do, buddy. Let's make this count."

We worked through some spins and stops, Copper's muscles flexing under me as he responded to my slightest touch. His precision was incredible. Cody had taught me well, but it wasn't just about the training. Copper and I had a connection, something that went beyond technique.

I heard footsteps behind me and glanced over my shoulder to see Cody leaning on the fence, watching me with that thoughtful look he got when he was sizing up my progress.

"You're looking good out there," he called, his voice steady. "Copper's really coming along."

I nodded, keeping my focus on the task at hand. "Thanks."

He was quiet for a minute, and I could feel his eyes on me. "You're thinking about Cole, aren't you?"

I pulled Copper up again, resting my hands on the saddle horn. "I don't know what to think anymore. How can you just stand by and let him leave us in the lurch like this?"

Cody nodded slowly, walking over to stand closer. "It's not easy when someone you care about is making a decision you don't agree with. But you can't control it. You can only control how you deal with it."

I sighed, looking down at Copper's mane. "I just don't understand why he's giving up."

"Whatever he's doing," Cody said, his tone gentle, "'giving up' isn't it. He's doing what he thinks is right for his family."

"I know." I ground my teeth. "But it doesn't feel right."

Cody rested a hand on the fence. "Sometimes people need to take a step back to figure out what they really want. Give him time, Emily."

"Time? We don't have time, not if he's going to change his mind in time to go to Vegas!"

Cody thinned his lips. "That's... that's not happening, Emily. You're going to have to accept that."

I nodded, though the knot in my chest didn't loosen. "Yeah, I guess."

"And I want you up on Lynx after this. We gotta get you two synced up."

"Cody, I..." I winced. "I can't ride her like Cole does. He can read her mind. I—"

"You'll do fine."

"Well, why aren't you showing her?" I protested. "You're the experienced one."

Cody shook his head with a slow grin. "Let's just say it's not about winning."

Chapter Twenty-Five

Emily

The trailers were nearly full, and the barn was buzzing with the kind of energy you could feel before a big show. I brushed the last bit of dust off Copper's coat, my hands moving automatically over the familiar spots. He leaned into the pressure, his usual lazy, calm self. His big brown eyes blinked slowly as he snorted, completely unfazed by the chaos around him.

"You ready for the road, big guy?" I murmured, patting his neck.

He flicked an ear as if to say, *I'm always ready.* I smiled and reached for his halter, my heart a little lighter, but still not quite settled. It was almost time to load up and hit the road for Vegas, the biggest show of the year. The excitement was there, somewhere in the back of my mind, but it was drowned out by something else—something that had been sitting in the pit of my stomach for days.

I tried not to look over at the empty space beside Copper's stall. Lynx's gear was packed up and ready, and she was already standing in the trailer, but it didn't feel right. Cole wasn't coming. He wasn't part of this trip, even though he should have been.

As I clipped Copper's halter on, my phone buzzed in my back pocket. I pulled it out, half expecting a text from Cody or Luke, but it was just Kate, sending me another encouraging message about the show. I smiled and quickly typed back a thank-you before shoving the phone away.

But it didn't help.

We were all heading out—the Walkers, their show horses, their team. The whole family was hitting the road with us to drive to the show, except for Blake and Meryl, who were flying in two days.

And Cole? He was staying behind. It just didn't feel like we were a team without him.

Cody walked past, clipboard in hand, double-checking the logistics. He paused when he saw me standing by Copper's stall, still holding the lead rope. "You good?"

I gave him a quick nod. "Yeah, just... making sure everything's packed."

Cody's brow furrowed, and he tipped his hat back, giving me a look like he knew there was more going on. "You don't have to worry. Copper's in good shape for this one."

I knew that. We'd been working day and night, putting in the hours, making sure he was sharp for Vegas. But my worry wasn't really about Copper, and Cody knew it. He studied me for a second longer before giving me a nod. "Don't let your head get in the way of what you've been working for, alright?"

"Yeah, I know," I said, forcing a smile. "We'll be fine."

Cody gave me a small nod of approval before heading toward the next trailer, calling out instructions to Luke, who was strapping down a flatbed full of hay for the horses. I took a deep breath and walked Copper up into the trailer.

Once I stepped down, I crossed over to the other trailer, the one where Lynx was poking her nose through the bars of the window. She already had a mouthful of hay, and she pressed her nostrils up against the bars when I put out my fingers to stroke her. She was ready, too—more than ready. I couldn't help but wonder what she understood about everything that was happening. Did she miss Cole, too?

With a sigh, I stepped away from her at the window and walked around the horse trailers to make sure all the doors were latched and everything was in order. The morning sun was climbing higher, casting long shadows across the yard. We were supposed to be on the road by now, but everyone was taking their time—checking, double-checking, loading, and reloading.

"You want to take a break?" Luke's voice startled me out of my thoughts. He appeared from around the side of the trailer, a grin on his face. "We've got enough hands here. Go grab a coffee before we hit the road."

I smiled weakly, shaking my head. "Nah, I'm good. Just finishing up here."

He gave me a knowing look, one eyebrow raised. "You sure? You look like you could use it."

"I'm fine, Luke," I said, trying to sound more convincing than I felt. "I just want to make sure the horses are all set."

"Alright, just making sure. You need anything, you holler."

I watched him walk away, disappearing around the corner with his usual confident stride. I wished I could shake this feeling—this knot in my chest that had been there ever since Cole told me he wasn't going. I should be focused, ready, but all I could think about was how different it was going to feel without him there.

"Emily, you about ready?" Cody called from the cab of his truck. He was already climbing inside, the engine rumbling to life as he checked his watch.

"Yeah, just need to double-check tire pressures on the trailers," I called back.

"Luke already did that. And then Jess didn't trust him, so she did it again. Come on, Em, it's time to roll."

I closed my eyes and sighed. No one was waiting? There was... no chance that last minute...?

But Cole was on the job site, working construction while we headed to Vegas. It didn't seem fair. We'd both worked so hard to get here, to get the horses ready for this moment, and now he was stuck swinging a hammer while I was going to Vegas without him.

I grabbed my phone again, almost dialing his number, but I stopped myself. What was I even going to say? He'd made his decision. He was doing what he thought was right for his family, and I couldn't blame him for that. But it didn't make it any easier.

I shoved the phone back into my pocket and stepped back around the trailer I was going to be driving, giving Copper a final pat on the nose as I passed. I climbed into the driver's seat, turning the key in the ignition and listening to the familiar roar of the engine. The road stretched out ahead of us, long and winding, leading us to Vegas. But as I pulled out of the ranch and onto the highway, I couldn't help but feel like something was missing.

Or someone.

Cole

The sound of hammers hitting nails echoed through the air, mixing with the hum of the saw cutting through planks of wood. Sweat dripped down my forehead as I lifted another beam into place, my muscles straining under the weight. The sun was relentless, beating down on us like it had something to prove.

I wiped the sweat from my brow, glancing at the other guys on the crew. They were all working in sync, moving quickly, efficiently. They belonged here—this was their world, their life. But me? I felt like an outsider, like I was just going through the motions.

I grabbed the nail gun, positioning the beam before driving the nails in. It was mindless work, something that usually helped me clear my head. But today, it wasn't helping.

All I could think about was the fact that Cody, Emily, and the rest of the Walkers were probably halfway to Vegas by now, the trailers packed with horses, the sun rising behind them as they hit the open road. They were heading to one of the biggest shows of the year, and I wasn't there.

I should've been there. Should've been guiding Lynx... cheering for Emily and Cody.

I let out a frustrated breath, driving another nail into the beam with more force than necessary.

"Hey, Langton, you wanna take it easy there?" one of the guys called. "We're building a house, not knocking it down."

I grunted, giving him a half-hearted nod before focusing back on the work. I had to keep my head in the game. This was my job now—this was where I needed to be.

But it didn't feel right.

I finished securing the beam and moved on to the next one, trying to push the thoughts of Vegas out of my mind. But they kept creeping back in, no matter how hard I tried to shake them. I could picture Emily, sitting in the driver's seat of her truck, Copper in the trailer behind her. I could see Cody checking the horses, making sure everything was ready. And Lynx... she'd be waiting, ready to show the world what she was made of.

My phone buzzed in my pocket, snapping me out of my thoughts. I glanced at it, seeing Chase's name flash across the screen. I sighed and hit decline, shoving the phone back into my pocket. I didn't have time for whatever was going on back at the ranch right now. Not while I was here.

But then it buzzed again. Trent this time.

"Come on," I muttered under my breath, hitting decline again.

The guys around me were giving me looks now, and I could feel the embarrassment creeping up my neck. I didn't want to be that guy, the one who was always taking personal calls on the job. But then my phone buzzed again.

Mom.

My stomach clenched, and I knew I had to answer it. Something must be up if she was calling me in the middle of the day. I glanced at my boss, who was busy looking over the blueprints, and then quickly pulled my phone out.

"Mom? What's going on?"

Her voice came through the line, excited and breathless. "Cole, you won't believe it!"

"What is it?" I asked, already feeling a knot forming in my chest.

"Fish and Wildlife just called! They're rescinding the restrictions on our grazing rights!"

I froze, the phone pressed against my ear as her words sank in. "Wait... what?"

"They said they're lifting the restrictions! We can keep the ranch, Cole. It's happening!"

For a second, I couldn't move. The world seemed to tilt, and everything around me faded into the background. My mom kept talking, but her words were drowned out by the pounding of my heart.

We could keep the ranch.

I dropped the phone.

I was still reeling from the phone call as I stepped into the house. The ranch looked the same—familiar and quiet, like it always had—but there was something different in the air. It was like the tension we'd been carrying for months had lifted, just a little. But not enough to let any of us really breathe.

The front door creaked as I walked in, and I found Mom and Chase at the kitchen table, their faces filled with the same confusion I felt. Trent was leaning against the counter, arms crossed, while Gage hadn't made it back yet.

"Hey," I said, still half in a daze. "Mom just called me at work. Is it true? Fish and Wildlife... they lifted the restrictions?"

Mom nodded, her eyes wide with disbelief. "That's what they said. It's like they just... changed their minds. I don't understand it."

Chase shook his head, rubbing the back of his neck. "I've never heard of anything like this. Those restrictions were supposed to be permanent. Once they decide an area is protected, that's it."

"Even when they're wrong?" Mom groused. "Ever hear of them backing down from *that*?"

"Nope. Never," Chase replied.

"That's what I thought, too." I pulled out a chair and sat down heavily, my mind racing. "So what now? What are we supposed to do with this?"

Before anyone could answer, the door opened again, and Gage stepped in. He looked tired, but there was a strange look in his eyes. He took his hat off and ran a hand through his hair before hanging it on the hook by the door.

"You get any more news?" I asked, looking up at him.

Gage nodded slowly, stepping into the room. "Yeah. I just got back from the forestry office. Had a talk with Ben Watson over there. It's true. The restrictions are lifted."

Mom blinked, still in shock. "But how? How did this happen?"

Gage shook his head, letting out a slow breath as he leaned against the wall. "I don't know. Watson said they did another assessment and found that our grazing land doesn't affect the owl nesting territory anymore—or it never did—he said a lot of things, really, but the bottom line is, we're off their radar. It doesn't make sense, but..."

I stared at him, feeling a suspicion creep up inside me. "Wait a second. Did you say Ben Watson?"

Gage frowned, giving me a funny look. "Yeah, he's the main guy we've been talking to. Why?"

I looked up, a spark of realization hitting me. "Blake," I said quietly, almost to myself.

Everyone turned to look at me, confusion on their faces.

"Blake Walker," I repeated, sitting up straighter. "He's friends with Watson... or says he knows him or something. I remember him talking about it once. What if... what if Blake had something to do with this? What if he pulled some strings to get our land reassessed?"

Chase raised an eyebrow, but there was a flicker of understanding in his eyes. "You really think he'd do that?"

Mom leaned forward, her face softening as she nodded slowly. "It wouldn't shock me," she said, her voice thoughtful. "Blake Walker seems to know everyone. He's helped so many people around here... Maybe he saw what was happening and decided to lend a hand."

I glanced at Gage, waiting for his reaction. He was quiet for a moment, then gave a slow nod. "It's possible. I mean, I didn't push for any reassessment. None of us did. But someone did, and it wasn't by chance."

I looked around the room, taking it all in. This was huge. Bigger than anything we'd hoped for, but it didn't solve everything. "Okay, so the restrictions are lifted. What does that mean for us now? We don't have any breeding cows left, Gage. We sold most of them off. How are we supposed to rebuild?"

Gage's face hardened, and he gave a short nod. "You're right. We can keep using the land, but we don't have the stock to make it worth anything anymore. The sale is still set to go through in three days. Lifting those restrictions... it's great, but it doesn't change the fact that we're running on empty, and we were even before we lost the grazing land."

The weight of his words crashed into the room like a stone, and we all sat there, letting it sink in. This victory, this thing we had been praying for... it didn't change the fact that we were out of time, out of resources. We'd fought to keep the ranch, but we might not have anything left to save.

My heart felt heavy, and I leaned back in my chair, staring at the ceiling. Everything we'd been through, all the sacrifices, and it still might not be enough. I looked around at my brothers, at my mom. They all had the same defeated look in their eyes.

Then, like a spark in the darkness, an idea hit me. It wasn't perfect, but it was something.

I stood up suddenly, pushing the chair back.

Chase looked up, frowning. "Where are you going?"

"I'm going to have a word with Blake Walker," I said, grabbing my hat from the table.

Gage and Chase exchanged glances, but neither of them said anything. Mom gave me a small, hopeful smile like she knew exactly what I was thinking.

Without another word, I stepped outside, stuffing my hat on my head as I made my way to the truck. There might not be much we could do, but I could at least thank the man who'd tried to help.

I stepped out of the truck and headed up to the porch, hearing the screen door creak open as I approached.

"Well, now, look who it is," Blake's voice carried out, warm and easy, but I could hear the surprise behind it. He stood in the doorway, arms crossed, looking at me with a raised eyebrow. "I figured you'd be off working with Mike Lindbergh. Heard you took that framing job."

I grinned sheepishly, tipping my hat. "Yeah, about that… I think I'm fired for running off the job today."

Blake's frown deepened, a serious look overtaking his usual relaxed demeanor. "Fired? And what would make you do a thing like that?"

I hesitated for a second, glancing past him to where I could see Meryl setting the table for dinner. "Can we talk for a second? It's... about the ranch."

Blake nodded, stepping aside to let me in. "Come on in, son. You're welcome anytime."

We made our way inside, the familiar warmth of the Walker home surrounding me. Meryl smiled as I passed, and I gave her a nod in return. She disappeared into the kitchen, leaving Blake and me alone in the dining room.

Blake gestured to the chair at the table, but I stayed standing, hands on my hips as I tried to figure out how to ask the question that was burning a hole in my gut.

"You see Ben Watson lately?" I asked, cutting to the chase.

Blake's grin came slow, but sure. He chuckled, leaning back in his chair. "I might've."

I cocked a brow. The old troublemaker. I *knew* it. "And... what did you say to him?"

Blake shrugged. "All I did was tell Ben to put his spectacles on and give the Langtons a fair shake. Figured it wouldn't hurt to have someone take a closer look."

I stared at him for a moment, letting that sink in. He hadn't just sat back and watched us struggle—he'd gone and done something about it, something I hadn't even dared to hope for. "You told him to reassess the land?"

Blake nodded, a twinkle in his eye. "Didn't take much convincing. Ben's a fair man, just needed a little nudge in the right direction. He's got his higher-ups to keep happy, you know how it is, but... well, I might've told him to get the wax out of his ears and push his pencil the right way for a change."

I exhaled, the tension in my chest loosening a little. "Well, I appreciate it. I really do. You might've saved our ranch, but..." I trailed off. "It won't do much good, Blake."

Blake's grin faded, his brow furrowing as he leaned forward. "Why not?"

I shifted from foot to foot, feeling like a fool for standing there. "We've sold off most of our stock. Even if we could buy the breeding cows back, we don't have the cash to do it. The money we got from selling them? It's already gone. Spent on the mortgage and keeping the ranch afloat." I rubbed the back of my neck, looking down at the floor. "We're stuck, Blake. No cows, no future."

Blake leaned back in his chair, nodding slowly as he listened. His eyes flickered with something—thoughtfulness, maybe, or that calculating way he had when he was sizing up a problem. He didn't say anything at first, just looked down at the table, like he was piecing something together in his mind.

I cleared my throat, feeling like I'd just wasted his time. "Anyway, thanks again for what you did. It means a lot, even if—"

"Hold on a minute," Blake interrupted, his voice quiet but firm.

I stopped, turning to look at him.

Blake stood slowly, one hand resting on the back of his chair as he looked up at me. "What if you could get your cows back? Right now."

My heart stuttered. "What do you mean?"

Blake tilted his head, a thoughtful grin forming on his lips. "Just... hear me out. What if you didn't have to start from scratch? What if I told you those cows you sold? They're not gone." He paused, letting that sink in. "What if you had an opportunity to get 'em back on an installment plan? Build your herd again, little by little."

I blinked, trying to process what he was saying. "Wait... Are you saying *you* bought our stock?"

Blake nodded, his eyes twinkling. "Evan did. Got 'em out on Cody's acreage right now. We, uh... figured they might come in handy."

My jaw dropped. I stood there, trying to find the words, but none came. Blake had been one step ahead of us this whole time, quietly buying back the future we thought we'd lost.

"You... you're serious?" I asked, my voice barely above a whisper.

Blake gave me a steady look. "I wouldn't be sayin' it if I wasn't. Now, you'll have to work hard—pay back what's owed over time. But it's doable. I trust your family can make it work."

"But... Blake!" I laughed, still disbelieving. "You have no idea how far behind we are. We can't even afford the interest we'd owe you, let alone—"

"I didn't say it had to be all at once, now, did I? And as for interest, I got something you can do for me instead."

I narrowed my eyes. "What can I possibly do for you?"

He grinned, removing his glasses and resting his hand on his knee. "You can make my horse win in Vegas."

I blinked. "Wh... what?"

He waved a hand. "Or just show her off. I don't care about the prize money or the laurels. I just wanna see a filly we raised drop some jaws down there, y'hear?"

"But... Emily's going to show her. I bailed on them, Blake. I can't—"

"Not if you don't get your rear on a plane, you can't. Meryl and I are flyin' out in the mornin'. You wanna get your job back, and your cows?" He chuckled, slapping a hand down on the table. "Better show up. We leave for the airport at eight tomorrow."

I stared at him, my mind racing. This was it. This was the chance we needed. We weren't done. The ranch wasn't done. *I* wasn't done.

"Blake, I..." I stammered, struggling to find the words.

Blake waved a hand, cutting me off. "Don't thank me yet. There's a lot of work to be done. But it's your family's legacy, Cole. Thought you'd like a chance to keep it going."

I stood there for a moment longer, then slowly nodded. "We will. Thank you."

Blake grinned. "Now, go home and tell your family." He patted my shoulder as he walked me to the door. "And don't forget—you gotta apologize to Mike Lindbergh for lettin' him down. You tell 'im I talked you out of swingin' a hammer."

I laughed, feeling a weight lifting off my shoulders for the first time in what felt like forever. "Yeah, about that... I might have some explaining to do."

Blake chuckled. "Good luck, son."

Chapter Twenty-Six

Emily

I led Copper into the arena, feeling his muscles bunch beneath me, ready for whatever I asked. The warm-up pen was buzzing with energy—horses trotting, trainers barking orders, and the low rumble of machinery from the vendors setting up around the grounds. The air smelled like hay and leather, with a hint of barbecue smoke drifting over from the food stalls.

Copper moved easily, his ears flicking forward, taking in the sights and sounds of the big arena. He had been through this before, but there was something about the Vegas lights, the grandstands stretching up into the sky, that made everything feel bigger, more intense.

I nudged him into a lope, keeping my seat light and my hands steady. His stride was smooth and relaxed, his hooves moving in a perfect rhythm on the freshly groomed dirt. I gave him a quick pat on the neck. This horse might not be greased lightning, but he was dependable. That was what counted right now.

"Easy, boy," I whispered, letting him stretch out a bit. We had a lot of work ahead tomorrow, and tonight was just about getting him used to the arena.

Cody leaned on the rail, watching us with that hawk-like intensity he always had when he was training. He nodded in approval, and I could feel the tension ease out of my shoulders.

"Looking good," he called, his eyes following every step Copper took. "Keep him relaxed, let him breathe. He's ready."

I smiled, feeling a rush of pride. Cody didn't hand out praise easily.

Copper and I did a few more laps before I slowed him down and brought him to a halt near the gate. Lizzy was standing by the gate with Dustin, and she stepped up to take him back to the stalls. I handed the reins over, patting Copper on the neck as he walked away.

Next up was Lynx. She was already saddled, and Morgan had been perched on the rail beside Cody, holding her reins. I grabbed her and swung into the saddle, and it was like she and I were speaking different languages from the second I touched her. Where Copper was steady, Lynx was electric. She was practically vibrating with energy as I guided her into the arena.

She tossed her head, her eyes wide and alert as she took in the scene. Her feet skittered to the side, her hips swaying against my cues. I nudged her into a trot, hoping to let her stretch out and get used to the space.

Cody's eyes never left us as we worked through some simple drills. Lynx moved like she was on springs, each step quick and light. She was sharp tonight—really sharp. Maybe a bit too sharp for me, because it seemed like every cue I gave her was too much.

"Stand her up," Cody said, his voice cutting through the noise. "Keep her shoulders square. And use smaller signals. Just think it—she'll feel it."

I backed off and felt the difference in her immediately. Lynx became a little less spastic and settled into a rhythm, her hooves tapping the ground in perfect time. Every move was responsive, crisp. It was like she was reading my mind, but some of it, I hate to say, was garbled.

Cody nodded again, more to himself than to me. "That'll do," he muttered. "Just take your time, Em."

We worked through a few more drills, and by the end, Lynx was breathing hard but steady, her coat shining under the arena lights. I couldn't help but smile. Even if we didn't quite "get" each other yet, she dazzled me. This horse was something special. More than special.

"Good work," Cody said as I brought Lynx to a stop near him. "Don't overthink it. Just stay calm, let her do her job."

I gave Lynx a pat, my heart still racing a little. "Thanks, Cody. She feels good. I just wish Cole was here to feel it."

He smiled. "Yeah. You and me both."

"I can't show her like he does," I reminded him. "She doesn't trust me like that. When the show jitters hit—"

"You'll do fine. Nobody expects you to be Cole. Just ride her like you know how." He sighed. "Better put her up for now. Keep her fresh for tomorrow."

He checked his watch, glancing toward the gate. "I'm going to make sure the rest of the horses are set for the night. Luke's heading to the airport to pick up Blake and Meryl, and I'm gonna hit the hay."

I nodded, swinging out of the saddle. The thought of Blake watching us tomorrow added another layer of pressure. He was the reason this whole program existed, after all. I couldn't let him down. I led Lynx back to the stalls, thinking about tomorrow and how everything we'd worked for was about to be tested.

But right now, the horses felt fit, the night air was cool, and for the first time in a while, I felt... sorta ready.

I was in the middle of brushing my hair when there was a knock at the trailer door. At this hour, I assumed it had to be Cody with some last-minute instructions about tomorrow, or maybe Morgan checking in about Nikki, because I was supposed to help watch her first thing in the morning until the rest of the family got to the show grounds. I tucked my brush onto the tiny counter and walked over, fully expecting some quick logistical conversation.

But when I opened the door, my heart nearly stopped.

"Cole?" I blurted, staring in shock. Before I could say another word, that tall cowboy pulled me into his arms. Without thinking, I launched myself into him, wrapping my arms around his neck in a fierce hug. "Cole, what are you doing here?!"

He laughed, the sound vibrating against me as he twirled me around in the small space by the door. "Surprise," he teased. "I flew down with Blake and Meryl."

I pulled back just enough to see his face, hardly believing he was real. "You came! But what about your construction job?"

His grin was as wide as I'd ever seen it. "I quit... or got fired. Still not sure about that, but it doesn't matter. With a little help from Blake, it looks like Ridgeview Ranch might have another season left after all."

I let out a whoop of excitement and hugged him even tighter. "Oh, Cole, that's amazing! But... how? After everything you said, I don't understand!"

"Neither do I. Bottom line, I owe Blake Walker a huge favor and a pile of money. I figured the least I could do was try to show his horse to the best of my ability. I... still get to show her, right?"

I laced my fingers into the hair at the back of his head, knocking his cowboy hat off, and leaned in for another kiss. "I sure hope so. She doesn't like me very much."

Laughing, he gently set me down, still holding me close. "I wasn't sure I'd even make it down here, but I couldn't miss this."

"I can't believe you're here! Hey, you need to come in and tell me everything," I said, tugging him inside. The trailer wasn't big by any means, and the dinette booth was cramped for just one person, so I stayed standing, still holding onto him. Cole casually leaned against the fridge, those blue eyes of his eyes sparkling in that way that made my heart trip over itself.

"So... what does your family think about you being here?" I asked.

He shrugged. "Mom's thrilled. She's got the horse training bug, too, you know. Always has, but her interests lie more in rehabbing horses that got a bad break."

"Like Morgan. Yeah, I've heard she's good, too. What about your brothers?"

"Chase is tickled pink for me. Gage just grunted and wished me luck, then started talking about the stuff we need to tackle as soon as I get back if we're going to keep the ranch. Trent seems pretty happy, but he's so distracted by his girlfriend that he hardly noticed I left."

"Oh? They must be pretty serious?"

He made a face. "No, the opposite problem. She's giving him headaches, but he won't admit it. But I don't... *really* don't want to talk about my brothers right now."

I crossed my arms, grinning. "Well, what *did* you want to talk about?"

Cole hesitated, then that huge cowboy grin took over his face. "How about how I spent all day talking to your mom?"

I blinked, and my arms fell. "My... my mom?"

"Yeah. She's real proud of you, Em. Almost as proud as I am."

My eyes narrowed, and I shook my head. "I don't understand. When did you talk to her?"

He shrugged. "It's a long car ride to the Boise airport. And I sat next to her on the flight, and in the van on the way back here..."

"I..." I gulped. "My mom is *here?* What? How!"

"Need you ask? Blake. He all but stuffed her in the car this morning when we were leaving town. Told her he already had a ticket for her and a room booked at the hotel. Never heard a grown woman squeal with joy like that."

I laughed. "I can't believe it! She's never seen me show before. She's really here?"

"Yeah." He reached out, cupping my shoulder until his hand slid down my arm. Oh, that felt so right... just touching him, being with him.

I sighed. "Cole, you have no idea how happy I am to see you."

His hand found mine, linking our fingers. "I'm happy to see you too, Em. Honestly, there's something I've been wanting to say for a while now."

My heart sped up as I watched him, waiting. "Yeah?"

"I'm crazy about you," he said, his voice quiet but sure. "And I'm sorry for all the times I pushed you away. I just... couldn't stand thinking I wasn't good enough for you. Don't have much going for me, you know, but—"

I cut him off with a kiss that made him gasp. "Shut up, cowboy. Don't ever let me hear you talking like that again, Cole Langton. You're already more than I could ever want, you hear me?"

He was breathing heavily, and he gave a shaky laugh. "I never thought you felt that way."

"Well, I do."

His smile grew braver again. "Thought I had to earn it. Thought if I just kept working, proved myself... But the truth is, I really want to build this dream with you. Even if I'm always the 'number two guy' to your shooting star... I'm okay with that. I just want to do life with you, chase our goals together."

I stood there, momentarily speechless, taking in every word. The depth of what he was saying sank in, and I felt my throat tighten. "Cole, you're not the number two guy. You never were." I cupped his face in my hands, leaning in to kiss him softly. "All I want is for you to be beside me, no matter what happens."

He smiled, pulling me closer. "That was the hardest part of walking away, you know? Knowing I'd be losing you, too. Losing the chance to chase that dream with you."

I felt tears sting the back of my eyes as I kissed him again, this time with more urgency, more emotion. His arms wrapped around me, strong and secure, and for a moment, the rest of the world faded away. It was just us, here in this tiny trailer, holding on to each other like nothing else mattered.

We pulled back slightly, laughing quietly, still holding each other. I reveled in the warmth and safety of his embrace, the feeling of being right where I belonged.

Then Cole stiffened slightly, his eyes widening in sudden realization. "Oh, shoot!"

I blinked, stepping back to look at him. "What? What's wrong?"

He scratched the back of his neck, looking sheepish. "Uh... I don't know where I'm supposed to sleep tonight."

I raised an eyebrow. "What do you mean?"

"Luke dropped me off here to see you, but I don't have a hotel room or anything. I mean, Morgan and Cody are staying in the other trailer with Nikki, but... I didn't exactly make a plan."

I couldn't help but laugh at the absurdity of it. "You're serious? *That's* what you're worried about right now?"

He nodded, clearly embarrassed. "Yeah. I mean, I'll be fine sleeping in a stall or something. I just wanted to be close to you and the horses."

I winced, trying to picture him curled up in the barn. "Well, we do have a tack stall by the horses. There's hay bales... doesn't sound very comfortable, though."

He grinned, kissing me again, his hands sliding up my back. "I don't care. I'd sleep anywhere as long as it's close to what's important." He kissed me softly on the forehead and added with a playful smirk, "But, uh... I might need to borrow a blanket."

I laughed, shaking my head as I hugged him tight. "I think I can manage that."

Cole

We'd settled into the booth, a deck of cards between us, and the familiar comfort of being with Emily wrapped around me like a favorite jacket. It was late, but neither of us seemed in a hurry to call it a night. After all the chaos of the past few weeks, just being here with her felt like some kind of reward.

Emily dealt the next hand, narrowing her eyes as she looked over her cards. "You're going down this time," she teased, a playful grin on her face.

I smirked, leaning back in the small booth. "We'll see about that."

We tossed lighthearted jabs back and forth as the game unfolded, but even with all the teasing, something lingered in the air.

"You're bluffing," I said, narrowing my eyes at her as I threw down my cards. "I can see it in your face."

Emily laughed, raising an eyebrow. "Oh, you think so? Maybe I'm just better at this than you think."

I smirked, leaning back in the booth. "Doubt it. You've got a tell."

She looked at me, her eyes sparkling. "And what's my tell, Mr. Langton?"

I tapped the side of my head with my finger. "You get that little crinkle right here when you're holding a bad hand."

Emily rolled her eyes and threw down her cards. "Whatever. You just got lucky."

I chuckled, picking up the cards and starting to shuffle them again. "Lucky? I think we both know I've got the edge tonight."

"Don't get too cocky," she said with a playful grin. "You know I've got a comeback in me."

But even with all the teasing, there was something else between us, something unspoken in the way her eyes lingered on mine, the way the smile stayed on her lips a little longer than usual. It wasn't tension, not exactly. More like... anticipation.

She caught me looking at her and tilted her head. "What?"

I shook my head, smiling as I shuffled the cards. "Nothing. Just thinking."

Emily narrowed her eyes, leaning forward a little. "About what?"

I shrugged, tossing a few cards her way. "About what comes next, I guess."

She paused, her hand hovering over the cards. "Yeah," she said softly. "Me too. So... what now? What's the plan going forward? What are you envisioning for... us?"

I kept my focus on the cards for a moment, considering the question. Honestly, I'd been thinking about it for a while, and it felt right. Natural. So, without looking up, I casually said, "I thought we'd get married this fall."

There was a pause, the cards frozen in Emily's hands. She blinked at me, her eyes wide like I'd just told her we were moving to Mars.

"Cole," she blurted, her voice half-laughing, half-disbelieving. "Are you pulling my leg? Is this another one of your jokes?"

I stopped shuffling the cards and looked her dead in the eye, all trace of teasing gone from my face. "When it comes to you, Em, I'm completely serious. I want it all—love, life, building a story together. We can wait until you're ready, but my mind's made up."

Her eyes widened even more, and then she burst out laughing, the sound filling the tiny trailer with a warmth that only Emily could bring. She reached across the table, grabbing my hand. "Wait, wait," she said, still laughing, "was that your idea of a proposal?"

I grinned, not breaking eye contact. "Why? Need a better one?"

"*Yes!*" she cried, her laughter infectious, her cheeks flushed.

Chuckling, I slid out of the dinette booth and down onto one knee, looking up at her with a grin that I hoped matched the seriousness of what I was about to do. I reached into my pocket and pulled out the little ringlet I'd made out of baling twine earlier—just in case.

"I'll get you a real ring when I get the chance," I said, "but for now, will you wear this one?"

Emily stared at the twine ring, then back at me, her laughter dying down as the reality of the moment hit her. Her eyes softened, and a smile tugged at the corner of her lips. "Cole Langton," she said, shaking her head, "you really did it, didn't you?"

I nodded, my hand still holding the makeshift ring up to her.

With a light laugh, she leaned forward, brushing a stray lock of hair out of her face. "Yes," she whispered, taking the ring from my hand and slipping it onto her finger. "I'll wear it."

I stood up, pulling her into my arms, and she kissed me, her lips soft and warm against mine. We laughed together, holding each other close, and for the first time in a long while, everything felt exactly as it should. Right there, in that little trailer, with Emily in my arms, I knew we'd found something real.

"Baling twine, though?" she teased, pulling back to look at the ring again.

I chuckled, brushing a thumb across her cheek. "Hey, it's got character. And just wait till you see the real one."

She grinned, her eyes shining. "I'll hold you to that."

Chapter Twenty-Seven

Emily

The crowd was already buzzing when I trotted Copper around the edge of the warm-up pen, keeping my hands light on the reins. The warm Vegas air seemed to vibrate with anticipation, and for a moment, I let myself glance up at the stands. I spotted my mom immediately, bouncing up and down in her seat next to the Walker family. Her bright smile and excited wave made something tight in my chest ease. We'd finally gotten to a place where she understood me, where we both fit into each other's worlds. And now, she was here—here for me.

But what really sent my heart racing wasn't just my mom's presence. It was Cole, sitting on Lynx just a few feet away, his eyes never leaving me. He caught me looking, and his mouth tugged up into that crooked grin of his, the one that made my stomach flip every time. He leaned over, his lips brushing against mine for just a second. "For luck," he whispered.

I smiled, feeling the warmth of his kiss spread through me, calming the nervous energy that had been churning in my chest. I tipped my hat at him and nudged Copper forward toward the arena gate.

As I entered the pen, everything else seemed to fall away. It was just me and Copper now, the world narrowing to the feel of the reins in my hands and the hum of the crowd in the background. I took a deep breath, settling into the saddle. This was it. Our reining class—his best event. Everything we'd worked for.

As we walked to the middle of the arena where we would start our pattern, I felt Copper come alive beneath me. His ears pricked forward, and his muscles shifted into focus, like he knew exactly what was about to happen. We'd trained for this moment—every spin, every slide, every lead change drilled into perfection. He was steady as a rock, and as we crossed the center, I let out a breath and caught another one, just so I wouldn't pass out. The judge gave the nod, and we were off.

I urged Copper into a large, fast circle, feeling the power beneath me as he hit his stride. His long, white mane flowed like a river, catching the arena lights. I sat deep, guiding him with my legs more than the reins, and Copper responded like he always did—steady, smooth, and perfectly in sync. We flew through the first set of circles, and my heart swelled with pride. This was everything I'd dreamed of.

I could feel Cole's eyes on me, watching from the side as we transitioned into our smaller, slower circles. I kept Copper's frame tight, and he slowed effortlessly, his movements fluid, like butter melting across a hot pan. He wasn't as catty as some of the other horses we were up against, but he didn't need to be. He was smooth, powerful—everything Cody and I had trained him to be.

The next set of circles came up, and I felt the adrenaline spike as we prepared for the lead change. I squeezed gently, giving Copper the cue, and he switched his leads perfectly, his body flowing underneath me as if it were the easiest thing in the world. We hit the next set of circles, and I couldn't help but grin. Copper was nailing it, every single movement crisp and clean.

Next came the spins. I gathered the reins just slightly, my heart racing with anticipation. "Come on, buddy," I whispered, sitting deep in the saddle. Copper knew what was coming, and the second I gave him the cue, he spun fast and sharp, his feet moving like clockwork beneath us. I counted the spins in my head, making sure to stop just at the right moment. Copper halted perfectly, his body still as a stone.

The final test was the sliding stops. I breathed in deep, settling myself as we galloped down the long side of the arena. This was Copper's favorite part—the part where he really got to show off. I pushed him forward, and just as we hit the perfect spot, I sat deep, giving him the signal to stop. Copper slid into the ground, his hooves cutting through the dirt like it was snow, his entire body sinking back with precision. It was smooth, clean, and perfect.

The crowd erupted, but all I could hear was the pounding of my heart. We galloped to the opposite side of the arena for the second stop, and Copper hit it just as flawlessly. His haunches dropped low, sliding us to a complete halt as if he'd done it a thousand times.

The final slide stop felt like we were flying, and when Copper slid into that last stop, I knew we had done it.

I patted his neck as I turned him toward the gate, my heart still racing, but with pride now. Copper had done exactly what he was prepared to do—smooth, clean, and dependable. He wasn't going to wow the judges with flashy moves, but he'd executed everything with precision and consistency.

As I exited the arena, the announcer's voice came over the loudspeaker. "Score for Emily Parker and Copper Spark: 72.5."

I felt a surge of relief and joy at the number. A 72.5 was solid—better than I'd hoped for. I knew we'd rank high in the reining scores, even if his cow work didn't end up being as strong.

I rode back toward Cole, feeling like I was on top of the world. His grin was wide, and I could see the pride in his eyes as I trotted up beside him.

"Not bad, Parker," he said, tipping his hat to me.

"Not bad?" I laughed. "That was the best reining class we've ever had!"

"Sure looked like it," he said, his eyes sparkling. "Copper's mane flying like you were riding a cloud."

I shook my head, still riding the high of the moment. "That was all him. He was perfect."

Cole reached over and squeezed my hand, his smile never fading. I squeezed back, feeling an overwhelming sense of contentment settle over me.

I smiled back, my chest swelling with pride. This was everything I'd dreamed of—the perfect run, the perfect horse, and Cole, right there beside me.

Cole

I sat in the warm-up pen, Lynx beneath me, her muscles coiled like a spring. Outwardly, she was calm, just flicking her ears back and forth, waiting for the signal to move. But I could feel it. That electric hum just beneath her skin—the one that told me she was ready. More than ready. I was the one who wasn't.

"Deep breath, Cole," I muttered to myself, trying to shake off the nerves that were threatening to choke me. We'd already nailed a 72 in reining, solid enough to keep us in third place. But Lynx had blown the boxing class wide open with her moves, bringing us into a tie for the lead and half a point ahead of Emily and Copper. Half a point.

But none of that mattered if we didn't get through this class. Cutting was where Lynx truly shone, but knowing that didn't calm my racing heart. Cody gave me a tip of the hat, but he didn't say anything. There wasn't really anything he could say, because he'd figured out... or maybe he knew before I even did... that the voice I needed to hear right now was Emily's.

Out of the corner of my eye, I saw her standing by the gate. I walked Lynx over to her, every step feeling almost skittery as Lynx started to wind up. She looked up at me, her clear blue eyes steady, and without saying a word, she leaned up and kissed me.

"Go get 'em," she whispered, her lips curving into that confident smile that always made my heart skip. Somehow, it was all I needed. The nerves that had been buzzing in my chest settled just a little. Emily believed in me, and right now, that was enough.

I straightened in the saddle, giving Lynx a pat on the neck as the gate swung open. It was our turn.

As we walked into the arena, the lights seemed brighter, the noise of the crowd sharper. My heart pounded in my chest, but Lynx was cool and collected. I glanced toward the stands and saw them—my second family. Meryl Walker was holding up her phone so my mom back home could watch the live feed, and Emily's mom waved and shouted "Good luck, Cole!"—she'd already started calling me "her son." All of them, here for me.

But I didn't focus on them long. It was Emily's kiss that still lingered on my lips, steadying me more than anything else.

The herd of cattle stood at the far end of the arena, their bodies shifting restlessly. I took a deep breath, settled my reins, and picked my cow. Lynx's ears perked up, her body already moving in sync with mine. I dropped my hand, and it was like a switch flipped.

Lynx shot to the right, cutting through the herd with an explosion that took my breath away. She was quick, cat-like, her hooves barely seeming to touch the ground as she blocked the cow from rejoining the herd. Every muscle in her body was focused, reacting faster than I could even think.

The cow made a sharp move to the left, and Lynx was there, mirroring it perfectly. The crowd let out a cheer, but I barely heard it. All I could feel was the surge of pride swelling in my chest as Lynx handled the cow with grit and precision.

"That's it, girl," I whispered under my breath, my hand still low, giving her all the room she needed to work.

The cow tried to dart to the right, but Lynx was quicker. She rolled to cut it off with a swift, snappy turn that made the crowd roar. My heart raced in time with her movements, but I didn't have to do much. Lynx knew what to do, and I was just along for the ride.

One cow down, two more to go.

I locked onto the next cow, a little tougher this time, its body tense and ready to test us. Lynx felt it too, her body humming beneath me, ready for the challenge. The moment I dropped my hand, she moved like lightning, cutting the cow from the herd in one smooth motion. The cow darted forward, testing her resolve, but Lynx didn't flinch. She was low, quick, her turns so sharp I could feel the whip of her mane as we pivoted. By thunder, I could feel the dirt hitting the bottoms of my boots, we were so low to the ground!

The crowd was on their feet now, the noise rising with every move. My focus narrowed, blocking everything out but the cow and Lynx.

She pushed harder, her feet a blur as she kept the cow in check, not letting it gain an inch of ground. The cow tried one last desperate move, but Lynx was too quick. She cut it off effortlessly, like she'd been doing this her whole life.

By the time we worked the last cow, I barely had to guide her. Lynx knew exactly what to do, her movements fluid and fast, cutting the cow with such style that even I was in awe. She wasn't just talented—she was special. This horse had something in her that I'd never seen before.

As we finished, I exhaled a breath and sucked in another before I passed out. The crowd roared, but I was only aware of one thing—Lynx, breathing hard beneath me, her body trembling from the sheer joy of the game. I gave her a pat, murmuring, "Good girl," and then turned to exit the arena, my heart still pounding from the rush.

We walked out, and the announcer's voice came over the loudspeaker.

"Cole Langton and Playin it Smart, score: 73.5."

I blinked, and my jaw about hit the saddle horn. 73.5. We'd done it! That score was good enough to win the entire futurity!

The crowd erupted into cheers, but all I could think about was Emily. I looked up at the stands, where my family was on their feet, clapping and shouting. But then I scanned the other riders at the in gate, and it was her face I sought out, her smile beaming at me like she'd known all along what we were capable of.

Lynx shifted beneath me, still breathing hard but steady, and I couldn't help but grin. We'd won. But better than the euphoria of victory was the girl who was waiting to kiss me as soon as I got out of the arena.

Keep reading for a preview of Chase and Kate's story in ***A Crossroads for the Cowboy!***

From our hearts to yours

Thank you for spending a little time with the family at Ridgeview Ranch.

I hope you've enjoyed getting to know everyone. I'd love it if you would share this family with your friends so they can experience life on the ranch with these swoony cowboys and sassy cowgirls. As with all my books, I have enabled lending to make it easier to share. If you leave a review for *A Home for the Cowboy* on Amazon, Goodreads, Book Bub or your own blog, I would love to read it! Email me the link at **TheCowgirlWrites@TessThornton.com**

Would you like to read Blake Walker's romance? Dive into Blake and Meryl's story, and stay up to date on upcoming releases and sales by joining my newsletter: https://mailchi.mp/11ce46b43f43/join-the-family

Keep reading for a preview of Chase and Kate's story in ***A Crossroads for the Cowboy!***

Epilogue

Kate

The day was already off to a busy start at White Pines. The sound of horses shuffling in the paddocks mixed with the occasional snort and whinny, and the familiar rhythm of saddles being thrown and buckles tightening filled the air. I'd just finished tacking up one of the therapy horses, a sturdy bay gelding named Jasper, when I noticed some movement over by the new mobile home at the edge of the property.

Cole and Chase were there, of course, getting everything set up for Cole and Emily to move in after the wedding next week. I knew about their plans—Morgan and Cody had mentioned offering the place to Cole and Emily once they got married, which was sweet and all, but... working together *and* living together? That was a whole new level of crazy, if you asked me.

I wiped the sweat from my forehead with the back of my hand, watching the guys for a minute. Cole was fiddling with some furniture on the porch, while Chase—oh, *Chase*—was bent over, messing with something in the back of his truck.

"I'll take that view any day," I muttered under my breath, barely resisting the urge to fan myself.

It wasn't the first time I'd seen Chase around, and definitely not the first time I'd noticed how ridiculously good-looking he was. The man was built like a cowboy out of a romance novel—broad shoulders, strong arms, and those blue eyes that made me feel like I needed to sit down. But the problem with Chase? He barely said a word to me. Every time I tried to get even a hint of a conversation going, he just grunted or tipped his hat and moved on.

And there he went again—head down, focused, like he didn't even see me standing there. I threw a glance at Jasper, the horse waiting patiently beside me. "You'd talk to me, wouldn't you?" I muttered, giving his neck a pat.

Feeling bold, I unhooked Jasper's lead rope from the post and led him over to where the guys were working. "Hey, Cole!" I called, my voice extra cheery as I approached. "Getting everything ready for the big day?"

Cole looked up and grinned. "Yeah, we're getting there. Just moving some furniture and fixing up a few things."

"Nice. The place looks great." I stole a glance at Chase, who, of course, was still focused on the bed of his truck like it was the most fascinating thing in the world. "Hey, Chase," I tried, keeping my tone casual but hoping he'd finally look up.

He gave me a quick nod, barely lifting his head. "Ma'am."

Ma'am? Really?

I bit back a sigh, throwing on my best polite smile. "Well, I just thought I'd come say hello while I had a minute. How's everything going?"

Cole, being his friendly self, chuckled. "Busy, but good. Still can't believe we're pulling this off."

I smiled back, but my eyes drifted toward Chase again, who had now grabbed a tool from the truck and was walking toward the house without another word. Great. Another missed opportunity. It was like talking to a brick wall, only less rewarding.

"Okay, Kate. Pull it together," I muttered under my breath, watching him disappear into the mobile home.

Cole must've noticed the look on my face because he shot me a grin, wiping his hands on his jeans. "Chase doesn't say much. Don't take it personally."

"I'm not," I lied through my teeth. "I'm just... you know... wondering if the guy ever speaks full sentences."

"He's just quiet," Cole shrugged. "But once you get him going, he's alright."

Right.

I was just about to make a snarky comment when I heard the sound of an engine roaring up the hill. Emily's car pulled up, and sure enough, there she was, stepping out with her mom in tow, the two of them chattering excitedly as they unloaded boxes from the trunk.

"Hey, guys!" Emily called, waving as she approached, her mom hurrying ahead toward the mobile home, clearly eager to help get things set up inside.

"Hey," I greeted, giving Emily a wave. "So... this is happening."

Emily laughed, her face glowing with excitement. "It's happening! Mom brought some stuff from the store to help set things up."

I nodded, glancing at the boxes Emily's mom was already hauling inside. "Yeah, I can see that. You ready for this? Like, *really* ready?"

Emily gave me a quizzical look. "For the wedding?"

I shook my head, smirking. "No, for working with Cole 24/7. You sure that's a good idea? You're never gonna get a break from him."

She grinned, glancing toward the mobile home where Cole had disappeared to help her mom. "I can't wait. Honestly, working with him has been the best part of this whole deal. He's not my rival anymore; he's my perfect partner."

I let out a low whistle, more in awe of her confidence than anything else. "You're brave. I'd probably kill him after the first week."

Emily just laughed and waved me off. "Nah, you wouldn't. He's great to work with."

"Yeah, yeah," I muttered, though I couldn't help the smile tugging at my lips. Emily had a point. Cole had come a long way, and seeing them together now, I could tell they really did make a great team.

As Emily walked back toward the mobile home, I let out a soft sigh, my eyes drifting toward Chase again. He walked out of the house with something in his hands, heading toward his truck, and as he passed me, he tipped his hat in my direction.

But he didn't say a word.

"Really? That's it?" I muttered to myself, watching as he walked away, not even sparing me a second glance.

I turned back to Jasper, shaking my head. "Well, at least you appreciate me, buddy," I said, patting his neck. "And hey, horses are less complicated anyway."

I led Jasper back toward the barn, grumbling to myself the whole way. Maybe one day I'd get more than a "ma'am" out of Chase Langton, but for now, I had horses to tend to and therapy clients who actually *did* talk to me.

Chase

I couldn't help but shake my head as I watched Cole haul a dresser, all by himself, up the steps to the mobile home. This was all happening so fast. One minute he's working construction and talking about getting me a job; the next, he's back to training horses, planning a wedding, and moving into a new place with Emily. Of all us Langton boys, Cole was never the one I figured for settling down so quick. But here he was, happier than I'd ever seen him.

He deserved it, though. He'd always had a bit of a chip on his shoulder, especially after Dad died. I guess it hit him hardest. Being younger, he missed out on more time with Dad than the rest of us. And now... seeing him like this, settled, content—it felt like he'd finally come into his own. Like he was finding peace. And yeah, I was proud of him. Even if I didn't always understand how he did things.

I carried another box toward the mobile home, and as I got closer, I couldn't help but notice some of the design flaws. The place was sturdy enough, sure, but the layout was all wrong. The porch wasn't properly supported, and that roof overhang? That was going to be a problem in a few years if the drainage wasn't fixed. My mind automatically went into planning mode, imagining how I'd change things, make them better. That's how I'd always been. I liked figuring stuff out, fixing things, and planning every little detail.

As I set the box down on the porch, I casually mentioned one of the things I'd noticed. "You know, you're gonna need to fix that drainage issue with the overhang at some point. Otherwise, it'll warp and cause all kinds of problems down the line."

Cole stopped mid-step, his brow furrowing before he broke into a laugh. "Seriously, Chase? It's a mobile home. You think we're going to be here long enough to worry about stuff like that?"

I shrugged, feeling a bit sheepish. "Well, you never know. Cody and Morgan might not want the place to fall apart in a year."

He shook his head, still chuckling as he walked past me with another load. "You're always overthinking things. It's fine. Nobody thinks this place will still be here in fifty years. It'll do just fine for a while."

I didn't respond, but as I stood there, looking over the mobile home again, I couldn't help but imagine all the ways I'd redesign it. That's the thing about me—I always saw potential. I'd had this crazy idea floating around in my head for years, one I hadn't told anyone about. Maybe not even fully admitted to myself. I wanted to be an architect. I loved the ranch, don't get me wrong. But there was something about planning, designing, and building things from the ground up that just made sense to me. Numbers and lines. Tangible things you could see and touch.

And maybe, deep down, I wouldn't have been devastated to see Ridgeview go. It felt wrong to think it, but the truth was, I'd pictured a different future for myself. I'd never said anything to the others, though. They all bled for that ranch. It was in their bones. And now that we'd managed to save it, I was relieved... but part of me still felt like I didn't belong.

As I headed back toward the truck, my thoughts wandered, but I couldn't help noticing Kate again. She was standing near the barn, chatting with one of the other hands, her thick curls catching the sunlight. They always seemed to defy gravity, those curls. It was... well, I didn't want to stare, but I caught myself doing it more than once today. She was beautiful, sure, but it wasn't just that. There was something else about her, something that made me curious. She had this energy, like she knew exactly who she was and wasn't afraid to be that person.

I thought about asking her if she wanted to help us haul the last few things, but then I figured, if she wanted to, she'd have offered. Besides, she was standing there with a horse. She probably had her hands full with the therapy stuff anyway. That whole program at White Pines had taken off, and it seemed like Kate had become a huge part of it. Not that I fully understood how that sort of thing worked—therapy with horses and all that "touchy-feely" stuff was beyond me. Give me numbers and blueprints any day. Something concrete. But whatever they were doing out there, it was helping people, and I had to respect that.

I walked past her again, and this time, I mustered the courage to offer a polite greeting. "Ma'am."

She glanced over, giving me a smile and a quick nod. "Hey, Chase."

Her smile was... well, I couldn't help but feel a little warm inside when I saw it. There was something genuine about it, like she didn't bother with fake pleasantries. But then, just as quickly, she turned back to her conversation, leaving me standing there feeling like an idiot for hoping she'd stick around.

Why would she? I thought, shaking my head as I walked back to the mobile home. She had work to do, and I had work to finish here. But still, it'd been nice, just for a second, to think she might've been interested in hanging around.

I bent down to pick up the last box, but as I straightened up, I glanced back toward the barn and watched as Kate walked away, heading back toward the therapy pens. And even though I tried to focus on what I was doing, my thoughts kept drifting back to her. Her smile. Those curls. And the fact that I couldn't figure her out for the life of me.

But hey, that's just how things go, right? Some things you can plan for, build from the ground up, and make sense of. And some things? Well, some things just leave you wondering.

Catch Chase and Kate's story in ***A Crossroads for the Cowboy!***

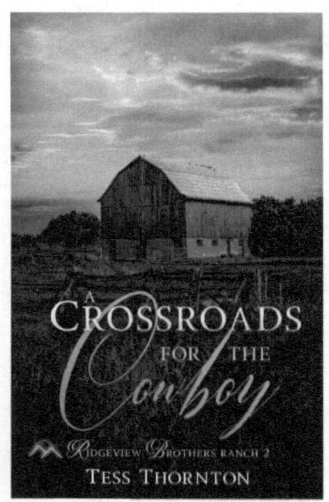

A Winter Surprise for the Cowboy

Blake Walker has built a legacy in his family and his ranch. His five boys are starting to find love and build their own lives, and he's beginning to wonder what adventures are left for him.

Meryl Justice has raised everyone's kids but her own, and now she's looking forward to retirement from the job she's had for thirty years. She loves her home and her farm animals, but is that all there is?

Find out when these two hearts set out to discover if wintertime might not just be the best time of all to fall in love!

Click HERE to get your story.

More from Tess Thornton

<u>The Walker Ranch Series</u>
A Home for the Cowboy
Cody and Morgan's Story
A Second Chance for the Cowboy
Marshall and Kelli's Story
A Winter Surprise for the Cowboy
*Blake and Meryl's Story
An Angel for the Cowboy
Dusty and Jess's Story
Taming the Cowboy
Luke and Audrey's Story
A Heart for the Cowboy
Evan and Meg's Story
**A Winter Surprise for the Cowboy* is a Free Novella available only to
newsletter subscribers

<u>The Ridgeview Brothers Ranch Series</u>

A Rival for the Cowboy
Cole and Emily's Story
A Crossroads for the Cowboy
Chase & Kate's Story
A Christmas Wish for the Cowboy
Trent & Lauren's Story
A Match for the Cowboy
Gage & Amber's Story
A Partner for the Cowboy
A Cowboy Buddy Book featuring Luke Walker and Gage Langton

www.ingramcontent.com/pod-product-compliance
Lightning Source LLC
Chambersburg PA
CBHW031658170626
46808CB00005B/1513